'What [...] kids doing it for themselves and kicking adult butt.' **CHARLIE HIGSON**

'One of those grab 'em by the throat thrillers that takes off on the first page.' **EOIN COLFER**

'A riveting read – with breathless action. **CHRIS BRADFORD**

'From the explosive beginning to the heart-stopping end, *The Haven* is a thrilling, gripping adventure. Simon Lelic has created a vivid underworld and a great hero faced by a truly twisted villain.' **SHANE HEGARTY, AUTHOR OF *DARKMOUTH***

'An action-packed book, rammed full of adventure and danger. I loved reading this book.' **BELLA RIX-CLANCY, AGE 11, LOVEREADING4KIDS**

'*The Haven* is exciting, captivating and unpredictable. I loved it!' **MADELEINE, AGE 12**

'Lots of unexpected twists, interesting characters and a thrilling plot. I would definitely recommend this book.' **CHARLIE, AGE 13**

'Adventurous, and thrilling.' **HARSH BUDHDEO, AGE 11, LOVEREADING4KIDS**

By Simon Lelic:

THE
HAVEN
DEADFALL

SIMON LELIC

HODDER

HODDER CHILDREN'S BOOKS

First published in Great Britain in 2020 by Hodder and Stoughton

1 3 5 7 9 10 8 6 4 2

A CIP catalogue record for this book
is available from the British Library.

ISBN 978 1 444 94764 9

Typeset in Adobe Garamond by Hewer Text UK Ltd, Edinburgh
Printed and bound in Great Britain by Clays Ltd, Elcograf S.p.A

The paper and board used in this book
are made from wood from responsible sources.

Hodder Children's Books
An imprint of
Hachette Children's Group
Part of Hodder and Stoughton
Carmelite House
50 Victoria Embankment
London EC4Y 0DZ

An Hachette UK Company
www.hachette.co.uk

www.hachettechildrens.co.uk

FOR BANJO.
(AND FOR THE *OTHER* LILY AND FLEA ...)

There wasn't much time.

Lily had only bought herself a twenty-minute window, meaning she had approximately six minutes left before the opportunity was lost. Either she found a way to hack the electronic lock on her prison-cell door, or she would remain trapped in this godforsaken pit – perhaps for ever.

The problem was, on top of the time she'd wasted simply trying to access the door's control unit, she couldn't be sure which circuit would release the lock, and which would secure the door permanently shut. And there was the danger she would electrocute herself before she had a chance to find out, simply by touching the exposed circuitry.

Realising she was sweating – from the nerves as much as from the sweltering heat inside the prison cell – Lily turned her attention back to the control board.

Top circuit or bottom? Which would open the door, and which would seal it? It was fifty-fifty. Lily had a small piece of exposed wire in her hand, which she'd swiped from the prison workshop, and she raised it nervously to the circuit board. Top or bottom? Heads or tails? In her mind she flipped a coin, and watched as it landed . . .

Tails.

She moved the wire towards the bottom loop on the control board, intending to bridge the metal solder and create a short circuit – but at the last moment she changed her mind and chose the top loop instead, for no other reason than her instinct telling her to do so. She flinched, expecting a shock, but there was nothing more than a light tingle, like pins and needles, spreading from her fingertips into her palm. There was a fizz as the circuit board fried itself, followed by a decisive-sounding click.

The door remained resolutely shut.

Lily cursed. Rather than freeing herself, she was now trapped inside. There would be no escape now. So much for her plan. She hadn't even got as far as the corridor outside her cell – and this was supposed to be the easy part!

All she could do now was sit and wait for the guards who'd been stationed in the corridor to come back, at which point there would be a full search of the entire cell block. When they found the damage to the control panel in Lily's cell, there was no telling what they would do to her. Beat her, torture her, *kill* her? Anything was possible, because this wasn't an ordinary prison, and the normal rules didn't apply. Lily had been here less than a fortnight – twelve days, according to the notches she'd marked on her cell wall – but already she'd witnessed first-hand how brutal the prison staff could be.

She swore again, and beat her hand against the door. She shut her eyes, furious with herself – and when she opened them, she saw the door had slid slightly ajar. Casting off her surprise, Lily hooked her fingers around the door and tried to open it further. It was like trying to prise apart the doors on a lift, but at least the lock had been disabled. She'd chosen the right circuit after all! The click she'd heard had obviously been the catch disengaging. It hadn't occurred to her that, to open the door, she would have to try to move it manually.

Using all her strength, Lily tugged at the door until there was a gap wide enough for her to squeeze through. She poked her head out first, fully expecting to turn and see Warden Bricknell. Either the warden or one of the guards, who as well as truncheons carried electric cattle prods.

But there was no one.

Lily slipped into the corridor and paused just long enough to try to gauge how much time she had until the guards returned. It was a matter of seconds now, surely. Lily could hear the commotion in the recreation area, which was only two corners away. The fire she'd set as a distraction would probably already have been extinguished, though with any luck the smoke would be lingering.

But even as she listened, Lily could hear the guards' voices getting louder, meaning they were on their way back.

It was time to go.

She darted to her right, away from the sound of the approaching guards. The prison was a maze of metal walkways and stairwells, like the interior of some futuristic industrial complex. Lily had to concentrate hard to recall the sequence of turnings she'd mapped out in her head, as every corner looked the same.

She veered left, right, left again, passing the endless parade of cell doors. The prison was *enormous*. And it was all completely off-grid, Lily was certain. There was no way her confinement here was legal, nor the way the prisoners were treated. It was some kind of *secret* prison, run by ... a spy agency? Some sinister private company? The government itself?

Lily didn't know. She couldn't even be sure where in the country the prison was located, because she'd been drugged before being transported here. Her best guess was that the prison was underground, because in all her time here she was yet to see daylight. And Lily was well aware that if you wanted to hide something in this day and age, beneath the ground was the best place to put it. As a member of the Council at the Haven, she spent much of her life in the secret city below London's streets – or had, before she'd lost her freedom.

She took another turning – the final one, if she'd counted correctly, before the *real* challenge would begin – and hurried to the hatch at the furthest end of the walkway. All around her was the same unremitting creaking sound she'd heard since her very first day in the prison, which had continued since then almost without interruption. It seemed to carry within the metal infrastructure, as though the prison were some huge beast that was constantly groaning in pain. It was hardly the worst aspect of life in the prison, but even so it was like some low-level mental torture, making it hard to sleep, or even think.

As Lily reached the hatch, however, the creaking sound was displaced by a piercing electronic screech. The alarm, she realised. Her escape had been discovered.

Now the chase was well and truly on.

Lily had loosened the screws on the hatch ahead of time, meaning it took only a few seconds for her to lift the metal cover free. Yet when she got her first look at the space behind the panel, she saw it was even tighter than she'd feared. Would she even fit inside?

A memory came back to her, of the narrow tunnel she'd been forced to crawl through to escape the dungeons below Forest Mount – the Gothic manor house turned boarding school that had since become the Haven's home. At least the shaft she faced now was made of metal, meaning there was no danger the tunnel would collapse in on itself. On the other hand, last time she'd only been required to wriggle forwards. Now she also had to *climb*.

She squashed inside. The metal ventilation tube was even hotter than her cell, and the sound of the alarm rebounded mercilessly off the gleaming aluminium. And there wasn't enough space for her to reach down to replace the panel behind her, meaning the guards would easily be able to tell which way she'd gone.

But it was too late to back out now. Lily pressed her shoulders against one side of the shaft, her hands and feet against the other, and began to inch upwards as quickly as she could. The going was painfully slow. Peering up into the darkness, she couldn't even be sure how far she had to climb. The prison seemed to be laid out over just two floors, and Lily couldn't imagine the lowest part of the complex would be more than fifty or sixty metres underground.

Even so, fifty-odd metres was a hell of a long way when you were crammed inside a metal tube, and no short distance were Lily to fall. Her hands were wet with perspiration, and the soles of her prison-issue shoes kept slipping. All it would take would be a momentary lapse of concentration, and she would plunge back where she'd come from, as though she were careering down a water flume – with no splash landing to soften her fall.

As Lily glanced below her, she was blinded by a beam of light.

'Here! She's in here!'

A guard had obviously spotted the displaced panel, and was shining his torch up the ventilation shaft.

'Well, pull her out!' came a voice from back in the corridor, and unless Lily was imagining things, she was certain it belonged to Warden Bricknell. The woman had a shrill, weaselly voice, as grating in its way as the alarm.

'I can't, she . . .' The guard was trying to reach Lily's ankles. 'She's too high up. And I can't fit inside!'

'*Out of my way*,' snapped the warden. The torch beam vanished, and the abrupt return to darkness was as blinding as the onslaught of light had been. Lily didn't stop climbing, though. She estimated she was twenty metres up now, meaning there was no way the guards would be able to seize her from below. But she still had to reach the top of the shaft before the warden could arrange for another team of guards to be there to greet her. She peered up, straining her eyes, and caught a glimpse of the top of the duct. She was nearly there. At most she had another ten metres to go.

Suddenly the torch beam reappeared, and Lily caught a flash of Warden Bricknell peering up at her.

'Your cattle prod,' the warden growled, to someone behind her. 'Give it to me!'

Lily hesitated in confusion. She'd felt the sting of one of those cattle prods several times before, and she had no desire to be shocked again. But what use was a metre-long cattle prod when Lily was already so far out of—

The realisation struck Lily like a fist into her stomach. The shaft. The *aluminium* ventilation shaft. Bricknell intended to electrify the entire thing. One short blast of the cattle prod against the wall of the tunnel down below, and the current would be conducted instantaneously through the metal and into Lily's body. Maybe the shock wouldn't kill her, but the resulting fall certainly would.

She doubled her speed, abandoning all caution. There were still another four or five metres to go to the top of the shaft. It was too far, surely. There was no way Lily would reach safety in time. She tried to move even faster, but her feet slipped and she slid, losing half a metre at least before she caught herself. Her heart thudding, she cursed her clumsiness, and tried desperately to regain the ground she'd lost.

There was a crackle, and Lily saw the warden once again gazing up, her face illuminated this time by the sparks at the business end of the cattle prod she'd been given by one of the guards. She touched the tip of the cattle prod against the metal, and pressed the trigger.

Desperately Lily looked up. Just above her now was a metal grille, marking the top of the duct. She couldn't tell whether it was in contact with the shaft itself, but it was the only option left open to her.

She leapt, propelling herself upwards by pushing at the side of the tunnel with her rubber soles. She felt the fizz of electricity in her fingertips, and realised she'd let go just in time. Her fingers hooked on to the grille, and for an instant Lily was certain she would be electrocuted anyway. But the grille must have been insulated from the duct itself, because the only pain Lily felt was from the wire lattice digging into the flesh of her fingers.

From below her, there was a roar of frustration, and a clatter as the warden tossed the cattle prod aside.

Lily clung on, grateful now for the fitness regime her friend Song had devised for all the members of the Haven's Council: a daily regimen of press-ups, ab crunches, and pull-ups – as many as you could do until you dropped. At first, Lily had barely been able to manage a single pull-up, but over the course of the past two months, she'd managed a personal best of fifteen. Which was all very well, but she'd never had to do one using only her fingertips – when the slightest slip would lead to her certain death.

Reminding herself to breathe, she heaved, raising herself enough that she could swing her heels on to the opening of the air duct where it kinked below the mesh, and carried on its course parallel to the floor below. The duct was bigger here, and when her legs were tucked safely inside, she had space enough to manoeuvre herself so that she was facing forwards.

She crawled, and a few metres on found herself facing another grille. She spun around again, kicking at the grille with her heels, and soon enough it was clattering to the floor. Lily slid gracelessly after it, landing in a bundle and bruising her back. But she didn't care. The room she'd tumbled into was one she'd never seen before, but through the windows on the wall opposite was the unmistakeable glow of *daylight*.

She'd made it!

With a glance to her left and right to ensure there was nobody waiting to seize hold of her, Lily found her feet and hurried forwards. The door beside the windows was locked, but she could tell from the draught of fresh air from beneath it that it would lead her directly outside. And after that? The reality was, Lily didn't know. She might emerge into the middle of a city, or somewhere on some distant moor. Her only priority had been to escape the depths of the prison. After that, she planned to do what Haven kids did best: she would improvise.

Lily took a step back and planted her feet. She wasn't as good at karate as Song was – no one Lily had ever met was a match for Song – but she had more than a few techniques in her arsenal. The most powerful was *ushiro geri*, a spinning back-kick, and after lining up her front foot with the keyhole, Lily whipped her hips around and slammed her heel into the door. There was a crack, and when Lily finished her rotation, she saw the wood panel around the lock was split in two. Now all she had to do was drive at the same place with her shoulder and she would be free. If only her cell door had been so easy to deal with.

The door had even less fight left in it than Lily had expected. It toppled like a domino, and Lily was rewarded by a terrific gust of fresh air, so powerful it almost blew her from her feet. She closed her eyes for an instant, drinking it in, unable to stop herself smiling. Then she was moving again. There was a wall directly in front of her, and she turned, ready to deal with any guards in the same way she'd dealt with that door. But there was no one, just another wall . . . and that was her first indication that something was wrong. Why was nobody trying to stop her? And that smell. What was that smell? So familiar and yet so unexpected. It was as though . . . as though . . .

Lily felt her pace slow. She sensed the smile slip from her face. Keeping her guard up, she turned another corner, and when she saw what lay in front of her, she stopped in her tracks.

'No,' she muttered. 'No, no, *no!*'

Her hands fell uselessly to her sides. And then the tears came. She couldn't stop them. It was all she could do to stand there weeping, as a shadow fell on her from the side and behind her came the unmistakeable sound of laughter.

TWO WEEKS EARLIER

1 PHONEY WAR

Ollie Turner swiped a shoe through the fallen leaves. The ground was a carpet of red and gold, the late autumn chill offset by the warmth of the sun that was filtering through the branches overhead.

It was the first time Ollie had ventured into the wood on the hill below Forest Mount and not immediately wished he was elsewhere. The last time he'd come this far in, he'd witnessed a man being murdered, before Ollie himself had been chased by a rabid beast over the edge of a cliff.

How different, in the sunlight, the wood felt today. In fact, it was almost idyllic: a tranquil retreat from the city, which sprawled all around them at the base of the hill. It was as though Forest Mount was an island, and London was the churning sea.

'This is perfect,' said a voice beside him. 'Just *perfect*. Oh, Ollie, thank you. Thank you so very much.'

His companion's arm was threaded through his. Aunt Fay couldn't see what Ollie could – the autumn colours and the dappled sunlight – but he knew that, even though she was blind, she was experiencing everything just as vividly: the sound of the birds in the trees, the scrunch of the leaves underfoot, the smell of the undergrowth and the air. The wood wasn't the garden Ollie had promised himself he would find for Aunt Fay, after her rooftop retreat in the original Haven had been destroyed, but from her reaction, it seemed she couldn't have been any more delighted. Not that Ollie could really claim credit.

'You were the one who found this place for us, Aunt Fay, remember? All I'm doing is acting as a guide.'

He veered to his left to avoid a low-hanging branch, gently tugging Aunt Fay with him.

'*Tsh*,' said Aunt Fay scoldingly. 'I did nothing more than ask for the help of a friend. It was thanks to *you* that Forest Mount became our home. And you've been counselled before about undervaluing your achievements, Ollie Turner. About the importance of allowing yourself to feel proud.'

He had indeed, by the prime minister of Great Britain herself. Ollie smiled at Aunt Fay's gentle rebuke, not daring to argue. Instead he thought back to how he and his friends had saved the PM's life, in the building that stood not two hundred metres behind him and Aunt Fay now.

'Will you be able to grow things in the wood?' Ollie asked. 'The way you did in the old Haven? I'm sorry it wouldn't be safe to plant vegetables and things out in the open.'

Aunt Fay dismissed his concerns with a wave of her hand. 'We'll absolutely be able to grow things,' she said. 'And the canopy will provide the perfect camouflage, protecting us from outside eyes.' She paused, and shook her head in silent wonder. 'Did you know, Ollie, there are such things nowadays as robots that fly in the sky? Jacqueline told me all about them. Apparently they have cameras that can track your every move!'

Ollie knew Jacqueline as Jack, the Haven's technical wiz. Like Ollie, Jack was on the Haven's Council – a slightly expanded version of the old investigations team, which ensured the Haven ran smoothly, and made all its difficult decisions. And by flying robots, Ollie presumed Aunt Fay meant *drones*. Aunt Fay was an old woman now, and for decades had been content living a simple life inside the Haven's walls, meaning she was somewhat out of touch with modern technical developments. Which, Ollie had come to realise, was exactly the way she liked it.

'Well,' said Ollie, smiling again, 'hopefully they won't bother us here. If your friend in the government has done all he said he would, everyone will assume Forest Mount has been condemned.'

'Monty is a good man,' said Aunt Fay. 'We can trust him to be true to his word.'

Ollie had to admit that so far everything had worked out exactly as Montgomery Ross – the prime minister's special assistant and an ex-Haven member himself – had promised it would. Forest Mount had been decontaminated following the release of a toxic nerve agent, and after that it had been boarded up, and the single pair of access gates sealed – allowing the Haven kids to move in through the tunnels below the hill completely undetected. Two and half months had passed since then, and there had been no sign of trouble, or even of outside interest – from drones or anything else.

The Haven's secret, it seemed, was safe.

Nevertheless, none of the Council members had dropped their guard. The Haven had enemies everywhere, from London's street gangs, to the police, to the British government. Even the prime minister herself would probably have ordered the Haven shut down if she'd known it existed.

And more worrying, as far as Ollie was concerned, was that the prime minister's position as the country's leader was growing more precarious by the day. Since 'Mad' Maddy Sikes had been allowed to escape with a notebook full of the cherished secrets of some of the most powerful people in the country, the government had been at war with itself. Sikes was using the home secretary, Sir Sebastian Crowe – father of Colton Crowe, the boy who'd died attempting to assassinate the prime minister – to undermine the PM at every turn. Sikes's endgame was obvious: she wanted Crowe to take over as PM, while she stood in the shadows pulling his strings.

'Ollie? What's the matter? You seem uneasy.'

They'd stopped walking. Ollie hadn't even noticed.

Nothing's the matter, he was about to say, because he didn't want to ruin Aunt Fay's enjoyment of their stroll in the woodland. But he knew Aunt Fay wouldn't be so easily deterred. She may have been blind, but she saw everything.

'I keep thinking about Sikes and that notebook,' Ollie admitted. 'It feels like . . . like a ticking time bomb. I mean, there's the worry about what will happen to the Haven if the prime minister and Montgomery Ross lose their jobs. More importantly, though, I keep wondering what it would mean for the entire *country* if Sikes were to somehow seize power. She's a monster, Aunt Fay. All she cares about is being in control, never mind who's standing in her way.'

Aunt Fay pursed her lips. She nodded gently.

'And the quiet . . .' Ollie went on, glancing at the peaceful scene around him. 'I know I should be grateful, and I am, truly – but I can't help thinking something's about to happen. Something . . . bad.' He looked up. The sky above them may have been clear, but he had no doubt there were storm clouds on the horizon.

Aunt Fay sighed, and folded Ollie's hand in hers.

'I share your concerns, Ollie. Of course I do.' She turned her unseeing eyes towards the sky, as though she were as wary as Ollie that the sunlight would soon be replaced by shadow. 'Do you know what this time reminds me of? The Phoney War. At the start of World War Two.'

Ollie frowned. He knew quite a lot about the Second World War, he thought – not least that it was during the Blitz that the Haven was first established, by Aunt Fay and a group of her friends. But he'd never heard of a war that had *preceded* it.

'What's the . . . "Phoney war"?' he asked Aunt Fay.

'There was a period after war was declared in 1939 when, for several months, nothing actually happened,' Aunt Fay explained.

'You mean there was no fighting? No battles?'

'That's exactly what I mean.'

'How long did it last?'

'For months on end. It was a very strange time, I can tell you. We lived in fear, but hope as well – that maybe the worst could be avoided.'

'But it wasn't,' said Ollie. 'Was it?'

Aunt Fay looked down. Her features clouded. 'No,' she said. 'After battle finally commenced, we entered what was perhaps the darkest period in humanity's history.' She squeezed Ollie's fingers. 'But my point, Ollie, is that there are *always* challenges ahead. The important thing is to be ready. And, just as crucial, to enjoy the happy times while they last.'

Ollie nodded, knowing that Aunt Fay was right. And he knew that the Haven was better prepared than it had been in months, certainly since he'd joined at the start of the summer. They had a proper home now, for one thing. Despite its unsavoury history and somewhat sinister appearance, Forest

Mount was a considerable improvement on the abandoned London Underground station that had been the Haven's home since the old library had burned down.

Plus, of all the buildings in London, Forest Mount was one of the most easily defended. Partly this was due to its position high on a hill, with a cliff edge at the hillside's back, and thick woodland skirting it to the front. Mainly, though, Ollie and the others had Jack to thank. She'd worked tirelessly since they'd moved in to overhaul and upgrade the surveillance systems in the tunnels that provided access, and to modify Forest Mount's defences. If someone – *anyone* – tried to bother Ollie and his friends here, the Haven would be more than ready.

'Oh,' said Aunt Fay, suddenly brightening. 'I almost forgot . . .' She reached into the pocket of her woollen overcoat. 'Here,' she said. 'Happy birthday, Ollie.'

Ollie blinked in surprise. Aunt Fay was holding out a small package, neatly wrapped in brown paper and tied with a purple ribbon. The reality was, Ollie had quite forgotten it was his fourteenth birthday today. He and Aunt Fay had ventured out on their walk while most of the Haven kids were eating breakfast, meaning he was yet to see any of his closest friends. Really, it was the first peaceful hour he'd spent awake in weeks, to the extent he'd completely lost track of dates.

'You've given me my present,' said Aunt Fay, gesturing to the woodland around them. 'Now it's my turn to give you yours.'

Ollie smiled, touched. 'What is it?' he said, accepting the package gratefully.

'Why don't you open it and find out?'

Ollie carefully unfastened the paper. Whatever it was, it seemed to be made of wood. Ollie removed the last of the wrapping and turned Aunt Fay's gift over – and when he did, he felt his breath catch in his throat. 'Where . . . where did you get this?'

'One of the younger children made the frame. It's oak, taken from some of the wood we salvaged from the staircase in the old Haven. It's beautiful, isn't it? I can tell from its feel. It reminds me of trailing my hand along that enormous curved banister.'

Ollie ran his fingertips around the photo frame, tracing the contours of the wood, and for an instant he, too, was transported back to the old library – he could almost smell the books. He studied the frame and noticed that in one corner, a small 'H' surrounded by a triangle had been inscribed: the Haven's symbol and secret emblem.

'As for the photo,' Aunt Fay went on, 'once again we have Jacqueline to thank. I asked her whether there might be some way we could find you a memento of the people you'd lost, and she wasted no time in setting to work. She said something about . . . social mediums, I think it was?'

'Social media,' Ollie corrected, smiling again, his eyes glued to the photograph of his parents. And it wasn't just of them. Nancy, Ollie's guardian, was in the photo, too, as well as Ollie himself. He was sitting on his father's shoulders, so he can't have been more than four or five years old. And unless Ollie's mind was playing tricks on him, he was sure he remembered the day first-hand – this very scene, in fact. His mother and father and their best friend, Nancy, were standing on the bank of the River Thames, the water glistening in the summer sun directly behind them. They'd been on a boat ride, and had been on their way to buy ice cream.

'Thank you, Aunt Fay,' Ollie said, meaning it from the bottom of his heart. He knew he would never forget the faces of his parents, or of Nancy – all of whom had been murdered by Maddy Sikes – but even so, his memories were all he had. Since the day he'd been snatched from his bed in the middle of the night, and inducted into the Haven's secret mission – to help kids in trouble, whoever they might be – he'd been forced to accept that everything he'd ever owned was lost to him for ever. The framed photograph Aunt Fay had given him represented the one and only physical reminder in Ollie's possession of his old life. 'Really,' he said again, 'thank you.'

Aunt Fay's smile was as bright as the sunshine she was standing in.

They walked on, savouring the early morning peace. There was the faintest sound in the distance of London's streets coming to life, but for that short while the real world seemed light years away – and all of Ollie's worries, as well.

Eventually they returned to the school. Forest Mount had been a manor house originally, before it had been turned into a private boarding school – one of the most exclusive in the country. Even so, it was as a school that Ollie and the others had first known it, and it was how they continued to refer to the main building. It seemed fitting: after all, the Haven was partly a school as well, and even though it was his birthday, Ollie had lessons to attend, as well as a class to teach.

'Happy birthday, Ollie!'

As he and Aunt Fay walked the building's corridors, the children they passed called out their greetings. Everyone had a smile on their face, and most seemed to know it was Ollie's birthday. He flushed at the attention, shyly thanking the well-wishers he passed.

'Such a wonderful atmosphere,' said Aunt Fay, gleeful at the jovial mood. Maybe the sense of occasion helped, but really it had been like this at Forest Mount since the day they'd moved in. People were just so pleased to be here. They'd never seen Forest Mount as Ollie and some of his friends had: as a place of fear and intimidation, where most of the pupils had walked around with their heads low and their eyes on the ground, desperate to avoid the prefects' attentions. As in the woods, and not for the first time, Ollie was struck by the contrast.

'And talking of things *growing*,' Aunt Fay said, referring to their earlier conversation, 'I hear certain affections have been blooming lately, too.' She turned to Ollie as they walked, a girlish glint in her expression.

'What do you mean?' said Ollie, his flush deepening.

'I mean *love*, Ollie Turner,' said Aunt Fay, unabashed, and something inside Ollie gave an uncomfortable wriggle. 'Some of the children have been gossiping in my presence. They seem to forget that, although I can't see, there is nothing wrong with my ears. And I hear relationships have been sprouting up all over the place. I believe Imani has a girlfriend now, as does Soloman. And even young Lily seems to have found a suitor.'

What Aunt Fay had said was true. Imani was dating a girl who'd once been her sworn enemy, from back when they'd belonged to rival gangs. Sol, Ollie's best friend, was going out with Keya, another one of Ollie's closest friends. As for Lily, Ollie had heard that she had started seeing Casper Sloane, a sixteen-year-old boy who ran the Haven's kitchen and food stores, and who'd recently been nominated to the Council. Not that it was any of Ollie's business. Why should *he* care who Lily chose to go out with?

'Will you come to the Council meeting?' Ollie asked Aunt Fay, changing the subject. 'I know everyone would love for you to be there.'

'Perhaps I will stop in and say hello,' said Aunt Fay. If she'd noticed the way Ollie had shifted the conversation, she made no comment. 'But I will make myself scarce before you settle down to business.'

Ollie wasn't surprised by Aunt Fay's answer. As the only adult at the Haven, she was conscious not to interfere in the way it was run, believing it was kids themselves who were best placed to judge other children's needs, and who should be trusted to make their own decisions. Still, Ollie was glad Aunt Fay would come along for the beginning of the meeting, which was due to start in the control room shortly. She was so determined to avoid becoming a nuisance, she was something of an elusive figure at the Haven, and nobody got to see her as much as they would have liked – Ollie included.

With Ollie still acting as a guide, they turned off the main corridor, and took a curving, stone-flagged passageway that would lead them to the East Wing. Forest Mount was something of a warren, but by now Ollie knew his way around intimately.

The control room was the old headmaster's office: a huge, extravagantly decorated room, with a large bay window overlooking the school's central courtyard, and a fireplace big enough to stand in. There was none of the fusty, gentlemen's club feeling that had marked out the room when Professor Strain had occupied it, however. Instead of leather-bound books on obscure Russian history, and gilt-framed photographs and

certificates, the room was packed with computers, printed maps
– some of which had been pinned haphazardly to the wall – and
handwritten flow charts. It was a vast improvement, as far as
Ollie was concerned. Strain's former office had become the new
Haven's nerve centre, as ramshackle and functional as the
control room had been in the old library.

When Ollie and Aunt Fay entered, Ollie was surprised to see
the seats around the central table were all empty. He was a minute
or two late, and he'd expected the meeting to already have begun.

He turned to his right, and saw everyone was present
nonetheless: Jack and Lily and Flea; Sol, Keya and Imani; as
well as Erik, Song, Casper Sloane and Errol, Jack's brother,
who'd been elected to the Council to represent the Haven's
younger members. But instead of debating the various items on
the Council's agenda, they were gazing in silence at the wall-
mounted television Jack had installed above the fireplace.

'Guys? What's going on?'

As one, the Council members turned, their eyes locking on
to Ollie. No one said 'happy birthday' or anything else. Instead,
their faces were white, and every single one of Ollie's friends
seemed lost for words.

Soon enough Ollie realised why. He looked at the television
himself – at the images that were playing out on the BBC's news
channel, and the headlines that were scrolling along the bottom
of the screen.

27

'Ollie?' said Aunt Fay. 'What's the matter, Ollie? What's happened?' From her expression, she'd clearly become attuned to the sudden shift in atmosphere, and the fear that permeated the room.

Ollie took her hand. 'It's over, Aunt Fay. The Phoney War.' He looked at the television again, and squeezed Aunt Fay's hand tightly. 'The real battle is about to begin.'

2 PUBLIC ENEMY

The debate around the Council table was as heated as Ollie had ever seen it. His friends sounded angry, but more than anything, Ollie knew, they were afraid. And he didn't blame them. From feeling relatively secure in their new home a few moments ago, it was as though they were suddenly under siege.

On the television screen above the fireplace, the news programme was reporting on the speech Sebastian Crowe had just made to parliament, with the scrolling tickertape at the bottom of the screen echoing sound bites of the policy the home secretary had announced.

'*Crackdown declared*,' ran the headline. '*Armed police to take to the streets to root out "undesirables" and "terrorist elements".*' It was hard for Ollie to hear over his friends' furious voices, but he could just about follow Crowe's words as the BBC showed clips of the home secretary's speech on repeat.

'. . . *country is under threat from terrorist organisations such as the one that was responsible for the* brainwashing *and* radicalisation *of my only son*,' Crowe was saying. Here he paused, and the camera drew tight as the home secretary pretended to wipe away a tear. It was all an act, of course. Ollie knew full well how much Sebastian Crowe had loathed and neglected his son, Colton, which was why in the end Ollie had felt some sympathy for the boy, despite everything he'd done.

'*The whole world was able to witness for itself the horrific consequences of this country's previous policy of inaction,*' Crowe went on. '*Of its excessive tolerance.*'

At the Haven, tolerance was a guiding principle, but Crowe somehow managed to twist the word into something evil-sounding – a concept to be ashamed of.

'*It was only through immense good fortune that the prime minister's life was spared during the cowardly attack last September, but that doesn't change the fact we have allowed terrorists to infiltrate our society,*' Crowe said. '*They have already forced the postponement of the general election, directly threatening the democratic process. More than that, they have gained such a footing that they are able to prey on society's most vulnerable, to poison their minds, and then hide in the shadows as they allow their poison to take effect. Exactly as they did with my poor, innocent son.*'

There was another pause, another fake tear.

'*But it* ends here,' Crowe declared, and his expression switched from sorrowful to angry – this time, Ollie could tell, the emotion was real. Probably he was furious at Colton Crowe for having put him in such a compromised position – in any other circumstances, his son's actions would no doubt have ended his career – but the home secretary was using that anger, and the situation, to his political advantage, twisting the truth so that both he and his son appeared as victims.

'*As of today,*' Crowe went on, getting to the meat of his new policy, '*and in the interests of protecting the freedom-loving citizens of this country, any organisation of ten or more people that fails to register and gain authorisation for its activities from a newly formed government committee will be declared* illegal. *Further, if such organisations choose to continue their operations rather than comply with the law, they will be declared* enemies of the state, *and will face the appropriate repercussions.*'

Ollie braced himself, knowing already what was coming next.

'*This applies to any group or association* irrespective of the age of its members – *and most particularly to the shadowy group of fanatics known as* the Haven.'

Crowe paused for effect, and Ollie noticed that the room had gone quiet, as his friends also tuned in to the repeat of the home secretary's speech.

Crowe said, '*The Haven is a secret organisation of radicals whose existence has only recently become known to the authorities. The organisation tricks the young and vulnerable into swearing allegiance in return for food and shelter, and the promise of a better life.* But it is all a sham. *Rather than being cared for, Haven recruits are forcibly coerced, and exposed to the vilest propaganda. This despicable organisation uses* children *to do its dirty work. Indeed, I have seen direct and irrefutable evidence,*' the home secretary went on, '*that the Haven is at the centre of the assault on our democracy. It was the Haven that was responsible for the brainwashing of my son, and the attempt on the prime minister's life.*'

There were mutters of outrage around the table, but Crowe's poisonous rant continued.

'*I will therefore make it my personal mission in my role as home secretary,*' he said, and here he turned to face the television camera, so that he appeared to be speaking to Ollie directly, '*to ensure that these Haven* terrorists *are hunted down and brought to justice,* however old they may be. *Moreover, anyone aiding or abetting the Haven and its associates will be deemed guilty of conspiring to commit treason against the state. This country is under attack, my honourable friends,*' Crowe thundered, addressing his fellow members of parliament, '*and it is time we finally struck back!*'

At that moment, the picture on the TV froze, and the news report cut back to the presenter in the studio. Sebastian Crowe's vengeful face – his dark eyebrows arrowed in fury, his black hair sticking out from his skull in angry tufts – was captured and framed in the top corner of the screen. He looked like a craggier, meaner version of Colton Crowe.

Below the image, the newscaster was delving into the details of the home secretary's draconian new policy: the so-called

'Emergency Action Plan'. Henceforth across the United Kingdom, the police would be authorised to carry firearms, with fewer restrictions on using them. Their stop and search powers would be expanded, meaning anyone could be detained in the street, without the police having to justify it. Immigration rules were to be tightened, with an immediate suspension of asylum applications, and anyone without a right to remain in the country, or without a permanent address, would be subject to arrest. Further, a curfew was to be put in place in the UK's towns and cities for under-eighteens, in response to what the government was calling the 'weaponisation' of the country's disaffected youth. No children would be allowed on the streets after 9 p.m., and no groups of four kids or more would be permitted to gather, even in daylight hours, unless a supervising adult was present.

'It'll be like living in a police state,' came a voice at Ollie's side. Ollie turned, and saw that his best friend, Sol, was watching the television screen as intently as Ollie, while the rest of the Council returned to its heated discussion.

On screen, the BBC was now showing footage of MPs in the House of Commons cheering the home secretary's speech. On the opposition benches, support appeared to be more muted. Some MPs sat there with stony faces and arms folded across their chests. Indeed, several looked as distraught as Ollie felt, and just as powerless to intervene. Conspicuous by her absence was the prime minister herself, making it clear what *she* thought of this new policy. On the other hand, it was clear too that she no longer had the power to stop it, meaning she had become as weak in her position as Ollie had feared.

Ollie turned from the screen, and instead tuned in to what his friends were saying. They were talking over each other, holding several conflicting conversations at once, so that Ollie only heard snatches of what was being said.

'. . . seriously blaming *us* for the assassination attempt on the prime minister?' Erik was asking, as Song threw her hands in the air. 'We *saved* the PM! If anyone should be branded a terrorist, it's . . .'

'. . . a crackpot – as deranged as his son,' another voice interrupted. Lily's maybe? '*He's* the one who needs locking up, not . . .'

'. . . like to see him try to hunt *me* down,' came Flea's voice. 'It would take more than a few cops carrying guns to . . .'

Ollie closed his eyes and shook his head. 'It's Sikes,' he muttered. 'It's all Sikes.'

'What was that, Ollie?'

Jack was seated in her wheelchair to Ollie's left, and when Ollie opened his eyes at the sound of her voice, he saw her frowning at him concernedly. Sol was looking on from Ollie's right. Ollie was about to repeat himself, but the din in the room was so loud that he only got as far as opening his mouth before he shut it again and shook his head.

Sol banged his fist on the table. 'Order!' he yelled. '*Order!*'

There was an abrupt silence, and everyone in the room turned Sol's way – including Ollie. Sol smiled at him and shrugged. 'It worked for the Speaker in the House of Commons,' he said, nodding towards the television screen. 'I thought I'd give it a go here.' Gently he nudged his elbow into Ollie's bicep. 'The floor's all yours, mate. You wanted to say something?'

Ollie looked around, and saw everyone was now looking at him: Jack, Sol, Lily, Flea, Song, Erik, Keya, Imani, Casper and Errol. The Council members were seated around Professor Strain's old desk, which was easily big enough to accommodate them all. There were a dozen mismatched chairs spaced around it, with Strain's huge old leather desk chair at its head. Generally Ollie tried to avoid that particular chair in Council meetings if he could, even though he was technically the chairperson, but today he found himself sitting in it, staring down the length of the table.

He cleared his throat. 'I said . . . I said, it's all Sikes,' he told his friends. 'Sebastian Crowe is just her puppet, as are half of those MPs who were cheering him on. Sikes is the one who told the authorities about the Haven – her version of what the Haven is, anyway – and she's the one who's instructed Crowe to hunt us down. *She's* behind this, and she won't stop until the Haven has been destroyed.'

There was silence around the table as the others digested what he'd said. They all would have known that Ollie was right, just as they knew that Sikes was a far more dangerous opponent than Sebastian Crowe would ever be. The Haven had defeated Sikes twice already, and *still* she seemed to be winning.

Ollie felt a flutter of despair, mirroring his friends' reactions, but then there was a touch on his arm, and he turned to see Aunt Fay standing at his shoulder. He felt a surge of warmth, and with it renewed confidence and determination.

'But the reality is,' he told his friends, his fractured voice becoming more resolute, 'nothing's changed. We knew this would be coming – this or something like it. We knew Sikes would use the secrets in that notebook to blackmail the ruling party into doing what she wants. And she's got at least one major television network on her side, too, remember, as well as the Metropolitan Police Commissioner. So it was always going to come to this at some point.'

Ollie glanced around the table.

'But,' he went on, 'this is how it's *always* been for the Haven.' Once again he met his friends' eyes. 'We've always had to hide. We've always had to fend for ourselves. We stand alone, but it's what we do best. We stand for freedom and tolerance and for helping people who can't help themselves. It's why the Haven was established. Nothing Sebastian Crowe says, or anything Maddy Sikes does, changes that.'

Ollie was heartened to see heads around the table begin to nod, and expressions of determination on his friends' faces that matched the way he was suddenly feeling.

'And I know that maybe it doesn't feel like it, given what we've just been watching, but really we're in a stronger position now than we have been in ages,' Ollie went on. 'We have a home now. A proper home. Sikes doesn't know where we are. Nobody does, thanks to Aunt Fay.' He had a brief flash of doubt, remembering again how precarious the PM's position was – and by extension, the position of their protector, Montgomery Ross – but he tried not to let it show. 'More importantly, we're *united*. Crowe and his lackeys are just a faction. Maybe they're the dominant force in the government at the moment, but it can't last for ever. It can't last as long as the *Haven* has lasted. Right?'

'*Right*,' Jack echoed, from Ollie's left.

'Hear, hear,' said Sol, grinning as once again he mimicked the MPs in the House of Commons.

But then someone started to clap – a slow, sarcastic beat from the far end of the table – and Ollie didn't have to look to know who was responsible.

3 COUNCIL CONUNDRUM

'Nice speech, PJ,' said Flea, still slapping his meaty hands together. Strain's old desk chair was Flea's preferred position at the Council's table, but second best was the seat directly opposite, at the *other* head of the table, which was where he sat now. 'It almost sounds as though you're making a bid to take over as leader again,' he said.

Ollie saw Lily, Flea's twin sister, roll her eyes. Everyone knew the question of the Haven's leadership had been settled. Lily had proposed the solution herself: they would *all* lead, through the Council. Ollie was chair, but that meant he was in charge of the agenda, nothing more. Flea was the only one who remained reluctant to accept the way things were now, mainly because he'd had designs on leadership himself – before, as he saw it, Ollie had come along and messed things up for him. Then again, Flea had taken against Ollie from the moment he'd first laid eyes on him, so he was always going to find some reason to criticise Ollie. He'd even refused to abandon the nickname he'd given Ollie: PJ, on account of the fact that the first time Flea had seen him, Ollie had been wearing his pyjamas.

'Did you have something you wanted to add, Flea?' Ollie asked, refusing to take the bait.

Flea stood up. 'Too right I've got something I want to add. I say, forget all this talk about *hiding*. PJ was right about one thing: we are stronger now than we have been for a long time. Our numbers are growing. We have the resources we need. So rather than cowering in a corner and hoping we outlast Sikes, and Crowe, and the rest of those deadbeats in parliament, let's *fight back*.'

'Fight back?' Sol said. 'As in, fight the *government*? The entire *police force*?' He gave a humourless grin and shook his head. 'I know you've taken some knocks to the noggin over the years, Fleabag, but I didn't realise you'd gone totally insane.'

'It's not insane,' growled Flea. 'It's common sense. We all know the PM is on her way out, right? She's losing her grip, and Crowe and his lackeys are on the verge of taking over.'

'Sikes, you mean,' said Erik. 'Maddy Sikes is behind this all, remember?'

'*Exactly*,' said Flea, as though Erik had argued his point. 'And when the PM falls, it will be Sikes who is effectively running the country. Meaning she'll be more powerful than ever. Untouchable, in fact.'

Ollie shifted uncomfortably in his seat, aware that Flea was right.

'At which point it will be too late,' Flea pressed. 'We have to stop her *now*, while there's still a chance we can get to her.'

'But *how*?' Lily asked. 'As far as I can see, she's untouchable already. And we don't even know where she *is*.'

There were one or two nods, Ollie noted – most vociferously from Casper Sloane, who reached and took Lily's hand. Ollie tried to ignore the tightening in his stomach.

'The book,' said Flea. 'The notebook. The one containing all the secrets that Sikes is using to blackmail people. If we can somehow get it back, we could . . .'

Jack was already shaking her head. 'Sikes has probably destroyed the notebook already. She already *knows* everybody's secrets. And if I were her, I'd have been busy collecting evidence to make sure nobody could try to deny what I accused them of. I'd tap people's phones. Probably set up some CCTV. Secret cameras – in people's homes, ideally. And what I'd do is, I'd build a database of everything anyone with any influence has ever done wrong, and I'd make sure they *knew* I knew about it, and then there'd be nothing anyone could do to stop me – secret notebook or not. *That's* how you build power. *Information* is the key – not money, which is what most people think.'

Ollie joined the others in staring at Jack.

'What?' said Jack, defensive.

'Nothing,' said Erik. 'Just . . .'

'You seem to have given it a lot of thought,' Sol finished for him. 'That's all.'

41

Sol looked slightly nervous, Ollie would have said. Everyone did. He watched as Jack surveyed the room.

'I don't have a database on *you* guys, if that's what you're thinking,' she said. There were smiles of relief around the table, before Jack added, 'Then again, that's what I would say. Isn't it?' She smiled, as though she were joking, but with Jack it was always hard to be sure.

'Look,' said Flea, getting back to business, 'all I'm saying is, we need to expose Sikes somehow. *Prove* she's been blackmailing people behind the scenes. And we shouldn't be afraid to take her on.' He stood tall, drawing back his shoulders. 'As the ancient Chinese philosopher Sun Tzu said, "If you know your enemy and know yourself, you need not fear the result of a hundred battles."'

There was a momentary, mystified silence.

'Sun *who*?' said Sol eventually.

'Sun Tzu,' said Flea tightly. 'He wrote *The Art of War*, if you must know.'

'As in a *book*?' said Imani.

'A book you *read*?' added Keya.

'Well, I . . .' Flea responded, shifting slightly.

'He didn't read it,' said Lily, rolling her eyes again. 'He started to when he found it in the library here, but gave up after the first four pages. Instead he went on Wikipedia and decided to memorise a few quotes.'

'That still counts as reading!' insisted Flea, over the laughter. 'And my point stands. Sikes is only going to get stronger. The more we wait, the weaker we become.' His eyes fixed on Ollie. 'I *know* you know I'm right, PJ.'

To his – and probably Flea's – surprise, Ollie found himself nodding. 'You are right,' he said. 'And there's nobody who wants to see Sikes defeated as much as I do. I *promise* you that.'

Flea crossed his arms, satisfied the argument was won.

'But I also agree with Lily and the others,' Ollie went on. 'I don't see how we can get to Sikes. More importantly, I can't help thinking that she wants us to try.' He gestured towards the TV. 'Crowe's speech, his Emergency Action Plan: it's Sikes making fun of us. Poking us with a stick. She *wants* us to react, to draw us out of hiding. She wants to destroy *us* just as much as we want to destroy *her*.'

Ollie felt a tap on his shoulder. Sol was pointing at the television screen.

'I reckon you're more right than you realise, Ollie,' he said. 'Look.' The news report had moved on, and Sol used the remote control to turn up the volume.

'. . . *already seeing signs of the government's tough new policy in action*,' a news reporter was saying. '*This group of illegal immigrants was intercepted crossing the Channel by Her Majesty's Coastguard*.' On screen, a group of kids ranging in age from around eight to sixteen were huddled in a makeshift prison cell.

They looked afraid, hungry and utterly exhausted. '*According to a Home Office minister,*' the news reporter went on, '*the children are suspected Haven sympathisers, lured to the country by false promises and extremist propaganda, and ferried here by adult people-smugglers who are in the Haven's pay.*'

There was an outburst of fury around the Council table, and Ollie was forced to call for quiet.

'*This man,*' the reporter went on, as a picture of Professor Strain appeared on the screen, '*has already been charged with being one of the Haven's ringleaders, and he and others like him – including a shadowy figure known only to the authorities as "Aunt Fay" – are suspected of building an army of vulnerable children to rival the biggest gangs in the country, involving them in all kinds of criminal activities, and who are likely to be used in future attacks against the state.*'

'Ridiculous!'

'Outrageous!'

'What a load of—'

'Quiet, everyone, please!' Ollie interrupted, as once again his friends' anger spilled over. Ollie knew every word coming through the television was based on lies, but he was intent on hearing the rest of the report. He wanted to know exactly what the Haven was up against.

'. . . *young refugees will be detained in this secure government facility, before being sent back to the countries they came from,*' the reporter was saying, and this time a picture of a building

44

surrounded by barbed wire filled the screen. '*The Home Office refused to be drawn on how long the repatriation process would take, saying only that the nation's security was the priority, and that the main focus in terms of resources was on stopping the influx of Haven sympathisers, not on the comfort and wellbeing of a group of young terrorists who should never have attempted travel to this country in the first place.*'

This time Ollie was unable to hold back the explosion of voices around the table. He looked at Sol, hoping his friend would again call for order, but Sol's eyes were fixed on the television screen, and the images of the terrified refugees. Sol's jaw was clamped tight, and there was an expression in his eyes of outright fury.

'Sol?' Ollie said. 'Are you OK?'

Before his friend could answer, Errol's voice cut through the commotion. 'How do they know about Aunt Fay?' he asked. 'How could they *possibly*?' He was looking at Jack, who laid a hand on her brother's shoulder.

'Dodge,' said Ollie, meeting Jack's eye. 'Dodge must have told Sikes everything.'

A quiet fell upon them, as the Haven kids remembered their former leader, who'd sacrificed his life to save them, but only after betraying the Haven to Maddy Sikes.

'What do you say now, PJ?' said Flea, breaking the silence. 'Do you still think we should sit here and hide? Those refugees will be just the beginning, you know. You heard it yourself: the government is already cracking down everywhere. There are kids out there who *need our help*.'

On screen there was an image of the refugees locked in their holding cell. With the wire mesh and the cramped conditions, it reminded Ollie of a pen for animals on their way to slaughter.

'We have to save them, Ollie,' came Sol's voice. 'We *have* to.' He spoke softly, but there was a fierce determination in his voice.

'But what about what Ollie said before?' said Lily. 'It *has* to be a trap. Sikes *wants* us to try to rescue those refugees. She's even allowing us to see where they're being held prisoner. She's taunting us, just like Ollie said.'

'So?' said Flea.

'So we shouldn't just rush in without thinking,' Lily pressed. 'We should—'

'What?' interrupted Flea. 'Leave them to rot?'

'No!' said Lily. 'Of course not! But we should sit tight for the time being, wait until things die down. If we try to rescue those kids *now*, we'll be doing exactly what Sikes wants us to, and then we'll *all* end up behind bars. And then we won't be able to help anyone! We have a responsibility to the kids already here not to compromise the Haven's safety.'

'So we wait,' said Flea derisively. 'And in the meantime, Crowe or Sikes or whoever's really in charge will lock up *more* kids – the very kids we swore to protect. Maybe Sikes is doing it to spite us, but that doesn't mean we shouldn't *act*.'

Lily appeared torn, and Ollie knew exactly how she felt. Flea was right: helping kids like the ones Sikes had locked up was the reason the Haven had been set up in the first place. On the other hand, there was the very real possibility that, by doing so, they would be putting the entire organisation at risk.

'I call a vote,' said Flea, cutting in on Ollie's train of thought. 'I can do that. Right?' His voice was laced with sarcasm. 'I mean, that is what this Council is *for*?'

Ollie nodded. 'Of course you can. Anyone can call for a vote at any time.'

'Right, then,' said Flea. 'Well, I say we rescue those kids *now*. Who's with me?'

'Wait,' said Ollie. 'Let's do this properly. All in favour of taking action immediately, as Flea suggests, raise your hands.'

Flea's hand was in the air before Ollie had even finished speaking. Sol shot his hand up, too. Keya's followed, as did Imani's and Song's.

'And who thinks we should hold back?' said Ollie. 'Play the waiting game. Leave it a few weeks before we do anything, hope that some of the pressure eases off.'

Lily hesitated, but hers was the first hand in the air. Unsurprisingly Casper raised his, too. Jack took longer, but eventually she held up her arm, as did Erik. Errol looked around uncertainly, then raised his hand nervously as well.

'That's five apiece,' said Flea. 'Looks like yours is the deciding vote, PJ.' He stared at Ollie defiantly. 'So what's it to be?'

4 OLD WOUNDS

'Sun Tzu,' said Sol, shaking his head. 'Honestly.'

He and Ollie were walking side by side along the corridor outside the control room. The Council meeting was over, and until Sol had spoken, Ollie had been focused on the floor, wondering whether he'd made the right decision.

'What I want to know,' Sol went on, 'is what Flea was doing in the library in the first place. I mean, it's hardly his natural habitat.' He thought for a moment. 'Maybe he got lost on his way to the toilets. Got trapped amid the stacks of books, and couldn't find his way out again.'

He smiled, and Ollie did his best to mirror it. Sol wasn't fooled, however. Noticing Ollie's uncertainty, Sol's smile dipped.

'You did the right thing, mate,' Sol told him, dropping his hand on to Ollie's shoulder. 'We can't just leave those kids to suffer. Old Fleabag was right about that much, at least.'

The rest of the Council members were further along the corridor. Jack and Lily were at the rear, heads down and whispering between themselves, as though sharing their misgivings about the Council's decision. Flea was at the head of the procession, clearly eager to lead the way now that his motion had passed.

'Yeah, well,' said Ollie, attempting to make light of the way he was feeling. 'That's what worries me most of all: the fact that, for the first time ever, me and Flea actually *agreed* on something.'

Sol laughed softly.

They walked on. After a moment, Ollie turned to his friend. 'Can I ask you something?' he said.

'Sure,' said Sol. 'But if you're looking for reassurance about Jack, you're asking the wrong person. The stuff she thinks about . . .' He shook his head. 'I guess we should be grateful she's on our side. She'd make one hell of an evil genius if she ever decided to put her mind to it.'

'It wasn't about Jack,' said Ollie, smiling again. 'I wondered . . . I wondered why, before, with the vote . . . why you were so sure. So . . .' Ollie recalled the look on his friend's face when they'd watched the pictures of the refugees trapped in their cell. 'So determined, I mean. So adamant we should help those kids, in spite of the risk.'

Sol's expression set firm. 'It's what we do, isn't it?' he said, in a voice that didn't sound like Sol's at all. 'It's the reason the Haven exists.'

'No, I know, but . . .' Ollie stole a glance at his friend, aware that he must have accidentally touched a nerve. 'It felt like more than that. That's all.' What he didn't say, but he was thinking, was that when he'd noticed the way his friend had reacted, it had seemed as though Sol was taking the refugees' imprisonment somehow . . . personally. He'd looked the way Ollie always felt whenever anyone mentioned Maddy Sikes.

'Sorry,' said Ollie at last. 'I shouldn't have asked. I didn't mean to pry.'

After a short, uncomfortable silence, Sol sighed. 'No,' he said. 'I'm the one who's sorry. It's not really fair, is it? I mean, I know all about your past. About how *you* got here.' He gestured to the walls around them. He cracked an unexpected grin. 'I was there, remember? The day we first brought you to the Haven? And if I recall correctly, you were wearing a delightful ensemble of dinosaur-themed sleepwear – skin tight, of course, with plenty of skin showing around the wrists and ankles – carefully smeared with sewer juice and rat's poo.'

Ollie nudged him as they walked, knocking Sol off balance. 'Yeah, well,' he said, grinning as his friend nudged him back. 'Maybe if I'd had more warning about what I was getting into, I would have dressed for the occasion.'

'And put on some shoes, maybe?' Sol suggested, referring to the fact that Ollie had also been barefoot.

They both looked down, and Ollie wiggled his toes inside his pair of Adidas trainers, remembering the squelch of sewage beneath his soles. 'Shoes would have been nice,' he conceded.

They reached the doorway that led into what had once been the dungeons below the building. The rest of the Council had already disappeared down the narrow staircase, their shadows ahead merging with the dark.

'Age before beauty,' said Ollie, gesturing Sol in front of him. They entered the gloomy stairwell, and started down the narrow stone steps. Ollie shivered at the chill in the musty air.

'What I was saying,' Sol began, not looking back at Ollie as they descended, 'was that I know about your past, but I've never told you about mine.'

Which was true, but wasn't unusual at the Haven. Everyone who ended up here had experienced misfortune of one kind or another. But few people spoke about their pasts if they could help it. Most preferred to focus on how fortunate they were to have found safety – to be among friends – than on the things they were trying to forget.

'You don't have to, you know,' Ollie said. 'I meant what I said about not wanting to pry.'

'Yeah, I know. But it's not like it's some big secret or anything. Compared to half the kids at the Haven, I consider myself lucky. But that doesn't mean . . .' Sol took a deep breath and expelled the air. 'That doesn't mean it doesn't bother me what my parents went through.'

Ollie waited for his friend to go on.

'They came here on a boat. Illegally, I guess, if that's the right word. I was six months old at the time, so I don't remember any of this, obviously. But their friend told me. After they got sent back.'

'Sent back?'

'Yeah,' said Sol, still facing forwards. 'They applied for asylum, the way you're supposed to do. You know, admit who you are, where you've come from, and ask the government for help. Just that. Just some *help*.'

'Where did they come from?'

'Sudan, Africa. And when my parents left, the country had basically been at war with itself for decades. They'd lost their home six times. *Six*. My father lost his hand. My mother, she . . . she suffered, too. And after they had me, they decided they would do whatever they could to get away. Because where they were, kids were getting snatched from their families.'

'How come?' said Ollie.

'To turn them into soldiers. To get them fighting in the stupid war.'

'So they fled to protect you?'

Sol nodded in the gloom. 'But it wasn't enough. What they went through. The things they experienced before they left, all the dangers they encountered on the journey. They almost *drowned* crossing the English Channel. But when they got here, the government said they couldn't stay. They said Sudan was *stabilising*.' Sol said this last word derisively.

'You mean it wasn't?'

'The old war turned into a new one. My parents sacrificed *everything* to try to get me a better life, to have the chance to raise me without waking up every night thinking the noise they'd heard was someone coming to murder them with a machete. But instead, they got put on the first plane back to the hellhole they'd just escaped from.'

'And they left you behind?'

Sol stopped and turned. 'They had no *choice*. What were they *supposed* to do?'

'No, I know . . . I didn't mean . . .'

Once again Sol sighed. 'Yeah,' he said. 'Yeah, I know you didn't. Sorry.'

Ollie was aware how painful it must have been for Sol to talk about his parents, and he realised now why his friend had been so adamant they should try to help the refugees who'd been imprisoned.

'They left me with a friend of theirs,' Sol went on. 'Someone who'd escaped the civil war, too. Zahir was his name. He was nice. Kind to me. He didn't have to take me in. But he died when I was ten. After that, there was no way I was going to take a chance on going to the authorities for help. Not after what happened to my parents.'

Sol started down the stairwell again, and Ollie followed him.

'Do you . . . I mean, you don't have to answer this. But do you know what did happen to your parents? Back in Sudan, I mean. Did they . . . are they . . .'

'I don't know. I don't know what happened to them. I don't even know if they're alive. Zahir tried to make contact with them, to let them know I was safe, to see if *they* were safe, but he never got word. Which means . . .' Sol shook his head. 'I don't know what it means.' He took another deep breath. 'All I know is, after I'd spent a year on the streets, Dodge found me and took me in. Into the Haven, I mean. And since then, I've made the best friends anyone could ever hope for.' He turned, grinning – a flash of the old Sol – and winked at Ollie. 'Present company excluded, of course.'

Ollie gave half a smile back.

'But anyway,' said Sol, clearing his throat and picking up the pace a little. 'That's why I consider myself lucky. And that's why I'm so certain that helping those kids is the right thing to do. It's like . . . when is helping other people *not* the right thing to do? You know? Even if it does involve an element of risk.'

Ollie stalled as he descended the staircase. Was it really that simple?

'And the other thing,' Sol went on, from up ahead, 'is that nobody has any idea what the people who come to this country are running from, how awful their lives were where they were born. Which is just an accident, right? Where you're born, I mean. So the way I see it, it's morons like Sebastian Crowe who should be locked up, not the people who are just trying to find a way to stay alive. To keep their *families* alive.'

Still mulling what his friend was saying, Ollie hurried to catch up.

'And while we're on that subject,' Sol added, turning, 'where *are* those kids' families? There must have been fifty or sixty kids locked in that room. No way they *all* came here without their parents.'

They'd reached the corridor in the old dungeons, and Ollie drew level with his friend. 'What are you saying?'

'I'm saying, the Haven is supposed to be this evil terrorist organisation that uses kids to do its dirty work. Right? According to Crowe, obviously. And hey presto, just as he announces his crackdown, a boatload of Haven "recruits" turns up in the English Channel.'

'You don't think that's what happened?' said Ollie.

'They're refugees all right. I'm sure of that. But because we know nobody is *actually* smuggling kids into the country on the Haven's behalf, it stands to reason that Crowe or Sikes or whoever has rounded up those kids from somewhere else. Snatched them from an immigration centre, probably, then chucked them in a cell as though they all arrived together, and then paraded them on screen. To bait us, just like you said.'

Ollie paused again. 'You think they've been separated from their parents? Just so Sikes can make her point?'

'I wouldn't put it past her,' said Sol. 'Would you?'

'So where are their families now? In a prison cell, too?'

'That would be my bet. You heard what they said on the news: all asylum applications have been suspended, meaning anyone coming to this country looking for help has basically been labelled a terrorist, too.'

Ollie could hear the anger in his friend's tone.

'As for that other stuff,' Sol continued. 'The curfew. The stuff about kids not being allowed on the streets. Who's to say Sikes isn't going to use that as an excuse to snatch up other kids as well? To do the *exact opposite* of what the Haven stands for. To show she can. To show us she's *winning*.'

Ollie felt a surge of fury, as well as renewed resolve. From being unsure he'd voted the right way, he was suddenly wondering how he could have considered voting for anything else.

He grabbed hold of his friend's arm and, ignoring Sol's expression of surprise, half dragged him along the corridor, towards the room in which the rest of the Council would be waiting for them.

'Come on,' he said. 'Let's get this done.'

5 EVIL GENIUS

'Nice of you to join us,' said Flea, when Sol and Ollie appeared in the doorway. 'What happened – did you get spooked coming down into the dark?'

Ollie didn't bother to answer. He moved past Flea, and into the room where the Council members had gathered. The kit room, they called it, in tribute to the underground chamber they'd used to prepare for operations back in the old Haven, but the truth was, their new kit room was much more suited to their needs. It was three times the size of the old room, for one thing, with a bank of computers against one wall, and the various maps and plans the Haven kids needed to navigate the city's underground tunnels on a table opposite. The computers controlled Forest Mount's defences: the CCTV network in the tunnels below the hill, as well as the system of tear-gas release valves, both of which the Haven kids had inherited when they'd taken over the building. There'd been some discussion at the first Council meeting as to whether they should disconnect the tear gas, but it was decided that, on balance, and with Maddy Sikes still out there, it would be foolish to decommission the single means of repelling invaders they had.

'What did we miss?' said Ollie, getting down to business. Sol, he noticed, moved next to Keya, and slid his hand discreetly into hers. He smiled at her, and she smiled back. Then she caught Ollie's eye, and dropped her gaze towards the floor.

'Jack's already found the building the refugees are being held in,' said Errol, unable to conceal how proud he felt of his older sister.

Jack was frowning at one of the computer screens. 'It wasn't hard,' she said. 'All I needed to do was isolate the picture of the building from the TV footage and run an image search on this government database I hacked into. It's as Lily said, Ollie,' she added, turning. 'They weren't trying to hide it. In fact, it's fairly obvious they wanted us to be able to find it.'

Ollie nodded. 'So we proceed on the basis it's a trap, as we suspected,' he said. 'Meaning our first mission is reconnaissance. After that, and once we know what we're up against, we decide how we're going to break in and free those kids.'

'Hang on,' said Flea. 'The vote was to take *action*, not to sit around *watching*.'

'Watching *is* action, Flea,' said Song. ' "Know your enemy",' she quoted, 'remember?' Ollie had a feeling that, even though Song would have been too humble to say it, she would have read *The Art of War* cover to cover, probably several times over.

'Right,' said Imani. 'And voting for action isn't the same as voting for a suicide mission.'

Ollie moved to peer over Jack's shoulder. 'So where is it?' he asked her.

'Here,' said Jack, pointing to the map on her screen. 'Foulness Island.'

'*Foulness Island?*' Erik echoed. 'It sounds like something from *Pirates of the Caribbean*.'

'It's a real place,' Jack assured him. 'And it's not actually an island. Or it is, but only just. It's cut off from the mainland by narrow creeks. It's right on the outskirts of London. Well, in Essex really, by the mouth of the River Thames.'

'Meaning we barely have to travel,' said Lily. 'They really *are* making it easy for us.'

Ollie saw her exchange a nervous glance with Jack. Ollie trusted Jack's and Lily's instincts as much as anyone's, and seeing them so anxious did nothing to improve his confidence that they were making the right decision. Ollie would have liked to have asked Aunt Fay for her opinion on the wisest course of action, but she'd deliberately made herself scarce after the Council meeting had ended. And anyway, Ollie knew what she would have said: that it wasn't her place to judge.

'So how do we do this?' said Flea. 'We get to this island – which isn't really an island – and then what? Spread a blanket on the floor and pretend like we're having a picnic?'

'I guess first we need to decide who's going,' said Ollie. 'And how many of us. We need to keep the team small to try to minimise the risk of detection, but on the other hand we need to make sure we cover the building properly. How many points of access does it have?' he asked Jack.

'There's one main entrance, here,' Jack replied, gesturing to the screen. 'But there's also a fire exit here and here, as well as a service entrance at the back. But in order to get through any of them, we'd need to break into the compound first.' She circled her finger around the edges of the computer screen to indicate the barbed-wire-topped fence that surrounded the building.

'A team of four, then,' said Ollie. 'One pair of eyes on each side of the building. How about I take the main entrance, and Sol takes the service door at the back? Then you two – ' Ollie gestured to Flea and Lily – 'can cover those fire doors, see if there's any chance we could—'

'*I'll* take the main entrance,' Flea cut in. 'This is *my* mission, remember?'

Ollie had only suggested covering the main door himself because it was likely to be the most dangerous of the assignments. 'Fine,' he said. 'Flea and Lily will take the front and back, Sol and I will cover those fire doors. It looks like the compound is surrounded by fields, so there might not be much in the way of cover. We'll just have to get as close as we can, and keep in contact using our phones.'

'Speaking of which . . .' said Jack, and she manoeuvred her wheelchair towards a table behind them. 'I've got some upgrades if anyone's interested.' She lifted the lid on a box that was on the table. Inside were a dozen brand-new iPhones, all the latest model.

'Sweet!' said Erik. He reached to pick up one of the phones, but Jack rapped her knuckles on the back of his hand.

'*Hey*,' said Erik, snatching his arm away. 'That hurt.'

'It was supposed to,' Jack answered. 'Nobody's getting one until they give me their old phones back. In *working order*,' she added, as everyone's hands dived into their pockets.

'Where did you get these?' said Sol, turning one of the new phones over in his hand. Ollie accepted one, too. The screen on the latest model was twice the size of the one on his old phone.

'We inherited them,' Jack explained. 'When Forest Mount was evacuated, the former pupils left most of their old belongings behind. I considered returning them, but figured those kids are so rich, they'll almost certainly have already bought replacements.' She picked up one of the phones and tapped the screen. 'You'll need to set up the facial recognition, but otherwise they're good to go. They're fully loaded with all the usual apps, some of which I've spent some time tweaking. The messaging app is the most important, obviously,' she said, referring to the bespoke communications app the Haven kids used to stay in touch. 'I've boosted the encryption level, and managed to

63

reduce the size of the shortwave antenna so that you can barely see it.'

Ollie flipped his phone and realised Jack was right. It was the specially installed shortwave antenna that allowed the Haven kids to talk to each other down in the tunnels, even when there was otherwise no signal. Once a bulky add-on, the antenna was so small now it was almost invisible.

'Oh, and the camera has a useful function,' Jack went on. 'You can use it to see around corners. Just point it straight ahead when you reach a junction, and it will show you what's waiting around the bend.'

'Wait,' said Sol, '*what*?'

Jack shrugged as though it was no big deal. 'It works in conjunction with the torch,' she explained. 'The torch sends out pulses of light, which bounce off the walls and then back again. It's how a mirror works, basically. It's easier when surfaces are reflective, obviously, but I was able to tweak the software controlling the camera so that it could construct an image based on the patterns of light that were bouncing back. The screen will only show you outlines, unfortunately,' she added, frowning as though slightly dissatisfied, 'sort of like a night-vision display. But it's better than nothing.'

'I'll say,' agreed Sol, studying his phone with renewed appreciation. Jack was moving on to another table in the room, and Sol nudged Ollie in the ribs. 'I told you, mate. Evil genius.'

'I heard that,' Jack said, even though she had her back to them.

Sol and Ollie exchanged grins, as the two of them moved with the others to follow Jack across the room.

'And this should help us as well,' said Jack. There was a dust sheet covering a smaller table in the far corner, and she whipped it off to reveal a contraption of metal and black plastic that looked a lot like an overgrown beetle.

'Is that a drone?' said Erik, reaching again. This time he jerked his hand away before Jack could rap it with her knuckles.

'It is,' said Jack. 'And I've extended its range, so that I'll be able to operate it from here while you lot approach the compound from the ground. It's got—'

'Wait,' interrupted Sol. 'Let me guess. It's got built-in high-definition cameras. And stealth capabilities. And miniature, laser-guided missiles.' He was smiling as he stretched out to spin one of the four rotor blades that would enable the drone to fly.

Jack frowned at him. 'How did you know?' she asked him.

Sol's smile dipped. 'Seriously?' he said. 'Laser-guided missiles?' He pulled his hand away from the drone, as though worried it might explode.

Jack kept a straight face for a moment longer, then rolled her eyes. 'Laser-guided missiles,' she muttered. '*Honestly.*'

Sol grinned again, in what Ollie took to be a mixture of disappointment and relief.

'I'm not saying I didn't look into it,' Jack went on, 'but missiles would have made the whole thing *way* too heavy.'

Sol's eyes widened. Like Ollie, he clearly couldn't tell whether Jack was joking.

She was reaching to pick up the drone. 'But you were right about the cameras,' she said. 'As well as the stealth capabilities. It's completely silent, so no one will hear it coming. And it can camouflage itself against the sky. There are camera lenses here and here,' she said, pointing. 'They film footage of whatever is above the drone, and simultaneously transmit the images to these screens on its underside.' She turned the drone over. 'That way, it's pretty much invisible from below. If anyone looking up notices anything, they'll assume it was a trick of the light.'

Jack replaced the drone on the table, and Ollie nodded his appreciation. Sol was right: they were incredibly lucky to have Jack on their side. Ollie didn't know where the Haven would be without her.

'So when do we leave?' said Flea, pocketing his phone. He was clearly itching to get going.

'No time like the present, I suppose,' Ollie answered. Sol and Lily nodded at him grimly. Even though it was a relatively simple mission, Ollie could sense their nervousness. He felt it himself. Indeed, the tension was palpable throughout the room, perhaps because the Council had never before been so divided on how to act. Until now, all the decisions they'd taken had been unanimous.

Plus, of course, there was the uncomfortable fact that they were knowingly heading straight into a trap.

'We'll cover your classes for you,' said Keya, attempting to sound upbeat. 'And anyway, with any luck you'll be back before anyone notices you're gone. Right?' Once again she took Sol's hand, and smiled at him reassuringly.

Casper Sloane had been loitering at the back of the group. He moved until he was standing next to Lily, his expression serious. 'Be careful,' he said solemnly. 'Won't you? *All* of you.' He kissed his girlfriend on the side of the mouth, and Lily raised her fingers to her face. Casper noticed Ollie watching, and Ollie quickly averted his eyes.

'Jeez,' said Flea, looking around at the sullen faces. 'You'd think we were heading off to somebody's funeral.' He grinned, clapping his sister on the shoulder and throwing a wink towards Casper. 'Don't worry, sis. This really will be a picnic in the park. You have the Flea's personal guarantee you'll be back here smooching your boyfriend by sundown.'

6 FOULNESS ISLAND

They travelled underground as far as the tunnels below London allowed – first through the passageways beneath Forest Mount, and then out through the crypt beyond the school's boundary walls. The chapel containing the crypt was a ruin, and was technically owned by whoever also owned the school, meaning the Haven kids had been able to clear and then camouflage the access point without having to worry about anyone spotting them, or asking any awkward questions.

From the chapel, they'd dropped down into the sewers, and taken the most direct route to central London, sneaking through an old ventilation shaft at Charing Cross Underground Station and on to a platform, and then riding the Tube as far as it would take them. After that they'd taken a train beyond London's outskirts, then covered the final few kilometres on foot.

Just as Ollie had expected, there was scant cover once they reached Foulness Island itself. It was mainly farmland, with few inhabitants and barely any roads. The cold grey sea lay to the south and east, adding to the sense of isolation. It wasn't lost on

Ollie that it was the perfect spot to spring a trap without the risk of unforeseen witnesses.

'There,' said Lily, pointing. The four of them – Ollie, Sol, Flea and his sister – were huddled beside a crumbling stone wall on the edge of a windswept beach. The detention centre was visible further along the coast. The squat, single-storey building was several hundred metres inland, but the barbed-wire fence surrounding the compound stretched almost to the craggy shoreline.

Ollie slid his arms from the backpack he was wearing, and carefully removed Jack's drone, setting it down on a flat patch of sand. He hit the power, and then waited for the red transmission light to glow green. An alert pinged on his phone.

Good to go, read Jack's message. *Stand back!*

Ollie and the others watched as the rotor blades on the drone began to spin, and then the strange bug-like contraption lifted itself silently into the air. It was caught by a gust of wind, but righted itself, presumably as Jack got a feel for the controls from her computer screen back at the Haven. The drone hovered for a moment, slowly rotating, and then, in a blink, it disappeared.

'Whoa,' said Sol, at Ollie's shoulder. 'I take it stealth mode is working then.' He was casting around, trying to catch a sight of the now invisible drone against the pale blue sky. And then he leapt back, as the drone reappeared at head height right in front of him. He cried out, startled, just as there was another ping on Ollie's phone.

Boo! read the message.

Once Jack had finished having fun, she sent the drone off towards the compound where the refugees were being held. Ollie and the others fitted the Bluetooth earpieces and microphones Jack had issued them with alongside their new phones, and switched their messaging apps to voice mode. Then they waited for Jack to give them the all-clear.

'That's weird,' said Jack into Ollie's ear. There was no phone reception on Foulness Island, they'd discovered, but thanks to the shortwave transmission capabilities Jack had developed, her voice came through crystal clear.

'What's weird?' said Ollie, not liking the sound of that at all.

There was a pause and, looking up ahead, Ollie caught a brief flicker in the sky. He wouldn't have noticed it if he hadn't been watching so closely, and he'd only spotted it for an instant, but if he'd been forced to guess, he would have said it was the sight of Jack's camouflaged drone doubling back on itself.

'Nothing, I suppose,' said Jack, to Ollie's relief. 'I was expecting the perimeter to be more heavily guarded, that's all. As it is, I can make out two guards in the booth beside the main gate, but that's basically it. There are security cameras at intervals around the fence, but I can run interference on those from the drone. If you stick to the dunes as you approach, there shouldn't be any danger of you being spotted.'

Flea had his finger to his ear as he listened. He grinned and hoisted his backpack on to his shoulders. 'So what are we waiting for?' he said. Before Ollie had a chance to respond, Flea was off. He stuck to the beach side of the dunes, using the contours and the waving grass for cover.

Lily and Sol looked at Ollie.

'Keep your eyes open,' Ollie told them, 'and your wits about you. I don't like the feel of this at all.'

They set off after Flea, ducking low as they moved. There was a cutting wind coming off the churning sea, offsetting the feeble warmth from the sun. Even so, Ollie was sweating, from the tension as much as the exertion.

They caught up with Flea twenty metres or so from the compound's fence. The building itself was a perfect rectangle, with the main entrance facing west – the direction from which they'd approached – and the fire exits on the north and south sides.

'I guess this is where we part company,' said Sol, as they huddled together in one of the sand dunes and peered at the detention centre over the edge of the grassy bank.

Ollie nodded. 'Lily and I will keep going along the beach. I'll take the fire exit on the south side, and keep watch as Lily heads on towards the rear of the building. Sol, you take the north side. Flea—'

'I know, I know. I've got the main entrance. I'm the one who suggested it, remember?' He made to move off, and Ollie grabbed his arm.

'Stay in contact,' said Ollie. 'And remember this is a reconnaissance mission. All we're looking for is a potential way in. That's *all*.'

Flea mock saluted. 'Yes, *sir*. Oh, wait . . .' He let his hand fall to his side. 'I just remembered you're not in charge any more.' He grinned then, and spun away, and once again it was all Ollie could do to watch as Flea darted off into the distance.

'Relax,' said Lily, laying a hand on Ollie's arm. 'My brother knows what he's doing. Even if he acts like an idiot when he's doing it.'

Ollie responded with an almost smile. He raised a finger to his earpiece. 'How are we looking, Jack?'

There was a short delay before Jack answered. 'The coast is clear, from what I can see,' she told them. 'It looks like Flea's already in position. There's not much cover on the beach, but there's a clutch of trees to the north that should help Sol.'

'In more ways than one,' Sol muttered, clasping his bladder. 'I've been bursting since we got off the train.'

He set off after Flea, moving as quickly as he had all day. Ollie and Lily continued along the windswept beach, ducking into the breeze as they ran. Once they drew level with the southern fire door, Ollie gave Lily a nod, and dropped into another dune. He watched as Lily continued on her way. Soon she was forced to cut inland, as she moved to take up her position at the building's rear.

Ollie found himself alone.

'Well, troops,' came Flea's voice in Ollie's earpiece. 'How are we doing?'

'Much better now, thank you,' Sol responded.

'All good,' put in Lily. 'Although what's with this wind? It's blowing a gale round here. I can barely hear you guys, and I've got the volume on my headset turned up to maximum.'

'How close to the building have you managed to get?' Ollie asked. 'Has everyone managed to find some decent cover?' Even as he spoke, he dropped on to his belly, and crawled to the lip of the dune.

'I've got half a forest to keep me hidden,' said Sol, 'but the truth is, I reckon I could be standing out in the open, and nobody would notice. There are no guards on this side of the building, and I can't even see any CCTV cameras.'

'Ditto,' said Flea. 'There are those two guards in the booth at the gate, but one of them is picking his nose, and the other one's fiddling with his phone. He's playing Temple Run, unless I'm mistaken.' Flea gave a snort. 'And he's really *bad* at it.'

Ollie felt himself frowning. He'd expected at least the *pretence* of high security. Were the rest of the guards waiting for them inside?

'Lily?' he said into his mic. 'How are things on your side?'

There was a shriek in Ollie's ear as Lily's audio kicked in, and at first Ollie was sure Lily was screaming. But after a second his heartbeat stilled, as he realised it was just the sound of the wind. It was blowy enough where Ollie was, but the wind was coming from the east, meaning Lily was experiencing its full force.

'Say again?' came Lily's voice. 'Seriously, I can barely hear myself think over here. I've got some cover, but there's not much to see. I could probably walk up and knock, and I'm not even sure anyone would answer. Other than those two guards at the front, the whole place feels deserted.'

'That's not a bad plan, you know,' came Flea's voice.

'Flea,' Jack warned, 'I'm not sure that's such a good idea.'

'What's not a good idea?' Ollie asked her, as he raised himself to try to see around to the front of the building. 'What are you up to, Flea?' From where Ollie was sitting he couldn't see the main gate, but he caught movement further out, and spotted Flea hunched over and darting towards the compound fence. '*Flea*,' Ollie hissed into his mic. 'Stay *back*. We're just supposed to be watching!'

'Chill out, PJ,' came Flea's response. 'If we'd been spotted, we'd already be in a cell by now. I'm just going in for a closer look.'

Ollie knew it would be pointless to try to argue. 'Jack?' he said, not even trying to keep the frustration from his tone. 'Keep an eye on him, will you?'

'I'm doing my best, Ollie,' said Jack. 'But the wind up here is a nightmare. It's as much as I can do to keep this thing steady.' Ollie saw a flicker in the air, as Jack's drone attempted to shadow Flea from above. And then both Flea and the drone disappeared from view, obscured by the corner of the building.

There was a pause, which Ollie told himself felt longer than it really was.

Then, all of a sudden, 'I'm in,' Flea announced.

'In?' Ollie echoed. 'What do you mean, *in*? I thought you were just going for a closer look!'

'I'm through the fence, not in the building itself. Although I do see a window up ahead that looks about my size . . .'

'Flea, don't!' Ollie cursed under his breath. He'd half wondered before what had been in Flea's rucksack. He'd obviously brought along his cable cutters, meaning he'd been contemplating sneaking inside the compound from the start, despite what the Council had agreed. 'Flea, just . . . just wait, will you? Stay exactly where you are. The rest of us will circle round and join you. And then we can decide what to do *together*. OK?'

There was a silence on the other end of the comms.

'Flea?' Ollie said again. '*Flea?* Did you hear what I—'

'Yeah, yeah,' said Flea eventually. 'Just make it snappy. I've got a window of opportunity here – literally.'

Ollie scrabbled to his feet. 'Sol, meet me at Flea's point of cover. Lily, hang tight. In the time it would take you to circle back around the building, chances are we'll be on our way out again.' Or so Ollie hoped, anyway.

He started to run, back the way he'd come along the beach, and then tracking the same route Flea had used towards the front of the building. There was an open field to his left; the main gate was directly ahead. Once again Ollie kept low, but as he passed the booth at the entranceway, he realised that Flea had been right. The guards weren't paying attention to anything other than their phones. And it didn't look like an act – they appeared genuinely bored. Ollie could have run up to the booth and rapped on the window, and the guards would probably have got the shock of their lives.

'Sol?' Ollie hissed.

'Over here, Ollie.'

Ollie heard his friend's voice through his earpiece. He looked ahead and spotted Sol crouched behind what appeared to be an old, rusting farmer's plough. Ollie signalled with his hand for Sol to cut in towards the compound's fence. They came together in what Ollie hoped was the guards' blind spot, and immediately Ollie saw the hole Flea had snipped in the fence. But there was no sign of Flea.

'Where is he?' Ollie asked Sol, as they slipped through the gap themselves. There was open ground between them and the building, and nowhere for Flea to have hidden.

'Come on in,' came Flea's voice over the comms, and Ollie saw him appear at a window off to Ollie's left. He was already *inside* the building.

'Damn it, Flea!' said Ollie. 'I told you to wait!'

'And I told *you*, you're not in charge any more. Besides, that wind was making me cold. It's much toastier in here.' As he spoke, he disappeared again, and Ollie cursed under his breath.

'Guys?' said Lily. 'What's going on?'

Ollie opened his mouth to respond, then looked at Sol. 'What do you think?' he asked him.

Sol shook his head. 'I think we should probably put Flea on a leash or something. But seeing as he's already inside . . .'

Ollie exhaled, and looked again towards the window. 'Lily?' he said. 'We're going inside.'

There was another shriek in Ollie's ear, and both he and Sol winced. '*Inside?*' came Lily's voice, over the sound of the wind. 'Inside the building, you mean? Are you *crazy*?'

'Relax, sis,' said Flea, from somewhere beyond the building's walls. 'From where I'm standing, it doesn't look like anybody's home.'

Ollie and Sol frowned at each other. Then Ollie started forwards, crossing the no man's land between the fence and the building. Seconds later they were pressed against the wall beneath the window. They checked the coast was clear, and then Ollie clambered inside. A second later, Sol dropped on to the floor beside him. From what Ollie could make out, they were in a storeroom of some kind, empty but for a set of metal shelves and some battered old boxes.

'Flea,' Ollie hissed. 'Where are you?'

The door into the corridor outside was open wide. Without warning, Flea appeared in the doorway. He stood tall, making no attempt to stay hidden.

'What are you doing, Flea?' said Ollie. 'Someone will see you!'

'Chill out, will you?' Flea answered. 'It's just us and those goons at the gate. Everybody else has already left the party.'

'What are you talking about?' said Ollie, rising from his crouch.

Flea hitched his thumb over his shoulder. 'Take a look if you don't believe me. There's nothing out there except empty—'

'Ollie!' Jack's voice cut in across the comm.

Ollie raised a finger to his ear. 'Jack? What is it?'

'You need to get out of there! Right *now*.'

'Why?' said Ollie, spinning towards the window. 'What's happening?'

'It looks like—'

But Jack's voice was drowned out by a crackle that sounded disturbingly like gunfire. An explosion rent the air, and Ollie staggered. He looked up through a cloud of dust, and then the ceiling came down on his head.

7 DEAD END

Lily saw the explosion before she heard it. There was a burst of light and rubble, and a second later a roar, as the noise of the detonation carried against the wind. It was followed by a piercing electronic shriek in Lily's headset, which needled from her ear into her brain.

She staggered, against the noise as much as from the force of the explosion, and ripped the comms unit from her head. The piercing sound changed pitch, but didn't diminish, and Lily knew the noise of the blast through her headset had damaged her eardrum. Wincing at the pain, and pressing a palm to her injured ear, she forced herself to turn back to face the building – and then dived to the floor at the sight of half a dozen men in black storming the entrance.

'What the . . .'

Lily scrabbled to retrieve her discarded headset. She spoke into the microphone, holding the earpiece as close to her good ear as she dared.

'Ollie?' she said, almost shouting against the wind and the echo of the detonation. '*Anyone?*' She looked up into the sky, searching for some sight of the drone. 'Jack? Are you there?'

There was no answer, just an empty hiss from the broken earpiece. The sheer volume of the explosion must have blown the circuitry.

Once again Lily tossed the headset aside. She tried tapping out a message instead, but it refused to send. After retrying several times, she gave up, and focused on what was happening in front of her. From her position in a ditch to the rear of the detention centre, she could see smoke rising from where the blast had ripped a hole in an external wall, somewhere near the building's main entrance. And the men dressed in black were entering the building through the doorway Lily was supposed to be watching. They moved with military precision, and carried what looked like automatic rifles. Who were they? Was this all part of the trap Lily and her friends had anticipated?

Desperately Lily scanned the air again, but there was still no sign of Jack's drone. Lily wondered if it had been fried by the explosion, too. Did Jack even know what was happening? Lily had heard her voice over the comms just before the detonation, but the wind had drowned out whatever she'd been saying. As for Ollie and the others, the last communication Lily had received from them was that they were heading inside the building. Were they still in there? The blast had come from their side of the building, and Lily just had to pray they hadn't been caught in the explosion.

She crawled from the ditch and started towards the building. She didn't know what she intended to do exactly – she didn't know what she *could* do – but her immediate priority was to find her friends.

There was a popping sound, harsh and metallic, and Lily saw one of the men firing his weapon. She looked to see where he was aiming, but as far as she could tell there was nobody in front of him. The bullets seemed to have ricocheted against the wall of the building, leaving a trail of holes in the crumbling plaster. Lily frowned, and watched the man disappear inside the building with his associates. Now there was no one between Lily and the open door.

She scaled the perimeter fence, using her jacket to cover the barbed wire at the top. Once she was on the ground again, she picked up the pace, covering her mouth and nose to filter out the dust. When she reached the entranceway, she saw the door had been knocked from its hinges. A battering ram lay discarded at the threshold.

Lily was just about to follow the men into the building when she heard voices from inside the doorway. She drew back, pressing herself against the exterior wall, and tried to peer around the corner. As soon as she moved, she heard the voices again, and quickly ducked back outside.

And then she remembered. The camera on her phone – its ability to see around corners.

She took it from her pocket and swiped to enable the camera function. She selected the appropriate mode and then pointed the camera directly through the entranceway. The image was grainy, distorted, and at first Lily assumed the phone must have been damaged by the blast, too. But gradually the image grew clearer and the men around the corner came into view. Just as Jack had said, it was as though Lily was looking at a night-vision display. She could make out three men, their outlines green but clearly decipherable, and they appeared to be looking Lily's way. If she'd stepped across the threshold when she'd first intended to, they would have spotted her immediately.

Silently thanking Jack, Lily watched and waited. Just when she thought the men would never leave, they turned and faded from view. Lily counted to three, then poked her head around the corner. The men were gone. Ahead of her was a corridor, empty but for the dust caused by the explosion.

Lily stepped cautiously inside. The corridor led both left and right, with no clue as to what lay in either direction. But the men in black had gone left, meaning the safest option was to turn right.

As she hurried along her chosen path, she tried to ignore the images that flashed into her head: of her friends' bodies lying trapped under the rubble from the blast. They would be OK, she told herself. They *had* to be.

When she reached the next junction, she used her phone once more to check that the coast was clear. Satisfied there was no one up ahead, she continued navigating as best she could towards the front of the building. She felt an urge to call out to the others, but knew she had to resist. There was no sight or sound of any of the gunmen, although that didn't mean they weren't nearby.

It was only after Lily had located what appeared to be the detention centre's main corridor she realised what had been bothering her since the moment she'd entered the building. She'd been so worried about her friends, all her other concerns had slipped to the back of her mind. But now she couldn't help wondering what had happened to all the people. There had been no sign of life within the building when Lily had been on the outside looking in, but she'd assumed the place had been in lockdown, with all the staff and detainees sealed inside. Yet all at once it was clear that there was nobody in the building *at all* – there was nobody running, no sign of panic, nobody to defend the place against the mystery attackers. The entire complex was deserted. In which case, what had those guards outside been protecting? And why was the detention centre under attack in the first place? None of anything that was happening made any sense.

Lily's phone vibrated in her hand, and when she looked there was a message from Jack.

Guys? it said. *Are you there? Comms went down for some reason, but I've switched us all to another frequency. What just happened??*

Lily scanned the corridor ahead, then tucked into an alcove, making sure she was out of sight before tapping her response.

I'm here, she told Jack, *but I've lost contact with the others. Do you have visuals?*

She had to wait for what seemed like an age before she received Jack's response.

No, it said plainly, and Lily felt her heart sink.

Another message followed swiftly after. *Where are you, Lily?* Jack asked her.

Inside the building, she messaged back. *It's EMPTY.*

Lily could picture Jack frowning as she read Lily's message.

Get out, Jack told her. *Repeat, get out. Find safety. Before the drone went down, I counted at least twenty armed assailants storming the building. They must have approached by boat!*

Scanning the thread, Lily could see that neither Ollie, Flea nor Sol had read any of the messages. She started typing her reply to Jack, shaking her head as she did so.

Negative. I'm going after the others. Will report back as soon as I have news.

She slipped her phone into her pocket. It buzzed again almost immediately, but Lily knew it would be Jack trying to convince her to fall back. But she couldn't. Not yet. Not until she was sure her friends were safe.

Further on she heard the sound of voices again, and this time Lily could make out some of what was being said.

'. . . waste of time. Three years in Iraq, seven in Afghanistan, and I've never been paid to storm an empty building before.'

'Who cares?' came the response, the voice just as gruff as the first. 'Money's money. I'd storm an empty phone box if the price was right.'

There was laughter and the sound of the voices faded. Lily checked her phone, saw no sign of communication from anyone other than Jack, and then continued the way she'd been heading. The air was so thick now it was difficult to see. She had to wrap the sleeve of her hoodie across the bottom half of her face to allow herself to breathe without coughing.

She took another turning. On the right hand side of the corridor, the wall seemed to be made of wire mesh, and Lily realised she was passing one of the holding pens, similar to the one they'd seen on television. Like the rest of the building, it was empty, with just a few discarded blankets and items of clothing scattered on the floor. Seconds later, she passed another pen on her left. She was still struggling to see through the smoke, but it was obvious that if the refugees had been held here, they'd been moved before Lily and her friends had reached the complex.

Abruptly Lily arrived at the end of the corridor. There was a door ahead of her, but when she tried the handle, it didn't budge. She looked closer and saw a numeric keypad beside the latch controlling the lock. Smoke was seeping through the gap around the doorframe, and Lily could see through the meshed security glass that the dust was even denser on the other side of the door. It swirled so thickly that Lily was sure that if she could just get through, she would find the site of the explosion and – hopefully – her friends.

She tried the handle again, but it wouldn't move. Randomly she punched sequences of numbers into the keypad, knowing that the chances of her guessing the correct code were thousands, if not millions, to one. There was no way through.

Lily swore, and tried barging the door with her shoulder. She hit it hard – once, twice – but the door just reverberated in its frame. And then, through the glass, she saw signs of movement. Instinctively, she ducked, hoping she hadn't unwittingly drawn attention to herself.

She waited, keeping low. Then, cautiously, she raised her head – and saw her brother's face on the other side of the glass staring back at her.

'Flea!' she called instinctively, before wrapping a hand across her mouth.

Her brother beamed. There was blood dripping down his forehead, and his hair was grey from the dust, but he was *alive*. Lily didn't think she'd ever been so pleased to see Flea's idiot grin. From his expression, he was clearly delighted to see her, too.

'Lily!' he called through the glass. His voice was muffled but clear enough that Lily glanced concernedly over her shoulder.

'Where are the others?' she asked her brother, raising her voice as much as she dared. She checked behind her once again, but there was no sign of any of the gunmen.

Flea shook his head, and cupped a hand to his ear. If Flea had indeed been at the site of the explosion when it had happened, his eardrums would have been even more rattled than Lily's were.

'Ollie,' she said, slightly louder. 'Sol.' And then she gestured a question mark with a shrug.

Flea jerked a thumb over his shoulder, then turned and called out behind him. Then he collapsed forwards coughing, splaying his hands against the glass.

'Flea?' came a familiar voice. 'I think I've found a way out. Hurry, though. Those men are—'

Sol appeared amid the dust cloud, his T-shirt hooked over his nose, and his head even bloodier than Flea's. He caught sight of Lily at the same time she saw him, and he rushed over to the glass.

'Lily! How did you . . .'

'Sol! Are you OK? You look awful!'

Sol touched his forehead gingerly. 'The ceiling and I had a little disagreement. But it's in a worse state than I am, I can assure you.'

Lily tried to see across his shoulder. 'Where's Ollie?' she said.

'He's alive,' Sol told her. 'But he's hurt. A lump of plaster knocked him out cold. The explosion sealed off our entry point, but I think I've found another way out. I just need someone to help me with Ollie and then—'

Lily started shaking her head. 'I can't get through,' she said. She rattled the door handle on her side to demonstrate, and the door barely shifted in its frame.

Flea frowned, and tried the handle from his side. Then he tried shoulder barging the door the way Lily had, with exactly the same outcome.

'Flea, don't,' Lily hissed. 'Someone will hear!'

As if on cue, Lily heard voices from somewhere beyond the corner behind her, and she spun around in a panic. It hadn't escaped her that she'd trapped herself down a dead end. The only doors between her and the approaching men were those leading into the holding pens.

'Someone's coming,' she hissed at Flea and Sol.

'Stand back,' Flea responded, and before Lily knew what was happening, he'd thrown himself against the security glass. Lily flinched, expecting it to shatter, but her brother bounced as though he'd hit solid steel.

'It's reinforced,' she told him. 'You'll never break it.'

Sol had vanished for a moment, but he reappeared at Flea's shoulder. Urgently he tugged at Flea's elbow. 'We've got company, too. We need to get out of here, Flea. *Now.*' Sol met Lily's eyes through the glass, and they both knew there was nothing more they could do. Lily was trapped, but Sol, Flea and Ollie still had a chance of getting away. And Ollie needed medical help.

'Go,' she said, even as the voices behind her grew louder. '*Go,*' she hissed again. 'Get to safety while you still can. And take Ollie with you!'

'But, sis . . .' Flea protested.

'Just do it!' Those men behind Lily were getting nearer. She took one more look at her brother, then fixed Sol's eyes with hers. She nodded at him, insistent – and then she turned and ran.

She didn't look back. She heard Flea banging on the door again, but she had to trust that Sol would bring him to his senses.

As she reached the first of the holding cells, she emptied her pockets, and tossed everything she owned – including her phone – into the furthest corner, hoping that nobody would discover it. Then she hurried on, and dived into the next cell as two men in black turned the corner. They hadn't seen her, Lily was sure, but in seconds they would be right on top of her.

'. . . told you before, it's a waste of time. The whole place is deserted.'

'Quit your moaning, will you? If our orders are to check for witnesses, we check for witnesses.'

It was the same voices as before, Lily realised, as she ruffled up her hair and wrapped herself in a dusty blanket. There was no doubt the men would spot her, but if she lay in a corner of the cell and acted like she'd been overcome by the smoke, there was a chance they would assume she was one of the refugees, overlooked during the evacuation. And after that . . . after that Lily didn't know what might happen to her.

She closed her eyes as she lay on the floor, her body angled towards the wall. She heard the sound of approaching footsteps, then tensed when they stopped outside the holding cell's door.

'Looks like we've found someone already.'

'That's just a pile of old blankets.'

'You should have gone to Specsavers, mate. Since when did blankets have hair?'

Lily heard a click as one of the men cocked his weapon. She screwed up her eyes, braced for the bullet in her back.

Instead, she felt herself being nudged by the toe end of a boot. 'On your feet! Hands where I can see them!'

Lily pretended not to have heard. The man kicked her again, harder this time, and Lily groaned and started coughing, as though she were slowly coming round.

'She's half-dead already. I say we put a piece of lead in her temple and finish the job. It would be kinder in the long run.'

Lily sensed, rather than saw, the first man raise his weapon. But then there was a clatter, presumably as the second man knocked the barrel of the weapon away.

'Use your brains, idiot. In half an hour this place is going to be crawling with cops. What are they gonna think when they find a pile of brains splattered across one of the holding pen's walls?'

'What then?' said the first man. 'We just leave her?'

Lily faked coughing again, then grew rigid when she sensed the second man crouch down beside her.

'Nah,' the man said, and Lily felt his breath on the back of her neck. 'We ain't gonna kill her, but we ain't gonna leave her here neither. We'll just have to deal with her the way we dealt with the others.' He grabbed her arm and wrenched up her sleeve. It took all of Lily's willpower not to pull away. 'Sorry, love,' he said to her. 'It's just not your lucky day, is it?'

And then there was a stabbing pain on the underside of Lily's forearm, as the man slid a needle into one of her veins.

8 COLLATERAL DAMAGE

'You should never have left her!'

Ollie was pacing beside the fireplace in the control room. Someone had lit a fire in the grate, and the flames crackled angrily, as though fuelled by the poisonous atmosphere in the room. The rest of the Council – minus Lily, of course – were slumped around the table, other than Song, who was sitting straight-backed and rigid. Erik's chin was practically on his chest. Casper had his head in his hands. Of the ten people gathered, Flea was the only other person on his feet.

'We didn't *leave* her,' Lily's brother spluttered. 'We couldn't reach her! Here, *look*.' Flea wrenched down his T-shirt and showed Ollie the bruises on his shoulder. The skin was so purple it was almost black. 'Sol's got them, too, in case you were wondering. We left dents the size of potholes in that door, but there was nothing we could do to get it open!'

'Yeah, well,' said Ollie bitterly, 'sometimes there are other ways to deal with things than by using brute force, Flea. You should have . . .' He shook his head, searching for some way to finish the sentence – even though he knew, deep down, that there was none.

'Should have *what*?' Flea countered. 'Left you to suffocate under that rubble? Allowed the three of us to get captured, too? Because that would have *really* improved the situation.'

'At least someone would have been with her! At least she wouldn't have been alone!'

Flea turned an even deeper shade of crimson than he had been already. 'In case you're forgetting, PJ,' he growled. 'We're talking about my *sister* here. Do you think I *like* the idea of her being dragged off by a bunch of trigger-happy thugs? That I wouldn't switch places with her in an instant if I could?'

Ollie looked at Sol, who dropped his eyes. Ollie could tell what his friend was thinking – that Ollie was being unreasonable. And he was. He knew he was. He knew as well that it wasn't really Flea he held to blame. More than anyone, Ollie blamed himself.

'And by the way,' Flea went on, holding up a finger, 'it was only because you were hurt that Lily insisted we get to safety. *She* ran away from *us*. To allow us to save *you*!'

Now Ollie was the one to lower his gaze. He gripped the mantel above the fireplace, feeling suddenly unsteady on his feet. He must have wobbled slightly, because all at once he felt a hand under his elbow.

'Easy, Ollie,' came Keya's voice. 'Take it easy.'

'You should be in the infirmary,' said Imani, who'd risen to help him, too. 'At the very least you're suffering from concussion.'

Ollie had closed his eyes for a moment, and when he opened them again he saw Flea throwing his arms up in despair.

'Oh sure!' he said. 'Treat *him* like he's the wounded war hero. It was me and Sol who almost choked to death saving his life. And that ceiling fell on our heads, too, you know. You don't see us acting all woozy, pretending like we're at death's door just to get people feeling sorry for us.'

Ollie felt his anger rising again. He wasn't *acting*. And the last thing he wanted was sympathy. Before he could respond, though, Jack slapped a palm on to the table.

'Enough! Both of you! Arguing isn't going to solve anything!'

'Look, why don't you finish telling us what happened?' suggested Erik. 'You got separated from Lily. I think we've established that much. But how did you three get off the island? How did you even escape the detention centre?'

Flea made a disgruntled noise and turned his back, flicking out a hand as he did so. He was clearly done talking for the time being.

'It wasn't easy,' said Sol. 'Ollie came to just in time. The explosion trapped us inside, but we managed to find another route out. After that we had to dodge a few soldiers, but all the dust and rubble from the explosion gave us cover. And actually, I think the soldiers were focused mainly on searching *inside* the building.'

Ollie moved to take a chair at the table across from Sol. Keya and Imani made to help him, but he wriggled free, conscious of Flea's derogatory sneer. Ollie found himself sitting next to Casper, who placed a hand on Ollie's shoulder, managing to simultaneously appear anxious for his missing girlfriend, and grateful to Ollie for his shared concern. Ollie shifted uncomfortably, disguising the movement with a cough he didn't entirely have to fake. He, Sol and Flea had come straight to the control room when they'd returned from their mission. They'd cleaned themselves up as best they could on the return journey from Foulness Island, which had also given Ollie some time to recuperate, but they were yet to get medical attention for their injuries, and their lungs were full of dust.

'By the way,' said Sol, 'I've . . . er . . . got a confession to make.' He slid his phone surreptitiously on to the table. He met Jack's eye, and winced an apology. 'My phone got kind of . . . totalled.' He flipped it so that Jack could see the screen. It was a spiderweb of cracks. Ollie stared at it, thinking it the perfect symbol for their failed mission.

'Mine, too,' huffed Flea, tossing down his own phone. Flea's was in even worse shape than Sol's, but at least they had something to return. Ollie had been holding his phone when the lump of plaster had clonked him on the head. As far as he knew, it was hidden somewhere amid the rubble that had almost buried him alive.

Jack shook her head dismissively. 'Forget the phones. Phones can be replaced. It's not the phones I'm worried about.' She looked at Ollie, Sol and Flea in turn, like an anxious parent. One by one they looked down, and Ollie's thoughts turned back to Lily.

There was quiet for a moment, and Ollie found himself staring out of the window. It had been dusk when he and the others had finally got back to the Haven, but now it was fully dark, with faint pinpricks of starlight visible above the London skyline. The younger kids would have been in bed by now. The older ones were probably huddled in the various common rooms, aware that the Council had gathered, and wondering what had gone awry. One or two of them would almost certainly have noticed that Lily had failed to return with the others, and rumours as to what might have happened to her would already have begun to spread.

'What do we know, Jack?' said Ollie at last. 'What did you see with the drone?'

Jack exhaled and shook her head. 'Not a lot more than you did, by the sounds of it. Most of what we've pieced together is based on the news reports.'

'The news reports?' echoed Sol, sitting straighter. 'What news reports?'

Flea had his arms crossed, but abruptly he turned towards the table, frowning his curiosity.

'You haven't heard?' said Errol. 'It's been all over the internet.'

'How would we have heard anything, pipsqueak?' Flea snapped, placing his hands on the table and leaning towards Jack's younger brother. 'In case you hadn't noticed, we've been a bit busy lately. And just for the record, it's hard to muck about online when you're stranded in the middle of nowhere, and your phone's just been blown up by ninjas.' He stuck a finger in his ear and waggled it. 'Plus, I'm finding it hard to hear much of anything at the moment. That explosion almost burst my eardrums.' He glared at him as though it was Errol's fault.

Errol recoiled in his chair. Flea noticed Jack glowering at him, and ceded his ground, as though wary of incurring Jack's wrath.

'The news stories, Errol,' Ollie prompted. 'What are they saying?'

'Well, just . . .' Errol had half an eye on Flea. He cleared his throat. 'Just that the detention centre was attacked. That there was an explosion, and that two people were killed, and—'

'Wait, *what*?' cut in Flea. 'Who was killed?'

Ollie felt his eyes widen, too, and immediately his thoughts went to Lily.

But, 'The guards,' Jack explained. 'Those two security guards. It was their booth that took the full force of the explosion. As far as we could tell, the explosives were planted on the outside wall of the main building, but that booth might as well have been made of cardboard. They . . . they wouldn't have suffered. They probably didn't even have time to realise what was happening.'

Ollie was shocked to hear that people had lost their lives. He'd assumed that, because the building had been empty, they could at least draw consolation from the fact that no innocent people had been hurt.

'They're saying the attack was down to terrorists,' Errol went on. 'And they're saying . . .'

'What?' Ollie asked, when Errol hesitated.

'They're saying it was *us*,' Errol finished. 'They're saying the *Haven* was responsible.'

Ollie saw Sol share an incredulous look with Flea. But to Ollie it all suddenly made sense. He closed his eyes and tipped back his head, bemoaning his stupidity. When he opened them again, he looked at Jack, and Ollie knew what was coming.

'It was staged, Ollie,' said Jack. 'The whole thing. It was a set-up. *That's* what the trap was. They waited for us to show our hand, and then they trumped it.'

'Let me guess . . .' Ollie said. 'They caught us on camera. The four of us. Me, Sol, Flea and Lily.'

Jack shook her head. 'Not Lily. She was at the rear of the building, away from all the action, so they must not have realised she was there. But you three . . . you're all over the evening news. It isn't quite possible to make out your faces, but they've spliced together footage of the three of you sneaking into the building, and then the explosion, and then the aftermath: the ruined building; the bullet marks on the walls. And the guards, of course. The body bags.' She looked down for a moment. 'All edited together in one simple, easy-to-understand narrative.'

'But what about those soldiers?' said Flea. 'The men in black. Is nobody bothering to ask who *they* were?'

Jack shared a glance with Song.

'What is it?' said Ollie, looking between them.

'I warn you,' said Jack, 'you're not going to like this.'

'Tell us.'

Jack sighed, and looked at Song again. Song reached beneath the table. She produced a folder and slid it along the surface, so that it spun and settled in front of Ollie. He opened it up.

'What the . . . What's *that* supposed to be?'

In the folder was a printout of an image: several printouts, in fact, all stacked together. They were stills, Ollie guessed, captured from one of the news reports Jack had been talking about. Ollie's attention was immediately caught by the picture on top.

It showed one of the men in black. Not his face. When Ollie rifled through the rest of the images, he realised none of them showed any of the soldiers' faces. Instead, they pictured markings on the soldiers' otherwise plain-black uniforms. A symbol, rather. On an armband on one of the men's sleeves. In what looked like a tattoo on the back of another man's neck. They were all the same: a capital 'H', framed by a triangle.

Flea reached across Ollie's shoulder, and snatched the picture he was holding from his hands. 'Are you *kidding* me?'

Sol was on his feet now, too, craning his neck to see the pictures on the table. 'But that's not even how it's supposed to look!' he said. 'The H is wrong, and the triangle is upside down. That's not *our* symbol.'

He was right, of course. At the Haven, they drew the triangle pointing downwards, and the cross section of the 'H' slightly longer than it needed to be. Probably when Dodge had described the symbol to Maddy Sikes, she'd simply assumed the triangle pointed upwards, which is how the men in black had ended up with the perversion of the design on their uniforms.

But Ollie knew it hardly mattered. The point was, everyone who saw the images would assume that the men in black were working for the Haven. Nobody would believe now that the Haven was just a bunch of kids, hoping to make the world a better place. Rather, they would see the Haven exactly as Maddy Sikes wanted them to: a group of well-armed, well-organised fanatics, who would stop at nothing in their bid to destabilise the country.

Flea tossed down the picture he was holding in disgust, and Jack slipped it back into the folder. 'Those men were almost certainly mercenaries,' she said, taking back the pictures Ollie was holding, too. 'Ex-soldiers, for the most part, who either left or were kicked out of the armed forces. They were pawns, in other words, working for money. They wouldn't have asked questions. Even if they knew what they were signing up for, they wouldn't have cared.'

'And the footage you talked about . . .' Sol prompted.

'They had cameras waiting for you, just like Ollie said,' Jack told him. 'Probably they had drones in the air like ours, high enough that we didn't spot them.'

'So *that's* why the building was empty,' said Ollie bitterly. 'The gunshots, the explosion – it was all for the cameras. And those two guards were collateral damage. To make it seem real. Before it was all just hearsay, but now Sikes has *proof* that the Haven is a terrorist organisation, willing to kill innocent people.'

'Some proof,' muttered Sol.

'Fake news at its finest,' put in Erik.

'And I'm afraid it gets worse,' said Jack, sighing. 'The official story coming from Sebastian Crowe's office is that we kidnapped the refugees who were being detained inside the building. They're saying we've taken them and recruited them to our cause.'

'But they weren't even there!' said Sol. 'Ollie just said it himself: the building was empty. Oh, wait,' he went on, 'let me guess. They conveniently forgot to mention that part to any news reporters?'

'As I said,' Jack replied, rolling a shoulder, 'Sikes and Crowe arranged everything to make it look like we're the bad guys, and they're using the media to convince the rest of the country.'

'So what have they done with the refugees *really*?' asked Ollie. 'Were they ever in the detention centre in the first place?'

Jack's expression darkened. 'That's what I meant about it being worse,' she said. 'Sikes is still holding them somewhere. And now she can do whatever she wants with them, because the world thinks *we* have them.'

Sol bit down, hard. Ollie watched him, wanting to offer some words of reassurance, but knowing there was nothing he could say.

Jack, in the meantime, glanced at Flea. 'As for whether they were ever there at all, we can't be certain. But for Lily's sake, we just have to hope that they were.'

'What do you mean?' said Flea, noticing the way Jack was looking at him.

Jack exhaled slightly. 'Because from what you described, when Lily left you, it sounded as though she had an idea. I pulled the schematics of the building, and I think I might have worked out what she was planning.'

The others waited for Jack to go on.

'You said you were caught either side of a security door. Right? And the only door like the one you described near the site of the explosion would have led you to the holding cells.'

'So?' said Flea, clearly impatient for Jack to make her point.

'Well, if Lily was smart – and we all know Lily is smart – I reckon she would have decided to take her chances hiding in one of the cells, to make out she was one of the refugees who got left behind.'

'You mean she let herself be found?' Flea blustered. 'Why the hell would she do that?'

'Because she didn't have a choice,' Ollie muttered.

The others looked at him, and a silence filled the room.

Ollie stared down at the surface of the table, trying to work out the chances of Lily's plan succeeding. And, if it had, where Lily might be now.

9 WORST NIGHTMARE

Lily sat upright with a start.

A bad dream. She'd been having a bad dream. But she was safe, she told herself. She was at the Haven, surrounded by all her friends. Except . . . she couldn't see. She was awake, or half awake at least, but for some reason she could barely open her eyes. And this place didn't *smell* like the Haven. It smelt damp and dingy and cold. And what was that *shrieking* sound in her right ear, like a dentist's drill burrowing into her brain?

And then Lily remembered.

The detention centre. The explosion, and the scream of her headset in her ear. And then the men, the holding cell, the hypodermic needle in her arm . . .

Lily slapped herself. Hard, with her right hand across her right cheek.

It hurt, but it did the trick. The heaviness lifted from her eyes, and with an effort she was able to open them fully. She was still groggy, and could feel the lingering effects of whatever sedative those men had pumped into her veins. She had a headache like an axe in each temple, too, as well as that constant

107

ringing noise in her damaged ear. But at least she was *conscious*, finally.

She looked around . . . and almost wished she'd never woken up.

She was in a box. Literally, that was what it felt like. A ceiling she could almost have banged her head on, walls too close together for her to be able to spread her arms. There was a blanket on the floor, muddied and dirty, the one she'd wrapped herself in back at the detention centre. Those men must have scooped her up exactly as they'd found her.

There was a single bulb caged in a plastic light fitting in the middle of the ceiling, emitting just enough of a glow for Lily to see that there was no way out. There was no obvious door, no windows. Just the blanket and the bulb – and a feeling that the walls around her had started closing in.

Panicking, Lily started banging her fists against the walls either side of her.

'Hey!' she shouted. 'Let me out! Do you hear me? *Let me out!*'

All the time her head continued to throb, and her ear continued to ring, and the more noise she made, the greater the pain she felt. But being in such a tight, confined space was worse, much worse, to the extent that after a moment or two, Lily felt herself gasping for breath. She was hyperventilating, and she knew she had to control it, or else she would pass out.

'Hey! *Hey!* Is anyone there? Does anyone hear—'

There was a grinding noise from behind her. Lily had been facing the opposite wall, and she spun, and shied at an onslaught of light. She covered her eyes with one hand and held the other out in front of her. Squinting, she saw a narrow door had opened in the wall across from her. She hadn't noticed it was there because on the inside there was no handle, no keyhole, nothing to indicate there was a doorway there at all.

Where the wall had been there now stood a figure, silhouetted against the light. The man – or woman – shifted slightly, and Lily realised they were holding something in their hand. A stick, it looked like, about a metre long, and with two small prongs at one end. And covering the figure's face was a mask. It was white, and completely featureless, except for two round eye holes, a protrusion for the nose, and a group of smaller holes where the mouth should have been, to allow the wearer to breathe.

The figure stepped forwards, raising the stick.

'Wait,' said Lily, 'who are you? Where am I? What do you—'

The end of the stick began to glow. It flashed, then flared, and though Lily tried to bat the stick away, the figure in the mask pressed the prongs into Lily's chest, and an explosion of pain racked her body. She felt herself convulsing, and though she knew what was happening she was powerless to stop it. She fell forwards, on to her knees. Her vision began to swim and she felt herself wobbling – and then she toppled face first on to the floor.

This time when Lily woke she came around suddenly, her eyes snapping open and her lungs clamouring for air. She gasped and immediately started spluttering, and she realised from the fact that she was dripping wet that she'd just been doused with a bucket of water.

She was on the floor again, lying on her side, and she rolled on to her hands and knees. Then another bucket of water hit her, and more than anything this time Lily noticed the cold. Instinctively she scrabbled backwards, shivering, and quickly collided with a wall. She looked up, around, and saw she was in a larger room now, though again it was nowhere she recognised.

Something touched her leg, and she flinched violently. She wiped the water from her eyes and realised that this time she wasn't alone. On the floor beside her, looking as wet and ragged as Lily felt, there was another girl. It was hard to tell, given the state of her, but she seemed about Lily's age. She had light brown skin and matted black hair that clung damply to her narrow shoulders. Her clothes were rags, and when she looked at Lily, there was an expression of outright terror in her eyes.

And then the girl screwed up her eyes and ducked her head, and Lily realised too late that the girl had seen what was coming. Another bucket of water hit them both, and Lily's hands slid from under her, so that she slipped and cracked her head on the floor. It should have hurt, but Lily barely noticed. Instead all she felt was a surge of fury, and she pressed herself upwards, staggering slightly as she found her feet. She turned in the direction the water had been thrown, and saw three figures standing in a line. The one on the left had an empty bucket beside them, but other than that they appeared identical to the man or woman who'd attacked Lily in the box: dark grey uniforms, white masks, truncheons tucked into their belts, and what Lily knew now was some kind of cattle prod in each of their hands.

The middle one, the largest of the three, stepped forwards. 'You! Get back on your knees!' The man's voice was muffled slightly by the mask, but it sounded thick and phlegmy, to the extent Lily could almost smell the cigarette smoke on his breath.

She stood taller.

The man drew his truncheon, and in one swift movement drove the butt end into Lily's stomach. Lily doubled over, once again gasping for breath. But if the man expected her to go down, he would have been disappointed. There was no way Lily was going to give him the satisfaction.

'I said, get back on your . . .' The man raised his truncheon, as though he intended to bring it down on the back of Lily's neck, but then another figure stepped out of the shadows.

'That's enough.'

III

It was a woman's voice this time: soft, but quietly authoritative. Lily turned and watched as the woman drew close.

She was short for a grown-up, barely any taller than Lily. She wasn't fat, but she wasn't thin either. She was round, almost matronly. She had plain brown hair, which she'd wrapped atop her head in a bun. And though she had on the same grey overalls as the figures beside her, she wasn't wearing a mask. Her lips were pale and dry looking, and her smile didn't reach her eyes.

'Do you speak English, my dear?' the woman said as she approached.

Lily opened her mouth, but didn't speak. She shook her head slightly, suspecting the question was some kind of trick. And then she cried out in pain, as from nowhere she felt a dagger in her leg. She fell to one knee as her leg crumpled beneath her. Lily saw one of the figures holding a cattle prod had edged in beside her as her attention had been on the woman. What had felt like a dagger was in fact another electric shock.

The woman's expression didn't change as she gazed down at Lily. 'I asked you a question,' she said mildly.

'What, I . . .' Lily noticed the figure holding the cattle prod start to raise it again, and she held up her hands. 'Yes!' she said. 'Yes, I speak English. Why wouldn't—'

Again the shock was completely unexpected. It came from behind this time, into the small of her back. After crying out again, Lily spun, furious, and was met by the impassive stare of one of those featureless white masks. A finger beneath her chin drew her attention back towards the front.

'I ask the questions, my dear,' the woman told her, her index finger hooked beneath Lily's jaw. 'Your role is to answer them. You'll find this whole process a lot less painful if you follow that simple rule.'

Lily jerked her head away, freeing her chin, and the woman's finger hung in the air, before curling back into something like a claw. She turned her attention to the other girl still cowering on the floor. A flicker of disgust crossed her features.

'My name,' she said, 'is Warden Bricknell. You will address me as such every time you speak to me – which will only happen if *I* first speak to *you*.' Her gaze moved back to Lily. 'Is that clear?'

Lily had a number of responses in mind, all of which she knew would get her nothing but another blast from one of those cattle prods. Instead, 'Yes,' she said, through gritted teeth. One of the masked figures edged closer, and Lily added, '*Warden Bricknell.*'

The warden considered Lily carefully, as though judging the degree of her insolence. But then her gaze moved on to the girl on the floor, who hadn't responded at all. Lily looked down, and tried to signal to the girl with her eyes – *Just answer! You haven't got any choice!* – but the girl looked back at Lily and shook her head. She appeared more afraid than ever.

Warden Bricknell nodded at one of the masked guards – the man who'd spoken to Lily first – and he fired up his cattle prod.

'Wait!' Lily cried, attempting to step between the girl and the guard. But the man shouldered her out of the way, and jabbed his cattle prod into the side of the girl's neck. The girl opened her mouth in a silent scream of agony, writhing and then collapsing on the floor. The guard withdrew his cattle prod, and Lily could see from the girl's shoulders that she was sobbing, but still she made no sound. And suddenly Lily understood. The girl didn't speak because she *couldn't*.

Warden Bricknell signalled to the guard once more, who moved to deliver another shock. This time Lily grabbed hold of the cattle prod itself.

'Stop!' she said. 'Don't you see? She's deaf! She can't speak! Shocking her isn't going to make any difference!'

The guard yanked the cattle prod from Lily's grip, and in one sharp movement drove the handle into Lily's jaw.

Lily staggered backwards, catching herself against the wall.

All the while the warden watched on. 'As I was saying,' she said, 'I am Warden Bricknell and this – ' she turned her palms towards the ceiling – 'is your new home.' She spoke as though she hadn't been interrupted, in the tone of an estate agent handing over a set of keys to a couple who'd just bought their first house together.

And then the blandness of her expression vanished, and her tone all of a sudden matched the cruelty in her eyes. 'Take them to the cells,' she said. 'Tomorrow, if they've learned their lesson, maybe we can let them eat and drink.'

Hands grabbed Lily from both sides. She found herself being dragged through a door she hadn't realised was behind her, and along a corridor that reminded her of one of the London Underground ventilation shafts she'd used so often to sneak around below the streets of the city. She didn't know what had happened to the other girl, but she thought she heard scuffling somewhere behind them.

Lily tried to concentrate on where the guards were taking her. She was obviously in some kind of prison, but she had no idea where, or why.

They turned a corner, into a corridor exactly the same as the last one: metal floor, metal walls, and pipes of various sizes running the length of the ceiling. Lily hadn't noticed it before, but all around them there was a constant metallic groaning sound, as though the building itself were alive. Lily tried to tune into it, hoping the noise would offer her some clue as to where she was, but before she had a chance she was hauled to a standstill. Roughly, the guards turned her to face the wall, and a door clicked open in front of her. Lily had time to register the cell that stood waiting for her, barely bigger than the box in which she'd first woken up, and then she was being thrust inside.

She staggered, colliding with the wall at the rear of the prison cell. The door slammed shut behind her, and dimly Lily caught the sound of laughter.

'Pleasant dreams, princess,' the guard with the smoker's voice called to her. And then his cackling faded as he walked away, leaving Lily trapped in her worst nightmare.

10 GREY DAWN

Ollie was with Song in the Haven's central courtyard.

It was early, and somewhere behind the mist that had sat for the past few days across the city, the sun had just come up. It filtered weakly through the greyness, bringing light but barely any warmth. There was no wind, though, and Ollie and Song were dressed in thick hoodies and tracksuit bottoms, meaning they just felt the chill on their exposed fingers and faces, and only when they stopped moving long enough to notice it. They were practising *kata*: the choreographed patterns of movements that sat at the heart of the style of karate Song taught at the Haven.

They had the courtyard to themselves. Probably it would be another hour at least before the building began to come alive. There would be breakfast in the refectory – with enough tables and chairs for everyone, which was more than most of the kids, including Ollie, had experienced at the Haven before they'd taken over Forest Mount. After that lessons would begin – in proper classrooms, no less – with the teaching conducted by the kids themselves, as had always been the case at the Haven. It would be just a regular day, in other words . . . in all respects except one. Because as much as Ollie was trying to concentrate on what he was doing, he couldn't forget for a moment that it would be another day without Lily.

'Relax, Ollie,' Song instructed. 'Soften your muscles.'

Ollie moved from stance to stance as the *kata* required, but every transition he made felt awkward and jerky.

'Smoother, Ollie. Let it flow. The movements should be like water tumbling down a rock face.'

Song looked on as Ollie struggled to the end of the *kata*.

'Sorry,' he said to her, struggling to recover his breath. 'I know the movements are supposed to flow, just like you said, but the problem is, I'm not exactly in a smooth frame of mind at the moment.'

Song pursed her lips. 'Which is exactly why we're working on this particular *kata*.' She sighed, and stared at Ollie appraisingly. 'Look, I know you're worried about Lily. I am, too. We all are. So if you don't feel like training, we don't need to be doing this. I just . . . I find it helps, that's all.'

'I do, too,' Ollie insisted. 'Really.'

Song looked at him dubiously, but Ollie meant what he'd said. If he hadn't been out here with Song, he would probably have been lying in bed, staring at the ceiling, his mind awhirl with useless thoughts. Either that or he would have been down in one of the common rooms, obsessively watching the news – alert for some clue as to where Lily might have been taken.

'Let's go through it again,' Ollie said, shaking out a chill. 'One more time, OK? You lead, and I'll do my best to follow.'

This time as they ran through the *kata*, Ollie concentrated on breathing, allowing his lungs to expand and contract in time with the movements. Partly because of this, and partly because Song was leading him through it, Ollie finished the *kata* much happier with himself than he had been before. And he *felt* better afterwards, too – his mind clearer, his body looser.

He bowed to Song when she turned to face him. Song, smiling, bowed back. Then something seemed to catch her eye, and when Ollie followed her gaze, he realised they were no longer alone. Casper Sloane was standing in a corner of the courtyard, watching them from the shadows.

'Maybe we should leave it there for the time being,' Song said to Ollie. 'It's always good to end on a high note.'

But the high Ollie had briefly experienced was already a fading memory. He found it awkward enough being around Casper even in normal circumstances, for reasons he didn't quite want to admit. But since Lily had been taken, just the sight of her boyfriend was enough to remind Ollie about how powerless they all were to rescue her.

Song slipped away, nodding to Casper as she passed him. Ollie lingered in the centre of the courtyard, slowly gathering his stuff, and watched out of the corner of his eye as Casper edged awkwardly towards him.

'I feel like I should clap or something,' Casper said. 'You're getting pretty good at that.'

He meant it kindly, Ollie was sure. From the encounters he'd so far had with Casper, he'd yet to hear Lily's boyfriend offer anyone an ungenerous word. And yet for some reason the compliment grated. Maybe it was just because Casper was two years older than Ollie. And taller. With perfect teeth and hair. Not like the mousy mop on Ollie's head, which refused to sit in any kind of style no matter how hard he coaxed it. Plus, of course, Casper could cook.

'Yeah, well,' Ollie said. 'I've got a lot to learn. That's why I was out here practising.'

Casper's face fell slightly. 'Sorry, I interrupted you, didn't I? I just . . . I'm not used to seeing anyone else up this early. I'll leave you to it, if you'd prefer?'

Ollie felt suddenly ungenerous himself. It struck him that if he was worried about Lily, her boyfriend was surely missing her even more.

'What *are* you doing up so early?' Ollie asked.

Casper gave something like a smile and hitched a thumb over his shoulder. 'I was in the kitchen heating up the ovens. In less than sixty minutes, about two hundred famished kids are going to be in the refectory demanding their breakfasts. That's a lot of sausages to cook in not a lot of time.'

'Right,' said Ollie, 'of course. Sorry, I . . . I guess I hadn't realised how much time you had to spend getting things ready. It *is* a lot of mouths to feed.'

Casper shrugged. 'Don't worry, you're not alone. I know they don't mean to, but after they've been at the Haven for a while, most people tend to take the food we make them for granted.' He laughed softly. 'They only seem to notice when we're serving something they don't like.'

Ollie flushed guiltily, recalling how he'd turned up his nose at the mushroom pizza that had been on offer one dinnertime just last week. Exactly as Casper had described, Ollie tended to go through meals guzzling his food, without thinking about how much effort must have gone into preparing it. And as he was effectively the Haven's head chef, Casper would have worked harder than anyone.

'What about you?' Casper asked Ollie. 'What are you doing down here at this time? I mean, you're training obviously, but why so early?' He turned his hazel eyes upwards, taking in the mist and the low-hanging sky.

'I haven't been sleeping much lately,' Ollie admitted. 'I was up anyway, and I knew Song would probably be up, too, so . . .' He finished the sentence with a shrug.

Casper bobbed his head. 'I can't say I've been sleeping much lately either.'

There was a pause, and both boys looked at their feet.

'Are you . . .' Ollie shifted and cleared his throat. 'I mean, how are you, you know . . . bearing up?' It was the closest Ollie could come to mentioning Lily's name. It wouldn't have been a problem if he'd been talking to Sol, say, or to any of the others in fact, but for some reason, with Casper, Ollie felt guilty for even *thinking* about Lily.

'I'm OK,' Casper replied, sounding grateful that Ollie had asked. 'At least running the kitchens keeps me busy.' He grimaced. 'And besides, I'm hardly in a position to complain. We're safe here, at the Haven, while Lily . . .'

He didn't finish the sentence. Mainly, Ollie suspected, because he didn't know how to.

'Do you know it was Lily who brought me to the Haven in the first place?' Casper went on, after a pause.

Ollie couldn't mask his surprise. 'Really?' He'd assumed Casper had been here even longer than Lily – for no other reason, Ollie realised, than that Casper was older.

'We kind of grew up together,' Casper said. 'Although maybe that's putting it too strongly. You know about Lily's uncle, right? Danny Hunter? The gangster?'

'We've crossed paths,' Ollie answered, recalling his encounter with Danny Hunter and his Razors, the name Danny had given to the gang of razor-wielding cutthroats at his command.

'Well, in that case, you'll know you're lucky to be standing here,' Casper said, with another grimace. 'Lily and her brother were sent to live with Danny after their mum died. She must have told you the story?'

'She told me some,' Ollie said. 'I know that their dad ran out on them when they were small. And that their mum got cancer.'

'Right,' Casper said, bobbing his head. 'So Danny ended up being their closest living relative. I don't think he particularly wanted to take Lily and Flea in, but, you know. Family's family. That's what Danny always said anyway.'

'You're talking about him as though you knew him,' Ollie said, frowning slightly.

'That's what I mean about us growing up together. I was one of Danny's Razors.'

'You were?'

Unexpectedly, Casper laughed. 'Although the truth was, I wasn't very good at it. I've never liked violence. And I kept dropping my razor blade. It's a miracle I've still got toes.'

Surprising himself, Ollie laughed, too.

'So they put me to work in the kitchen of Danny's casino,' Casper continued. 'He only had one casino at the time, though I hear he has several now. I was basically a dogsbody, running around doing what people told me. There was a guy, Danny's cook – Angus was his name – who took against me for some reason. He didn't like the fact that I was always watching what he was doing. I just . . . it was the highlight of my day. Seeing how he took a pile of ingredients and turned it into something completely different. And he wasn't even that good at it! I realised after a while that he could barely tell a pestle from a mortar.'

Ollie wasn't sure he could have either. He smiled to cover his confusion.

'Sorry,' said Casper. 'Cooking joke. The point is, I was only trying to learn, but Angus must have figured I was trying to take his place or something. Also, I don't think he liked it that I was getting better at cooking than he was. Like, he used to give me stuff to do when he couldn't keep up on his own. Just simple stuff at first, but more and more complicated. He was trying to catch me out, force me to make a mistake, but my stuff always turned out better than his did.' Casper flushed. 'I don't mean to sound arrogant or anything,' he said. 'Cooking is just one of those things I've always seemed to have a knack for. The only thing actually. Do you know what I mean?'

Ollie felt a twinge of envy. He'd never really had anything like that – a talent he could call his own. The way some people were amazing at drawing, say, without even having to try, or a natural at football, or playing an instrument – or awesome at karate, the way Song was.

'Anyway,' said Casper, 'Angus decided to make my life a living hell. He used to hit me, which was one thing, but he used to blame me for all his mistakes, too. And that meant everyone *else* started blaming me, and they just laughed when Angus punished me. He shut me in a freezer once. One of those big walk-in ones. Another time he held my hand on the table and made me splay my fingers, and then he used one of his great big kitchen knives to stab down faster and faster between the gaps. Treated it like a game. Like my tears were the funniest thing he'd ever seen.'

'That's awful,' Ollie said, horrified.

Casper shrugged again, as though yeah, it was, but he knew there were others at the Haven who'd suffered worse. 'To cut a long story short, Lily was the one who came to my rescue. She found me crying once and I told her everything that had been happening. I didn't want to. I was too ashamed, like it was my fault, you know? But when I started talking I found I couldn't stop. And then, after Lily and Flea ran away, Lily came back for me. Told me they'd found a place. *This* place. The Haven. And I went with her and I've never looked back.'

He looked Ollie in the eye, and Ollie found himself at a loss for what to say. He felt bad for not having taken the time to find out about Casper's history earlier. The truth was, Ollie had *wanted* to not like him, when really he should have been glad for Lily that she'd got together with someone she was obviously so close to. Apart from anything, she'd not exactly had the best of luck when it came to boyfriends.

'The point is,' said Casper, 'I owe Lily my life. Literally. So I want you to know that I'm here if there's anything I can do. I mean, I'm not sure what exactly. I can't do . . .' He gestured to the middle of the courtyard, where Ollie and Song had been practising karate. 'I told you, I'm not very good around violence. And I'm not like the rest of you guys on the Council. About the most dangerous thing I've had to deal with since I joined the Haven was a gone-off avocado.'

Ollie smiled in spite of himself.

'But if I can help,' Casper concluded, 'then I will. In any way I can.'

'Thanks,' said Ollie, nodding his appreciation. 'Although you're helping already. Just by being here, doing what you're doing. Keeping everybody fed, their strength and morale up. The truth is, you're probably doing more to help than anyone at the moment.' Ollie sighed heavily. 'The rest of us keep hitting dead ends. We might as well be sitting on our hands.'

'You mean there's no news? No leads on where Lily might be?'

Wearily Ollie shook his head. 'We're doing everything we can. Checking with all our contacts on the street, scouring social media – basically hunting for any kind of clue about where she might have been taken. But there's been nothing. Literally, *nothing*.' Ollie heard his frustration carrying in his tone.

Casper dropped his eyes towards the floor.

'But we'll find her,' Ollie told him. 'We will. Even if we have to—'

He was cut off by a shout from somewhere inside the building – what sounded like a scream of somebody in pain. There was a crash after that, as a door flew open and hit the courtyard wall, and Song appeared from behind one of the pillars.

'Ollie!' she yelled. 'Come quickly!' She gestured frantically, and didn't wait to see if Ollie followed her. She turned and dashed back the way she'd come.

Ollie exchanged a glance with Casper, and then both boys set off at a run.

11 RAT CATCHERS

'What *happened*?' blurted Casper.

When Ollie and Casper had entered the building, Song had already disappeared. They'd hesitated for a moment, unsure which direction they were supposed to be heading, when they'd heard another yell. Just like before, it had sounded like a scream of agony. They'd dashed towards it, and had found themselves following a trail of blood.

Now, looking at the scene in front of him, Ollie could only stare in shock and horror. Keya was lying on the floor, half slumped against the wall. They were in the East Wing, and from the trail Keya had left, she'd clearly crawled as far as she could up from the tunnels, before her strength had finally given out. Ollie was amazed she'd even made it this far. A shard of glass the size of a carving knife was half buried in her thigh.

'Got . . . cornered,' she managed to say. 'Had to jump. Landed in a . . . a skip. On a sheet of . . . glass.'

Song was crouched beside her, and she placed a hand on Keya's shoulder. 'Don't try to talk,' she said. 'Save your strength.'

By the look of things, Galen, the Haven's medic, had arrived just before Ollie and Casper. She was already examining Keya's wound, tilting her head to the left and right.

'Well, it's missed the artery,' she said, frowning, 'otherwise there'd be a lot more blood.'

More blood? Ollie looked again at the trail leading down the corridor, and noted the state of Keya's trousers. They were sodden all the way to the ankle.

'But the muscle's almost certainly been damaged,' Galen went on. 'And you're going to need stitches. A *lot* of them.'

'Just . . . get it . . . *out*,' Keya growled, and with tightened eyes she tried to reach and pull out the shard of glass herself. Her bloody fingers failed to find purchase on the glass, and when they slipped, Keya screamed again.

'*No!*' Galen insisted. 'The glass stays in, at least until we get you to the infirmary. If you'd managed to pull it out when you were on your own, you would almost certainly have bled to death before you'd got here.' She looked at Song. 'Can you fetch a stretcher? There's one in the infirmary.'

Song gave a single nod, and then she was gone, dashing off along the corridor. Moments later she was back, with one of Galen's assistants in her wake. Carefully they loaded Keya on to the stretcher. They were about to lift the stretcher from the floor, when they heard a door slam further along the corridor. There was a frantic pound of footsteps, and Imani appeared around the corner. She didn't appear to be as badly hurt as Keya, but her jacket was torn, and her face was scratched and bruised.

'Keya!' she yelled, when she saw her friend lying on the stretcher. 'Are you OK? What happened? How did you make it ba—' She skidded to a standstill when she saw the glass sticking out of Keya's thigh. 'My god!'

Galen held up a palm to reassure her. 'She's going to be OK. But we need to get her to the infirmary. Right now.'

Open mouthed in shock, Imani nodded, and backed against the wall to allow them to carry Keya through. Song bore one end of the stretcher, Galen's assistant the other, as Galen kept pressure on Keya's wound. Keya's eyes were barely open, but she smiled up at Imani weakly.

Once they were gone, Ollie, Casper and Imani were left standing either side of the corridor, Keya's blood in a splattered line between them.

'Ollie, I'm sorry, I . . .' Imani was staring after Keya, slowly shaking her head.

'Were you with her, Imani?' Ollie asked her. 'Where did you go? And what the hell happened out there?'

'Ollie!'

Ollie turned, and saw Jack propelling herself towards them.

'I just had a message from Song,' she panted. 'Where's Keya? Is she all right?' She noticed the spatters on the floor and her own blood drained from her face.

'Galen's with her,' Ollie reassured her. 'She needs stitches, but Galen says she's going to be OK.' He turned back to face Imani. 'Keya said something about being cornered. Did the two of you get separated?'

Imani looked ashamed. 'It's my fault,' she said. 'We went out last night to try to find out where Lily might be. To see if there were any rumours on the street worth following up.'

'You went out after the government's curfew?' Ollie said. 'I thought we'd agreed to lie low. Not to do anything that would attract attention.'

'We didn't attract attention,' Imani countered. 'At least, not at first.' She flushed and bowed her head. 'We took the sewers, obviously. We were on our way to see Keya's brother. He still runs the Forzas down in Brixton. Keya was hoping he might have had word somehow, or at least that he might be able to find something out. But I made us take a detour.'

'Where did you go?'

'I suggested we try my old gang on the way. The Free Souls, in Kennington. But when we got there, they . . . they weren't exactly pleased to see us.'

'What do you mean?'

'It turns out they've lost people, too. Kids who've been arrested for breaking the curfew, or sometimes for no reason at all. A bunch of them got picked up for loitering – hanging around on the street listening to music, basically. One kid got nabbed for tossing his burger wrapper into the gutter. He hadn't meant to. He'd been aiming for a litter bin, but missed, and a passing cop happened to see him. Then, when he couldn't provide a home address, the cops bundled him off and no one has seen him since. That's what Paws told me, anyway.'

'Paws?'

'He's one of the kids I used to run with. Me and him, we always used to get along. But he was the most angry at me out of any of them.'

'He was angry at *you*?' said Casper. 'Why?'

Imani looked at Casper, Jack and Ollie in turn. 'They blame us. They blame the Haven. For the curfew, for the government crackdown – for everything. They say the police would have left them alone if we hadn't gone around starting trouble.'

'*Starting* trouble?' Ollie echoed. 'You mean they believe all that rubbish Sikes has got the news channels showing on TV? That we're a bunch of brainwashed fanatics, who stormed a government detention centre? With automatic weapons? And *explosives*?' It was so ridiculous Ollie found himself smiling.

'Not Paws,' said Imani. 'But some of the others believe it, I could tell, and even those who aren't sure either way figure we must have done *something*. Maybe they don't know what exactly, but frankly they don't much care. All they really know is, the police are making their lives hell, on the government's orders, and as far as they can tell it's all because of *us*.'

'But that's like . . . like blaming turkeys for Christmas,' said Jack.

'I know,' said Imani. 'I tried to reason with them, but they wouldn't listen. They had us surrounded almost the second we popped out of the sewer, and it was only because Paws was with them that they didn't rip us to pieces there and then. But Paws said he owed me. I've helped him out of a scrape or two in my time. So he gave us a ten-second head start.' Imani sniffed, and shook her head bitterly. 'Ten poxy seconds. In return for all the times I've saved *him*. And what he said was, after that, if the other kids caught us, he couldn't be held responsible for what they'd do.'

'What would they have done?' said Casper, aghast.

Imani gave him a look, as though to say, *You really don't want to know*.

'So they were the ones chasing you?' said Ollie. 'It was the Free Souls who cornered Keya? She said she had to jump into a skip, and that she landed on a sheet of glass.'

'At *first* they were the ones chasing us,' said Imani. 'And if it had just been them, we would have got away. Keya's quicker than a greyhound, and me . . . Well. I'm no slouch. And we're both smarter than those Free Souls losers, Paws included. We double-backed on ourselves at the first corner we reached, sent the lot of them charging off into the night. But then, the second we broke cover, we got spotted by a squad of Rat Catchers.

Somehow they got between us, and we ended up running in different directions.'

'Did you say *Rat Catchers*?' said Ollie.

Imani nodded. 'That's what the gangs are calling the goons who are out there enforcing the curfew. They're the ones snatching up all the street kids. The beggars, the rough sleepers, too, from what I heard. The *undesirables*, basically. Isn't that what Crowe called us? The riffraff.'

'You mean it's not the police?' Casper asked.

'The Rat Catchers call themselves police, but they're not really,' Imani said. 'The actual police are out there, too, but mainly during the day, and only in the most public areas. Trafalgar Square, Covent Garden, places like that. But at night – on the back streets, down the alleys – it's the Rat Catchers who have got free rein. They wear all brown, and from what I've seen of them, they aren't exactly worried about keeping things legal.'

'What do you mean?'

'They're basically roving bands of thugs. They already had one kid in handcuffs when they ran into me and Keya, and the poor boy had been beaten black and blue. I'm sure the Rat Catchers would claim that he resisted arrest, but from what Paws said, they can claim what they like, because nobody is going to challenge them *whatever* they say.' Imani gave an angry sniff. 'It's as though they're above the law.'

Ollie looked at the floor. 'So this is how they're doing it,' he said, half to himself. 'Sikes. Crowe. This is how they're seizing control. First they make it look like the country is under attack, next they pass a law that allows them to arrest whoever they want to. Meaning they'll be able to lock up all their enemies, or anyone who dares to speak out against them. They've even started to build themselves a private army.'

'Well, Sikes isn't in control yet,' said Imani. 'Crowe isn't even prime minister, even if he's basically the one running things. And some of us are still trying to stop them. Right? I mean, that's why me and Keya were out there in the first place. Even if . . . even if it didn't work out quite how we intended.'

'Did you manage to find *anything* out?' Ollie asked her. 'About Lily, I mean. About where she might be?'

Imani looked at her feet. 'We didn't even get a chance to ask,' she said. 'Not that anyone would have told us if they knew. From what everyone's been saying, Sikes has got regular people thinking we're a bunch of terrorists, and she's got people like Paws – people who should know better – blaming us, too. I mean, we know the gangs out there have never liked us, but now they actively *hate* us.'

'Meaning that, whatever happens next, we're on our own,' said Jack.

Ollie had to admit, Sikes's plan was brilliant. On the one hand she was using Crowe to attack the Haven by undermining everything it stood for, rounding up the very kids it was the

Haven's mission to protect, at the same time as destroying the Haven's reputation. And she was simultaneously tightening her grip on power, making the public so afraid that they actually *supported* Crowe's policies.

'What about you, Jack?' Ollie asked. 'Have you made any headway?'

For the first time, Ollie noticed how tired Jack looked. Ollie knew that, like him, Jack had barely slept since Lily had gone missing, and that she'd been spending almost every waking hour scouring social media, or going over and over the footage of the attack on the detention centre that had been captured by her drone – anything that might yield the slightest clue as to where Lily had been taken.

But when Jack shook her head, Ollie knew it had been to no avail. 'Nothing,' she said. 'There's not a hint on social media. Just a lot of guff about what a great job Crowe's doing, and how the police should have been given extra powers years ago. It's as though people *want* to live under a dictator.'

Ollie felt his jaw tighten. It was like Jack had said: they were on their own. But they weren't entirely out of options yet.

'Ollie?' said Imani. 'What are you thinking? You're wearing that expression Song gets in the dojo, just before she clobbers you with a roundhouse kick.'

'Things have gone far enough,' Ollie said. 'It's time to act. *Now*. Before Sikes assumes total control, and we lose Lily for ever.'

'But what can we do?' said Casper. 'Jack and Imani just said it – we've no idea where Lily is.'

'We don't,' said Ollie. 'But Sebastian Crowe does.'

'Sebastian Crowe?' said Casper. 'The *home secretary*? Maddy Sikes's stooge – the person who controls the police force, and the Rat Catchers, and that bunch of mercenaries you ran into at the detention centre? The most powerful man in the country, who basically wants us dead. You're suggesting we ask *him*?'

Ollie smiled grimly. '*Asking* him wasn't exactly what I had in mind,' he said. 'But if we do this, we're going to need some help.'

12 FEEDING FRENZY

Lily had no idea how much time had passed when her cell door finally opened again.

She hadn't slept. There was only a thin, uncomfortable mattress to lie on in the cell, but she knew she wouldn't have been able to fall asleep had there been a king-sized feather bed on offer. Whatever drugs those men back in the detention centre had injected her with (how long ago that seemed now!) had well and truly worn off, and now only fear and adrenaline coursed through Lily's veins.

So when the door clicked and cracked open, she leapt immediately to her feet. She backed against the wall furthest from the door and raised her hands, so that she would be ready to fight if she needed to.

But no one appeared, and Lily realised that the door must have been opened remotely.

She edged forwards. Despite having been soaking wet when the guards had thrown her into the cell, she was in danger of overheating. With its metal walls and floor, the cell was like an oven set on low, and any lingering dampness in Lily's clothes was now mainly sweat. She was desperate for something to drink, which was the only thing distracting her from her hunger.

At the door she paused, and peered through the gap. Other prisoners were filing along the walkway outside. And unless Lily was mistaken, they were all *kids*. It was like watching the morning dash for breakfast back at the Haven. The difference was, nobody here was smiling. There was no laughter, no conversation even. Every single one of the children she saw looked as wretched as Lily felt.

She stepped outside the cell, and found herself buffeted by the steady stream of people.

'Hey,' she said, reaching for a girl who was passing, and who must only have been nine or ten years old. 'Where is everyone go—'

But the girl shrugged Lily's hand from her shoulder, and when she spun she practically hissed. '*Shh*,' she said. 'Are you *stupid* or something?' Her narrowed eyes took in what Lily was wearing and rolled skywards, even as the girl continued on her way. Lily looked down, and realised she was the only person not wearing an orange jumpsuit. She was dressed in the clothes she'd been wearing when she'd broken into the detention centre, though now they were so grubby they were barely recognisable. It occurred to Lily that she probably stuck out like a sore thumb. The girl had noted her clothes and had her marked down as a new arrival.

'You! Get moving!'

Lily looked up, and saw several guards watching from the walkway above. They were all holding cattle prods, and their masked faces were tracking the movements of the children down below. One set of hollow eyes had latched on to Lily, and the guard pointed his cattle prod menacingly.

Lily felt her fingers clench into fists, and she stared back furiously at the guard. But she recognised it wasn't a fight she had any chance of winning. The guard was armed, and there were a dozen others nearby ready to back him up. Lily was famished, thirsty and exhausted, and *her* friends were a million miles away.

She fought back tears. The stream of children all around her was thinning, and soon Lily would be left standing all alone. She looked up once again at the guard, then at the dwindling flow of prisoners. Her only option was to follow.

They trudged along walkway after walkway. The entire complex seemed to be made of steel, and there was no escaping that constant groaning sound she'd noticed before. Lily wondered if it was perhaps a symptom of her damaged eardrum, but when she covered up her right ear, she found she could hear the noise with her left ear, too. More than that, she could almost feel it vibrating in her bones.

She wondered if perhaps they were in a factory of some kind, and the noise was the sound of some great machine. She'd heard before about prisoners being forced to work, but if that was the case here, what would they have been making? And why was there no daylight? No windows, no skylights – no link to the outside world. The air smelt damp and musty, with a tang of oxidised metal. Lily had thought before that one of the corridors reminded her of a London Underground ventilation shaft, and her best guess was that the entire prison was buried beneath the ground.

After a while the sound began to change. On top of that background drone and the ringing in her right ear, Lily heard a noise that once again reminded her of the Haven. The further she walked, the louder the noise became, and soon she recognised chairs scraping, pots clanging and cutlery scraping plates.

The smell changed as well, and Lily caught the unmistakeable whiff of school dinners. Not the good kind, though. The odour made Lily think of vats of boiled cabbage and soggy, overcooked vegetables. But it was still *food*, and even the pungent, slightly gone-off stench was enough to make Lily drool.

Following the children in front of her, she turned a corner, and saw a set of double doors up ahead. The doors flapped as children filtered through them, and as Lily approached she caught only glimpses of what lay beyond. Then it was her turn to enter, and after catching the door as it swung back at her, Lily pushed it open.

And immediately stopped in her tracks.

In front of her was a vast, elongated room, almost the length of a football pitch, though only about half as wide. At the far end was the food counter Lily had anticipated, with a queue of kids bearing trays. In between were dozens of tables, all of which had been bolted to the floor. And around them sat the children in their orange jumpsuits: hundreds of them. Possibly as many as a thousand.

Lily felt her mouth fall open. Who were they all? And what were they all doing *here*?

'Move it, newbie,' came a voice from behind her, and Lily found herself being shoved into the room. The flow of kids carried her towards the queue snaking from the counter, and Lily did her best to survey the scene as she wandered through it.

Some of the kids appeared as young as six or seven, others were as old as seventeen. There were white faces, black faces and every hue in between. Most of the kids seemed to be speaking English, in accents from all over the UK, but Lily could also hear French and Arabic, as well as several languages she didn't recognise.

For the most part the prisoners kept their heads down, muttering into their food as they ate. One or two looked at Lily as she passed, and everyone who noticed her narrowed their eyes. Lily had to fight a rising sense of paranoia. *It's just because*

I'm new here, she told herself. *Because I'm the only one still dressed in their own clothes.*

Although when she surveyed the room more closely, she realised that wasn't strictly true. Dotted among the children were others dressed like her: more new arrivals, Lily guessed, from the way they were casting around as anxiously as she was.

As she joined the end of the queue, Lily noticed the guards. In their white masks and grey uniforms, they stood around the perimeter of the room at approximately five-metre intervals. There must have been thirty or forty sentries at least.

There was a squeal of electronic feedback, and then Warden Bricknell's voice filled the air, addressing the prisoners over a PA system.

'Good morning, children,' the warden said. 'I trust you had pleasant dreams.' There was a pause, as though Warden Bricknell was allowing herself time to smile. 'You will note some new faces among the group this morning. Please make them feel . . . welcome.' Again, a pause, and when Lily looked at the children around her, she noted one or two of them were smiling at her nastily. The rest of the kids nearby looked sympathetic, and somehow this was worse.

'After breakfast has concluded, the new intake will report to Administration for assignment of roles and the allocation of uniforms. That is all.'

With another squeal of feedback, Warden Bricknell was gone, and Lily was left casting around numbly. She shuffled forwards, idly following the boy in front of her, and searching around for some clue as to where 'Administration' might be, when once again she was nudged from behind. The younger girl who'd been queuing behind her had tripped forwards, as a group of five or six kids of about sixteen shoved their way towards the front of the queue.

Lily didn't recognise anyone in the group, but they looked like gang members: the type of kids the Haven had to contend with on the streets of London almost every day. Two thickset boys were leading the way – the bouncers of the group, Lily guessed – with a taller girl with bleached, cropped hair and a tattoo down the side of her neck just behind them. She had a shorter boy at her side, shrewd and sharp looking, and then another two bouncers following behind: two girls, this time, who if anything looked meaner than the boys in front.

As the group drew closer, Lily raised her chin and stood firm, instinctively slipping into *sanchin dachi*, hourglass stance, in the way Song had taught her. One of the boys bumped her with his shoulder, attempting to knock her out of the way, but Lily didn't so much as stagger. Instead, it was the boy who bounced away. He looked at Lily with a mixture of surprise and anger, and she glared at him. And then she found herself meeting the narrowed gaze of the girl with the tattoo: the leader of the group, clearly.

'Watch yourself, newbie,' the girl warned. 'You don't want to start making enemies before you have a chance to decide who your friends are.'

'I've got plenty of friends already, thanks,' said Lily.

The girl smiled, displaying a set of teeth that appeared to have been sharpened into points. With her long limbs and almost regal posture, she looked almost feline. Not like a house cat, though. More like a leopard or a cheetah – something vicious and wild.

'Not in here, you don't,' she replied.

And then her predatory smile broadened, and she walked on, slipping past Lily into the gap that had been created for the girl by her bouncers. The shorter boy who walked at her side looked back, appraising Lily coldly.

Lily surveyed the room again, conscious that eyes all around were trained on her. It was suddenly obvious to her that the prison wasn't quite the melting pot she'd first assumed it was. Rather, the inmates had clearly arranged themselves into groups – gangs, basically, some of which would have had more power than others. It was the natural thing to do in a place like this – people always felt safer in numbers, never mind that being in a gang also put you right on the front line. It was exactly like it was out on the street, and it occurred to Lily that as well as finding herself in prison, she'd also landed slap bang in the middle of a turf war.

Not feeling quite so hungry any more, she collected a plastic tray from the pile and edged towards the food counter. It was being manned by other prisoners, with one huge masked guard on the kitchen side of the counter watching on. When it was Lily's turn to be served, the girl behind the counter noted Lily's clothes, and sneered at her disdainfully. She slopped a ladleful of something yellow on to Lily's tray, not seeming to care that half of whatever it was spilled on to the floor, then raised her eyes to Lily in an obvious challenge. *Got a problem?* her expression seemed to say.

'Thanks,' said Lily, under her breath, before moving on to the next stop along the counter. By the time she reached the end of the serving line, she had four equally disgusting-looking dollops on her tray, and was none the wiser about what any of them were. The yellow stuff might have been scrambled eggs, cooked to the consistency of congealed potato, and the orange splatter was probably supposed to be baked beans, though if there were any actual beans involved, they were drowning under the thin, bubbly sauce. As for the green and brown splats, Lily didn't even want to think about what they might be. The one recognisable component of her breakfast was a single triangle of burnt, unbuttered toast. Lily thought of the kind of breakfast they would be eating at the Haven right about now, and *that* made her think of Casper, which in turn filled her with a strange and uncomfortable mix of affection, sadness and . . . guilt?

Lily shook her head and focused on the tray in her hands. Even though she'd lost her appetite, she knew she would need to eat. Given the ordeal that no doubt lay ahead of her, it was important she keep up her strength.

'Better watch your step in here, newbie,' came a voice in Lily's ear.

She felt a foot hook around her ankles, as whoever had spoken shoved her forcefully from behind. She staggered forwards, catching her balance in time to prevent herself face-planting into the floor, but there was nothing she could do to save her tray. It flew out of her hands, and landed in an explosion of noise and colour. At the same time, a cheer went up around the room, and as Lily recovered her balance, she felt herself flush with both shame and fury.

She spun to see who had tripped her, and wasn't surprised to see the bouncer boy who'd bumped into her a few moments earlier leering back at her. His friends were standing in a cluster beside him, with the cat girl watching on from one side. Her arms were folded and her chin raised, and the expression on her face was a warning. *Don't even* think *about trying to retaliate*, was the message to Lily.

Even so, and despite the fact that it would have been six against one, Lily couldn't help herself lunging forwards, determined to land at least one good blow on the boy who'd cost her the first meal she could remember having since she'd left the Haven. But a hand on her shoulder held her back, and when Lily spun to see who had hold of her this time, she was confronted by a warning look of another kind. It was the girl from the day before, who Lily had last seen cowering on the floor in front of Warden Bricknell. The deaf girl's eyes were wide, and she shook her head at Lily firmly. Then she showed Lily her own tray, seeming to indicate that Lily could share *her* food.

Lily hesitated, caught between the girl's act of kindness and the anger that continued to boil within her. But any decision about her next move was taken from her as another confrontation broke out elsewhere in the room. There was a shout, and then a clatter, and when Lily turned towards the source of the commotion, she saw that a fight had erupted at a nearby table.

And then, like a Mexican wave, the violence seemed to cascade towards Lily and her new friend. Chairs were shoved back, and trays upended, and the entire mess hall was consumed by a brawl. It was exactly as Lily had suspected – a single disagreement somewhere had escalated into a full-blown gang war.

Lily stood rooted to the spot, uncertain which way to turn. The cat girl and her followers had disappeared into the crowd, but where they had been standing there was now a group of boys swinging chairs at whoever was in their way. The path in front of Lily was blocked by fighting, too, as was the way she'd come. She looked behind her, and saw the prisoners who'd been serving behind the counter dashing towards the kitchens.

A siren kicked in, so loud and piercing, Lily had to cover her ears.

She faced her new friend. 'This way,' she insisted, uncertain whether the girl could lip-read. Just in case, she took hold of the girl's hand, and yanked her in the direction of the kitchens. If they could just get over the counter, they could duck out of sight until the fight diminished.

But this time when Lily turned towards the kitchens, she saw a squad of guards charging towards them. Like those boys swinging chairs, the guards were thrusting their cattle prods at whoever was standing in their path, and within seconds they would be right on top of Lily and her friend. They were trapped.

'Hey, newbie! Over here!'

Lily spun, braced for someone to attack her . . . but there was no one there.

'Down *here*, newbie!' came the voice again, and this time Lily felt a hand seize her wrist. When Lily looked, she saw a girl, who couldn't have been older than nine or ten years old, tugging at her from beneath one of the bolted-down tables.

She yanked on Lily's wrist again, with surprising strength, and Lily found herself ducking down underneath the table, dragging her new friend with her. Seconds later, the three girls were huddled out of sight, and the phalanx of guards broke around them like a wave against a rock.

The little girl grinned at Lily. She extended her hand. 'I'm Ember,' she said. 'It's a shame you didn't get to eat your breakfast, but you didn't miss much, I promise.'

There was a thud as something – or someone – fell on to the table above them, and Lily ducked instinctively. She looked at the girl, and held out her own hand. 'Lily,' she said. 'And this is . . .' She turned to the other girl, and realised she didn't know her new friend's name.

The deaf girl smiled, and made two short motions with her hands. Most kids at the Haven knew some sign language, and though Lily wasn't exactly fluent, she thought she recognised the movements.

'Aya?' she mouthed to the girl, who nodded and smiled.

There was another thud on the surface of the table, and this time all three girls ducked.

'Well,' said Ember, smiling again. She spread her hands. 'Welcome to your first day in the Pit.'

13 GHOST TOWN

A pall hung over Westminster, and to Ollie's mind it had nothing to do with the miserable weather. As soon as they'd broken cover, he'd noticed it: a dense atmosphere of fear and mistrust that was almost as visible in the air as the autumn fog. Ollie wondered if it was just here it was possible to feel it, so close to the nation's seat of power, or whether it was the same all over the country.

Ollie looked at his friends, and he knew they could sense the poisonous atmosphere, too. Because of the new government rules forbidding children to gather publicly in groups of four or more without adult supervision, it was just Ollie, Erik and Flea. Sol had wanted to come, too, but in the end he'd decided to stay with Keya, and Erik had taken his place. Sol's girlfriend was on her way to making a full recovery, but still needed help just hobbling around.

Neither Ollie, Flea nor Erik had talked much on their way through the tunnels. Even when they'd emerged through a sewer hatch on the edge of St James's Park, they'd stood in silence for a moment as they'd taken it all in.

Several things had struck Ollie right away. There were no tourists, for one thing. Ordinarily, and even so early on a miserable day in November, there would be visitors taking selfies with Buckingham Palace in the background, and on the footbridges that crossed St James's Park's central lake. But the park was virtually empty, and the only people outside Buckingham Palace were the ones guarding it. In fact there were far more armed police outside the building than usual, suggesting the palace was in lockdown.

The roads were less busy than usual as well, with traffic crawling at a strangely subdued pace. There seemed to be checkpoints preventing cars driving too close to the palace, and there were several helicopters hovering in the air. One looked like a police helicopter, which appeared to be monitoring the nearby streets for signs of trouble. The other two helicopters that Ollie could see looked like military aircraft, suggesting Crowe had gone as far as to mobilise the army against the supposed 'terrorist' threat.

It was the strangest atmosphere Ollie had ever experienced in central London. Normally the city made him feel alive, with its noise and its buzz and even its stench, all of which contributed to the sense that the city was the beating heart of the country.

Now, though, it felt more like a ghost town – less of a beating heart, and more like something that was dying.

It wasn't the first time the city, or indeed the country, had faced up to threats – imaginary or otherwise – but from what

Ollie knew of London's history, its people invariably came together in times of crisis. During World War Two, for example, there was the famous 'Blitz spirit', which refused to be dampened even by the steady downpour of Nazi bombs. And after the supposed terrorist attack that had claimed the lives of Ollie's parents, among others, there had been an outburst of public defiance, which had culminated in hundreds of thousands of people from all sorts of backgrounds marching through the streets of London to proclaim their unity. Ollie had been too caught up in his grief to pay much attention to what was happening at the time, but he'd read and heard about the march afterwards.

What was different this time, he wondered?

But of course he knew the answer already. By proclaiming there was an enemy in the country's midst – a secret, subversive organisation, intent on maiming and killing – Sikes had sown seeds of paranoia. She had people checking across their shoulders, seeing shapes they didn't trust in every shadow. There was no great external enemy the population could unite against, because the enemy – if Sikes was to be believed – was within.

'Ollie, look.'

Ollie turned in the direction Erik was pointing. On the wall of a nearby building, there was a graffitied version of the fake Haven symbol, with a red-painted line across it that looked like a slash of dripping blood. 'Down with Haven scum' had been scrawled beside it, in letters almost a metre high.

It was three days since Keya and Imani had returned from their ill-fated meeting with Imani's old gang, and in that time other Haven members had reported seeing similar graffiti, in places all over the city. There'd been more run-ins with gangs, as well as with the Rat Catchers, and even lonely street kids had taken to refusing the Haven's offers of help, fearing they were being lured into an outfit of radicals in exactly the way Crowe had described.

So Ollie wasn't surprised to see the writing on the wall. Still, it made his heart sink. It was an illustration of what the Haven was up against: not only Sikes and Crowe, but a pervasive hostility that had completely undermined morale at the Haven, to the extent that most kids had stopped leaving the sanctuary of Forest Mount at all. It was a stark contrast to the upbeat mood that had bubbled along the Haven's corridors after the kids had first moved in to their new home.

'Come on,' Flea growled. 'Let's get this done. We can worry about redecorating later.'

Ollie checked his watch. They were ahead of schedule, as they'd intended – partly in case they ran into trouble on the journey, partly because they wanted to get to the rendezvous point early, so that they could be sure they weren't walking straight into a trap. 'This way,' Ollie said, leading off, and they started across the road towards the park.

They kept their hoods up and their heads down, but even so Ollie caught the suspicious glances of the few people they passed along the way. A father with a buggy and a young girl walking beside him veered away from Ollie and his friends when he saw them coming. A businesswoman scowled at them, and the second they'd crossed paths, she raised her mobile phone to her ear. Maybe she was just making a call to her office, but Ollie didn't like the way she then looked back at them. Technically there was nothing they were doing that was illegal – they were just three friends going for a walk in the park – but who was to say whether that would be enough to save them if they were challenged? Maybe it was a mistake coming in a group. Maybe this whole plan was flawed from the beginning. But it was as Ollie had told his friends before: he didn't see that they had any other options.

Doing their best to avoid other passers-by, Ollie, Erik and Flea followed the walkway along the bank of the lake until they reached the eastern end of the park. In front of them was Whitehall, the very centre of the government of the United Kingdom. From where he was standing, Ollie could see both the Ministry of Defence and the Cabinet Office, while just beyond the vast stone buildings was the Palace of Westminster itself. Elizabeth Tower, which housed Big Ben, rose above them through the fog. Ollie had always considered it beautiful, but today the tower seemed somehow diminished. It looked old, and fragile, and incapable of standing up to the approaching storm.

'Where's the meeting point?' said Erik.

Ollie took his eyes from the looming structure, and cast around. 'There,' he said. 'By that coffee stand on the edge of the lake. But we've still got another – ' He checked his watch again – 'twenty minutes. Let's find somewhere to lie low. We'll keep a lookout until it's time, make sure it isn't a set-up.'

They turned towards a clutch of nearby trees – and straight into a wall of Rat Catchers.

'Well, well, well. What have we here?'

Somehow they'd sneaked up on Ollie and his friends. Ollie, for one, had been so intent on worrying what lay ahead, he'd forgotten to check behind him.

There were four of them, all men, each almost as broad as they were tall, and dressed in their trademark brown shirts. 'Civil Defence League' was emblazoned on badges across their breasts. They weren't carrying guns, the way the police were allowed to under Crowe's Emergency Action Plan, but they had fearsome-looking nightsticks tucked into their waistbands.

The one who'd spoken leered down at them.

'Get lost on our way to school, did we?' he said in a thick, east London accent.

Ollie saw Flea's fingers bunch into fists. Surreptitiously, Ollie placed a palm on his friend's forearm, willing Flea to stay calm.

'It's only eight o'clock in the morning,' Erik answered. 'School hasn't even started yet.'

'Exactly,' said the Rat Catcher. 'So maybe you can explain what you lot are doing up and about so early? Here, Horace,' he said, turning his chin towards the man next to him. He kept his eyes fixed on Ollie and the others. 'How many teenagers do you know who get out of bed these days without being crowbarred? Who are out on the town an hour before they're due to start school?'

'Only the ones who are up to no good,' replied Horace, in a thin, nasally voice that was entirely at odds with his barrelled belly and tree-trunk arms.

'What school do you even go to?' said the first man, who Ollie decided looked like a gorilla. 'There ain't none on this side of the park. Just these here governmental institutions, which are out of bounds for the likes of you.'

'We go to . . . St Jerome's,' said Ollie quickly, quoting the name of the school he'd attended before he'd joined the Haven. 'But today's an inset day. We're just here visiting the Houses of Parliament.'

'You know,' chipped in Flea, 'that big brown building over there. The seat of *democracy*. Where *laws* are made. The kind that guarantee individuals' *rights*.'

Briefly, Ollie closed his eyes. When he opened them again, the man who seemed to be in charge – Gorilla – had turned a vivid shade of red. He drew his nightstick.

'Names and addresses. All of you. And if you haven't got some ID on you to back it up, you can forget about visiting anything other than the insides of a prison.'

'That's not fair!' said Erik. 'We're not doing anything wrong. We've got as much right to be here as you have.'

Gorilla edged closer. 'Resisting arrest, are we, sonny? Failing to comply with the demands of an officer of the law? That's an automatic two-week sentence.' He grabbed Erik's arm, as with his other hand he produced a set of handcuffs.

'No, wait! Here!' Ollie dug into his pocket and pulled out the fake passport Jack had made for him, as she had for every member of the Council. It had been her idea, too, that they all carry the passports with them whenever they left the safety of the Haven, for precisely such occasions as this one.

Releasing Erik's arm, Gorilla snatched Ollie's passport from his hand. Ollie widened his eyes at his friends, and they handed over their passports, too.

Gorilla frowned at the photo pages, his eyes darting from the mugshots to the faces of the boys standing before him. His frown deepened, as though he were realising the passports checked out, and that he'd be forced to let Ollie and the others go.

Ollie shared a look with Erik, and saw the same relief in his friend's expression that he was feeling internally himself.

But then Gorilla's frown became a sneer. He held the passports out in front of him, and slowly tore them in two.

'Hey!' said Ollie. 'You can't do that!' He lunged, meaning to grab the passports from Gorilla's meaty hands, but another of the Rat Catchers held him off.

Gorilla stuffed the ripped-up passports into his pocket. 'I guess you'll have to tell mummy and daddy that you lost your passports somewhere on your journey. Assuming you ever see your parents again, that is.' The man's eyes tightened, and he gestured to his associates. 'Take them away, lads. It's the cells for these three.'

The Rat Catchers surged forwards, overpowering the three boys easily. Gorilla stood in the background and folded his arms. He smiled at Ollie. 'Take a deep breath, boy. It's the last fresh air you're going to be tasting for quite some time.'

14 BLACK OPS

'Oliver! Fletcher! Erik! *There* you are!'

The Rat Catchers were struggling to secure a pair of handcuffs on Ollie's flailing arm when Ollie heard the shout from behind them.

He turned, as best he could with his other arm wrenched behind his back, and saw the man he and his friends had come to the park to meet striding up the bank of the hill towards them.

'*Thank* you, er . . . officers,' said Montgomery Ross – the prime minister's special assistant, and former member of the Haven, who'd been personally responsible for securing Forest Mount as the Haven's new home. The first time Ollie had met him, Ollie had assumed Ross was an enemy, but despite his stuffy appearance and pompous manner, he'd since proven himself a genuine friend.

'Truly, I've been worried sick,' the man blustered as he drew closer. He waggled a finger at Ollie and the others. 'Didn't I tell you not to go wandering off? Honestly,' Ross added, looking at the Rat Catchers now and shaking his head, as though hoping to elicit some sympathy, 'children these days. They seem to have the attention spans of goldfish. I blame technology, if you want the truth. All that time staring at tiny little screens seems to have shrunk their brains.' He stood up straighter and took hold of Ollie's sleeve. 'Well, no harm done, I suppose. Come along now, boys. There's no sense wasting any more of these fine gentlemen's time. Thank you again, officers.'

Ross tried to lead Ollie and the others off, but Gorilla hauled Ollie back, so that for a moment he was caught in a tug of war. 'Here,' Gorilla said, 'where do you think you're going? We're not done with these three yet. They're under arrest for causing a public disturbance, and for failing to comply when questioned.'

Ross turned. To Ollie's surprise, the man laughed. 'Under arrest? No, no, no. That wouldn't do at all.'

'Wouldn't *do*?' Gorilla echoed, and this time he was the one to laugh. He turned to his friends, whose thievish smiles mirrored Gorilla's own. 'I'm not sure you realise who you're dealing with, friend.' He said this last word disparagingly, and he looked Montgomery Ross up and down. Ross was a head shorter than the leader of the pack of Rat Catchers, and half as wide. If it came to a physical confrontation, Gorilla could no doubt have squashed Ross with a single stamp of one of his size twelves – and both men quite clearly knew it.

Even so, Ross didn't back down. He let go of Ollie's arm and carried his smile closer to Gorilla, so that they were standing almost toe to toe. 'With all due respect, *friend*,' Ross said, 'I'm not sure you realise who *you're* dealing with.'

Ollie looked at Erik, whose eyes widened at Ross's unexpected show of nerve.

'This boy,' said Ross, and once again he grabbed Ollie's arm, dragging him so that he was by Ross's side. Ollie could feel Ross's hand shaking, and he could see the sweat that was bubbling on the man's forehead. Ross may have been acting tough, but Ollie had no doubt that he was as afraid as Ollie was. 'This boy,' said Ross again, 'is Sir Sebastian Crowe's godson. You do know who Sir Sebastian Crowe is, I take it?'

For the first time in the whole encounter, Gorilla appeared uneasy. 'Sebastian Crowe? You mean . . .'

'That's right,' said Ross. 'The *home secretary*. Your *boss* if I'm not very much mistaken. Sir Sebastian has charged me with escorting these boys to his private office. He's arranged for young Oliver and his two friends here to enjoy a behind-the-scenes tour of the Palace of Westminster. What do you think the most powerful man in the country would say if he learned that you'd decided to take his godson into custody for . . . what was it now? "Failing to comply when questioned"? I'd imagine the first thing he'd want to know is what you were doing challenging his godson in the first place!'

Somehow throughout his little speech, Ross had managed to grow taller, as Gorilla seemed to shrink.

'Well, I, er . . . I didn't realise who . . . That is to say, we . . .'

'And now look at the time!' interrupted Ross, with a theatrical examination of his watch. 'Thanks to you we are going to be late. And Sir Sebastian takes even less kindly to tardiness than he does to public servants who overstep the limits of their responsibility. Which is lucky for you, otherwise I would surely be taking a note of each and every one of your names, to deliver to Sir Sebastian *personally*.' Ross looked at the four Rat Catchers in turn, like a headmaster scolding an errant group of pupils. And, like naughty schoolboys, the Rat Catchers bowed their heads.

'Come along now, children,' said Ross, turning to Ollie and his friends. 'We have an appointment to keep.'

This time when Ross led Ollie and the others off, nobody tried to stop them. Ross took long, deliberate strides, and Ollie found himself scurrying to keep up. None of the four dared to look back, and it was only when they were safely around the corner, behind the coffee stand where they'd originally arranged to meet, that Ross slumped forwards and expelled the breath he'd evidently been holding.

'Oh, my,' he panted, clutching a nearby bench for support. The fear Ollie had detected in him earlier had obviously caught up with him in a rush.

Ollie moved to help him. 'Mr Ross? Are you OK?'

'*OK?*' Erik echoed. 'I'd say that was more than OK. That was *awesome!*' He clapped Ross on the back, with enough force that Ross staggered forwards. '*Crowe's godson*,' Erik enthused, oblivious to Ross's reaction. 'Did you *see* the look on that Rat Catcher's face? I swear to god he was about ready to run crying to his mummy. Or to fall on his knees and start begging for mercy!'

'They were nothing but a bunch of bullies,' said Flea, swinging a fist through the air. 'I *hate* bullies.'

Ollie was focused on Ross. The man had turned alarmingly pale, and the perspiration was running from his forehead in little rivers. 'Um . . . Mr Ross?' Tentatively Ollie put a hand on Ross's shoulder, but the moment Ollie made contact, Ross reared upright and shrugged him off.

'In answer to your earlier question, Ollie Turner,' Ross said, '*no*, I am not OK! Do you know what those men would have done to me if they'd found out the truth? If they'd realised who I *actually* was, and that I'd used Sebastian Crowe's name in vain? They would have locked me up! Tossed me into a prison cell and thrown away the key!'

Ross was pacing now, puffing in and out but clearly struggling for breath. He seemed to be in the middle of a panic attack.

'But they *didn't* do any of that,' Ollie said. 'We got away with it. You *saved* us.' He edged forwards, palms out, as though he were trying to placate a frightened animal.

Ross stopped walking. 'I did?' he said, and for a moment he seemed to recover himself. 'I *did*,' he said again, with more certainty this time. But then he shook his head and resumed pacing. 'But that's not the point. The point is, you should never have put me in that position in the first place. I shouldn't even *be* here. It was only because Felicity asked me to meet you that I agreed to come. But it was a mistake. *Clearly* it was a mistake.'

Abruptly, Ross turned, and started walking away. He didn't even pause to say goodbye, and it took Ollie a second or two to work out that he was leaving.

'Wait!' he called. 'Mr Ross, please! We need your help!'

Ross continued on his way. He didn't look back. He just raised a hand above his shoulder, signalling that there was nothing more Ollie could say.

Ollie turned to the others in a panic. Without Ross, there was no way they would be able to get what they needed, meaning they'd have no chance of rescuing Lily.

Ollie looked at Ross's retreating back. He opened his mouth, and said the first thing that came into his head. 'It's not just us,' he said. 'The *country* needs your help, Mr Ross! Your *prime minister* does!'

For a moment it seemed it would make no difference. Ross was leaving and there was nothing Ollie or anyone else could do to stop him.

But Ross slowed, and then stopped walking altogether. He hung his head, as though chastising himself for what he was about to do. And then he turned.

They crossed one of the footbridges so that they were on the other side of the lake. They'd spotted the pack of Rat Catchers heading off in the opposite direction, but even so, Ollie wasn't the only one to check periodically across his shoulder.

'I thought the Rat Catchers only came out at night,' said Erik, as he scanned the bank on the far side of the water. 'What were that lot doing patrolling during daylight hours?'

'They're getting bolder,' Ross replied. He was walking with his head lowered, and his eyes didn't settle for an instant. He didn't want to be there, clearly, but what Ollie had said to him had obviously struck a nerve. He'd evidently decided to at least hear Ollie and the others out – though how Ross would react when Ollie told him what they needed from him, Ollie could only imagine.

'The only reason they let you go is because I mentioned Sebastian Crowe,' Ross went on. 'But if they recognised me, and they decide to check out my story . . .' He dug a finger behind his tie to try to loosen his shirt collar.

'Relax, would you?' said Flea. 'The big, bad men have gone away. You're *safe*.' He turned to Ollie and Erik. 'Are you *certain* this guy was a member of the Haven?' he muttered. 'Because he sure as hell isn't acting like one.'

'Don't you understand yet?' Ross blurted, either not hearing Flea's aside or choosing to ignore it. '*Nobody's* safe! Not any more!'

'What do you mean?' Ollie asked.

'I mean, everything's changed now. Those . . . Rat Catchers, did you call them? They're basically Crowe's private army. Civil

Action Groups, he calls them. They report to him and *only* to him. And because of his Emergency Action Plan, he can lock up anyone he likes. All he has to do is accuse them of inciting terrorism!'

Ross was shaking his head. 'He's even got the press on his side,' he went on. 'They're spouting the same garbage Crowe is, that the country is under attack, and they're actually praising Crowe for the way he's dealing with things. Meaning the public are supporting Crowe, too.' Ross gave a full-throated, half-crazed laugh. 'Do you know, if a general election were held tomorrow, with Crowe on the ballot, I have no doubt he'd win by a landslide. Civil rights groups have been muzzled or disbanded, and the only opposition of any note is from within his own party. From the prime minister, in fact, who's growing more isolated by the day.' Ross shook his head again. 'Truly, I don't know how he's doing it. It's surely only a matter of time until Crowe mounts a leadership challenge. Until he takes over as prime minister himself.'

Once again Ollie looked at his friends. If Crowe were to become prime minister, that would mean Maddy Sikes would be pulling the strings of the highest politician in the land.

'Maddy Sikes,' Ollie said, looking at Ross. 'That's how Crowe's doing it. She was using Forest Mount to gather secrets on all the most important people in the country. The head of the police. Judges. The people who control the media. MPs, too, including

Sebastian Crowe. She's using what she knows about them to blackmail them into doing what she says. Crowe is just Sikes's puppet. Everything that's happening is happening because of *her*.'

Ross stopped walking. He looked at Ollie intently.

'I told you about Sikes before,' Ollie said. 'After what happened with Crowe's son. But, well . . .'

'I didn't believe you,' Ross said, sounding ashamed. 'I apologise, Ollie. I apologise to you all. I was wrong not to listen to you. And now it's too late to do anything about it.' He dropped his head and shook it.

'But it's not too late!' said Erik. 'That's why we're here.'

'Right,' said Flea. 'Sikes and Crowe may be planning on taking over, but we intend to stop them.'

Ross looked at Flea, incredulous. '*How?*'

Flea opened his mouth, but didn't answer. He turned to Erik, who looked at Ollie.

'We . . . we don't know yet,' Ollie admitted. 'But the first thing we need to do is find our friend. She was taken and we don't know where. And that's why we need your help.'

'But how can *I* help?' Ross said. 'Crowe doesn't confide in the likes of me. I'm on the prime minister's side, remember? As far as Crowe is concerned, I'm one of his enemies. Someone to be . . .' Once again he tugged at his collar. 'To be got rid of.'

'But you can help us find out where all the people being snatched are being taken. All we need to do is—'

Ross was already shaking his head. 'No one *knows* where they're being taken. People in the public eye – political opponents, journalists – are being charged under tough new anti-terrorism laws, and processed through the courts, but others are simply disappearing. If they're being detained somewhere, they're being held outside of the established prison system. If they've been deported, they've been done so secretly – and illegally, I might add. Crowe might be unpicking the constitution in this country, but he can't bypass *international* law. There are *rules* about how people are treated, which every country in the world has to follow.'

'So why hasn't Crowe been arrested?' said Flea. 'If there are laws, and he's breaking them, why doesn't someone do something about it? Your pal, for instance. The prime minister. Isn't she supposed to be Crowe's boss?'

'Right,' said Erik, nodding his head. 'Can't *she* find out where Lily is? Put a stop to what Crowe's up to?'

Ross shook his head again. 'I told you, she's too weak. She could count her allies in the cabinet on one hand, and the people around her who she actually trusts on the other. And she . . . she . . .'

'What?' said Flea.

'She's afraid, too,' said Ross ashamedly. 'She knows exactly what will happen to her if she crosses Crowe. If she attempts to limit his authority. Crowe will engineer some scandal – something that will end the PM's career or, worse, result in her being arrested, too.'

'So why hasn't he done that already?' said Erik. 'If he wants power, and the PM is already on the edge, why doesn't he just shove her out of the way?'

Ollie spoke before Ross could answer. 'Because Sikes has told him not to,' he said. 'She's biding her time. She's good at that, remember? But she'll finish us all off when the moment is right for her.'

'And besides,' said Ross, into the silence that followed, 'there's nothing the PM could do anyway. There's nothing *anyone* can do. There's no *evidence* about what Crowe is up to. Most of the people who are disappearing are the sort nobody can prove existed in the first place. Just like your friend. She's missing because nobody is trying to find her.'

'We are,' said Erik. 'The *Haven* is looking for her. And for all the other people, too.'

'And that's how we stop him,' said Flea. 'Right? That's how we stop Sikes. We prove to the world what they're up to, that Crowe is breaking international law. We just need to find my sister, and then we'll find everyone else who's being disappeared, too!'

Which sounded simple, Ollie thought, but in reality took them right back to the point at which they'd started.

'But that's just it,' said Ross, who was clearly thinking the same thing as Ollie. 'That's exactly what I've been trying to tell you. Crowe has covered his tracks. Anyone who knows what's happening is completely loyal to him. There's no way even a *hint* of where your friend has been taken would leak without—'

Ross stopped talking. His eyebrows joined at the middle.

'What is it?' said Ollie.

Ross raised his head. 'Deadfall,' he said.

Ollie and the others looked at each other.

'Did you say . . .' Erik began.

'*Deadfall*,' Ross repeated. 'It's . . . it's something I heard. Overheard, rather. Several times, from some of Crowe's closest allies – I just didn't know what it meant at the time. I still don't, but the way they were talking about it – *whispering* about it – it's obviously a code word for something. Or a . . . a secret operation or something. Which *has* to have something to do with the people who are disappearing. Doesn't it?'

Deadfall. Ollie turned the word over in his head. It did indeed sound like a code name for some kind of covert operation, though what it might actually mean, Ollie could only have guessed.

'Mr Ross,' he said. 'I told you before that we needed your help.' He looked across Ross's shoulder, towards the Houses of Parliament. 'Well,' Ollie went on, 'this is what we need you to do . . .'

15 THE PIT

'There must be *some* way out,' Lily said. 'There's always a weak point in the system. *Always*. No matter how foolproof its designers intended it to be.'

Ember and Aya were standing alongside her. They were in what could loosely be described as a workshop, though there was very little being done that could be classified as actual 'work'. In a regular prison, Lily knew, inmates were encouraged to acquire new skills that they might be able to use to earn a living once they were released back into society. Here, the prisoners were required to break up old computer equipment into its component parts, right down to the smallest screw. And rumour had it that other groups of prisoners were tasked with putting it back together, in other workshops similar to this one. None of the other kids had actually seen this happening, but Lily didn't doubt that it was true – she would have sworn she'd disassembled the same machine more than once in the week she'd now been incarcerated. It was the equivalent of digging holes and then filling them up again: mindless, mind-numbing work that simultaneously kept the prisoners busy, and ensured they were so exhausted by the end of the day that they lacked the energy to cause the guards any trouble.

At least, that was the theory, Lily imagined. Since the chaos in the mess hall, she'd personally witnessed two more full-blown riots, both of which had started as fights between rival gang members. There were at least a dozen competing groups in the prison, though in truth there was little that was actually worth fighting over. Unlike in normal prisons, no contraband came in, and there seemed no way of getting anything out – a letter, say, or a message to a loved one. There were no perks on offer – no extra exercise time, for example, because the only exercise the prisoners got was traipsing around the labyrinth of walkways. There wasn't even any turf worth battling for, because every corner of the prison looked identical: from the box-like cells to the metal corridors and stairwells. Even the orange jumpsuits worn by the inmates were indistinguishable, and the same bland food was served in the mess hall every day.

All of which meant that the gangs fought purely for bragging rights, for the chance to say they'd won. Not that any of them could hope to lay claim to top position in the prison hierarchy because that spot was unquestionably occupied by Kitty Xu. Kitty was the cat girl Lily had identified in the mess hall, who came as close as any of the inmates to legitimately being able to claim they ran the place. She was sixteen, and was apparently the daughter of one of the biggest gangsters in Glasgow

– indeed, in the whole of the UK. Half the kids in the prison seemed to have heard some story about her from before their time inside, and everyone feared her. At least, they feared the wrath of her father if they ever got out of here, and word was leaked that they had crossed Kitty while they'd been in prison.

Which seemed a nonsense to Lily, because it was perfectly obvious to her that *none* of them were getting out – not unless they escaped.

'What about tunnelling out?' said Ember. 'You know, the way they always do in the movies. *The Great Escape*, *The Wooden Horse*, even *The Shawshank Redemption*. Ooh, ooh, and *Escape to Victory*. That's one of my absolute favourites.'

Lily paused in unspooling a particularly tightly wound metal coil. 'How old did you say you were?'

'Nine,' Ember replied. 'Why?'

'Shouldn't you be watching kids' films? *Finding Nemo*, stuff like that?'

'I've seen that, too,' Ember replied. 'I've seen pretty much *all* the movies.'

Aya signed something with her hands.

'She wants to know how that's possible,' Lily interpreted. 'You know, going back to the fact that you're only nine.'

Ember shrugged. 'There wasn't much else to do in the foster home where I grew up. The only good thing about the place was that there were two TVs back to back in the living area. You

177

know, so that the kids didn't fight so much if nobody could agree on what to watch.'

Lily glanced at Aya, and saw her following what Ember was saying by reading her lips.

'Anyway,' Ember went on, 'if nobody else was around, it meant I could watch two films at a time. What I'd do was, I'd put both TVs on one of the movie channels, and walk around them in a circle. That way, I'd double my viewing *and* get some exercise.'

Aya smiled and dipped her head.

'Well,' said Lily, 'digging might have been an option if the entire complex weren't made out of steel.' She stamped her foot on the floor beneath them to demonstrate, and there was a dull, metallic clang. 'Plus, everyone calls this place the Pit, right? Because as far as anyone can tell, we're already below ground. Meaning if we were to dig our way out, who knows how far we'd have to tunnel up again before we reached the surface?'

Ember frowned, clearly disappointed by Lily's logic. They carried on working for a moment, conscious of the attentions of a passing guard. There were fifty or sixty kids around the workbenches in this particular workshop, and perhaps half a dozen guards circling the room to maintain order.

'Wait,' said Lily, raising her head, and checking to make sure the guard had moved on. She leant in closer to the others, keeping her eyes fixed on Aya so that the girl could see Lily's lips. 'Rather than dig, we could *climb*.'

Now Aya's eyebrows joined in a frown.

'Climb what?' said Ember.

'I don't know,' Lily admitted. She looked around the workshop, as though the answer would present itself. 'But if we *are* underground, the air down here must be coming from somewhere. Right? If we can access one of the ventilation shafts, we wouldn't need to dig a tunnel to the surface. We'd have a path laid out for us.'

Ember shuddered. 'I don't like the sound of that. You know, being squashed inside a metal tube. Like toothpaste.'

Lily had to fight off a wave of claustrophobia herself – not so much at the thought of the ventilation shaft, but at the knowledge she was *already* trapped. Maybe there was space to walk around down here, to stretch out as far as her limbs would allow, but that didn't mean she wasn't sealed inside what was effectively a metal box – one quite possibly buried under thousands of tonnes of earth.

'And anyway, the only time we aren't being watched is when we're locked in our cells,' Ember went on, and as if to prove it, another guard passed them by. 'Before you break in to a ventilation shaft,' Ember whispered, when the guard was gone, 'you'd have to break out of your personal sweatbox first.'

Lily considered for a moment. She looked at the metal coil she was unwinding, and thought of the electronic lock on her prison-cell door. After quickly checking again over her shoulder, she snapped off a section of wire, and tucked it up the sleeve of her jumpsuit.

Aya noticed her doing it, and looked at Lily fearfully. Lily glanced from Aya to Ember and back again. 'Don't you two *want* to break out?' Lily asked them, reading the expressions on their faces.

Ember and Aya looked at each other.

'Well . . .' Ember said. 'I realise this isn't exactly the Hilton, but it beats being out on the street. And there are regular meals, too. I mean, I'd kill for a KFC, but even at the foster home before they kicked me out, I never ate as well as I do here.'

'Really?' said Lily, placing a hand on her stomach, and trying to suppress the memory of the thin, grey slop they'd been served for lunch, which more than anything had tasted of rotten fish.

Aya waved a hand to catch Lily's attention, and then began signing. *I'm not leaving without my parents*, she said. *They're here somewhere, I know they are.*

It had turned out that Aya was one of the refugees Lily and her friends at the Haven had seen being paraded on TV: the so-called Haven recruits she and the others had been attempting to rescue from the detention centre. According to Aya, she and her mother and father had arrived in the UK after smuggling themselves aboard a lorry in northern France, having fled the war in Syria. After they'd presented themselves to British authorities to claim asylum, immigration officers had dragged Aya from her mother's arms, even as her father had begged the officials to let his family stay together. Now Aya was here, and she was convinced her parents were being held captive somewhere in the same complex.

It was entirely possible, Lily supposed. *Someone* was putting the computer equipment back together, after all, and there was no telling how big this place really was. Where they were, it was just kids – a sort of anti-Haven, Lily had decided, knowing full well that was precisely what Maddy Sikes had intended – but she knew that adults were being caught up in the government's crackdown, too, and they obviously had to be taken *somewhere*.

So Aya's reasoning made sense, sort of. She was convinced her parents would come for her, and she was terrified that if she escaped without them, they wouldn't be able to find her, and the three of them would be separated for ever.

'What are you so desperate to get back to, anyway?' Ember asked Lily. 'I thought you said you lived on the streets, too?'

'I did,' said Lily, looking down to cover her lie. Initially it had been instinct that had stopped her from telling anyone she was from the Haven – even the two girls who'd become her only friends in here. Lately, though, she'd come to realise how prudent that decision had been. More than that, it had probably saved her life. It had turned out that, almost without exception, the kids in the prison *hated* the Haven. They blamed it for the government's crackdown, and for the fact they were locked up in the first place.

And it wasn't just the inmates she had to fear. Warden Bricknell was on the hunt for Haven members, too. Seemingly at random, inmates would be dragged off, often disappearing from the prison's general population for days at a time. They were taken to solitary confinement, which was apparently in the depths of the complex. And when they returned, they invariably came back starving, desperate for water, and with visible signs they'd been interrogated. According to their reports, they were only ever asked one thing: *Where was the Haven?* Of course none of the other prisoners would have known, so Lily could be certain the warden wasn't getting any answers – none that would have led her where she wanted to go. But the fact that she was torturing inmates in a bid to discover the Haven's secrets only made Lily's situation more perilous.

'So what then?' Ember persisted. 'Is it the *cold* you're missing about being homeless? The constant *hunger*? The *fear* that you're never completely safe?'

'No, of course not.' Once again Lily flushed, feeling bad for not telling her new friends the truth.

But misinterpreting the rush of colour to Lily's cheeks, Ember's smile stretched. 'I know, I know!' she sang. 'It's because of a *boy*, isn't it! Like in *Clueless*. Or *Love, Actually*.'

'No!' Lily protested, loudly enough that some of the other kids looked across. 'It's not because of a boy,' she hissed. She spoke more sharply than she'd intended, but she was more angry at herself than she was at Ember – mainly because, rather than thinking about Casper when Ember had mentioned boys, the first person Lily had thought of was Ollie.

'Listen,' Lily said, sighing. 'There's something I should probably have told you days ago.'

'What?' prompted Ember, when Lily stalled. Aya was frowning her curiosity.

Lily leant closer. 'I'm . . . I'm from the Haven,' she whispered.

'You're *what*?' exclaimed Ember, and Lily flapped at her to keep her voice down. Aya's eyes had gone wide.

'It's not like you think,' Lily told them, in a rush. 'We *help* people at the Haven. We're not a terrorist organisation, the way the government is saying. They're just setting us up as the enemy, so that the public turns against us. They need to be able to justify all the evil stuff they're doing. Like separating refugees from their parents, for example,' Lily said, looking at Aya, 'and locking up hundreds of street kids in an illegal, underground prison.'

'But . . . the *Haven*,' Ember echoed, gobsmacked. 'Why didn't you tell us before?'

'Because I didn't know you!' Lily answered. She looked at her two friends in turn. 'You believe me, though, don't you? That we're the good guys?'

The other two girls exchanged glances. Tentatively Aya raised a shoulder.

'I guess,' said Ember, turning to Lily. 'I mean, if *you* say so. And I suppose it kind of makes sense. Given, well . . .' She cast around, at the metal walls and ceiling. '*This*.'

Lily almost melted with relief: that her friends believed her, but also that she no longer had to carry her secret all alone.

'You're from the Haven,' Ember muttered, as though testing the sound of the words. She looked at Lily with a kind of awe, but then her expression turned to one of concern. 'You know, I'd keep that quiet in here if I were you.'

'No kidding,' said Lily, with another quick glance across her shoulder. 'But *that's* why I'm so eager to get out of here. My friends will be looking for me. And if I can get back to them, there's a good chance we'll be able to help everyone else who's been imprisoned. Including your parents, Aya, if they're really here.' Lily looked at Aya pleadingly. 'So what do you say? Are you with me?'

For a moment Aya held Lily's eye. But then she looked down at the workbench, and gave a quick shake of her head. *I can't*, she signed. *Not without my parents.*

Lily exhaled deeply, unable to conceal her disappointment. 'What about you, Ember?'

But the younger girl didn't get a chance to answer. Her eyes widened at the sight of something over Lily's shoulder. Before either girl could speak, Lily was grabbed from behind. She caught a flash of metal, and felt something sharp being pressed against her throat: a knife perhaps, or some kind of shank. She wriggled, trying to break free, but there were two people holding her, and when she moved, the shank bit deeper.

'Hello, ladies,' said a voice, and even before the girl stepped into Lily's line of sight, Lily recognised the soft Scottish purr of Kitty Xu. She was showing those teeth of hers, sharp like daggers, and yellow, like her tightly cropped hair. The tattoo on Kitty's neck was of a lioness, and Lily didn't need to wonder why she'd chosen it.

At Kitty's side, as always, was the shorter, shrewd-looking boy Lily had first noticed in the refectory. Physically, he appeared almost stunted: a sixteen-year-old trapped in a twelve-year-old's body. Apparently, though, there had been nothing wrong with his brain's development. Connor Ward's IQ was reportedly off the scale. He was Kitty's closest confidante and adviser, and he reportedly saw and heard *everything*.

'How is everyone settling in?' Kitty asked. Beside her, Connor picked up a computer chip from Ember's workbench. He kept his narrow eyes on Lily as he turned it over in his fingers.

'What do you want, Kitty?' Lily growled. The two goons who were holding her tightened their grips on her wrists. They were standing so close, Lily could smell the fish from the lunchtime gruel lingering on their breath.

Kitty smiled at her. 'There's plenty that I *want*,' she said. 'But very little, unfortunately, that you can give me.'

Kitty's goons had hold of Aya and Ember, too, and Aya let out a silent shriek as one of them yanked her head back by her hair.

'Let's just call this a friendly reminder,' Kitty told Lily. 'Just so none of you forget who runs this place.'

The goon who was holding the shank pressed it into Lily's neck, and Lily felt it pierce her skin. She glanced out of the corner of her eye, and saw that the guard who was standing closest had turned his back, so that he was conveniently blind to what was happening. Kitty must have had even more clout in the prison than Lily had realised.

'Also,' Kitty went on, 'I have a ... request, let's call it. Warden Bricknell and I have an arrangement. She allows me certain privileges, and in return I give her what *she* wants.'

'Yeah?' Lily said through gritted teeth, and conscious of the blade against her throat. 'And what's that?'

Kitty spread her hands, as though the answer should have been obvious. 'The only thing I can offer that's of any value. *Information*.'

Lily gave a humourless laugh. 'You're a *snitch*, you mean.'

She braced herself for a reaction, because there was nothing worse among gang members – or inside a prison – than being called a snitch. At Kitty's side, Connor visibly tensed, but Kitty herself just shrugged.

'Call it what you like,' she said. 'Though I would advise you to watch your tone.'

Once again the shank pressed deeper, and Lily became aware of a warm trickle running down her neck.

'The fact is, the warden likes to know what's going on within these walls. Names, relationships, *associations*,' Kitty said.

Lily didn't need to ask Kitty to spell out what she meant. It was obviously Kitty who helped the warden decide which inmates to drag off and torture. She really *wasn't* someone you wanted as an enemy.

'You've heard of the Haven, I take it?' Kitty said, and she took the expressions on the three girls' faces as her answer. 'Well, should you come across anyone who might have information that the warden would find . . . valuable, be sure to come to me with it first. I wouldn't want anyone else claiming credit that is rightfully mine.' Kitty smiled again, just enough to show the points on her teeth. 'Is that understood?'

Lily had to suppress an urge to tell Kitty where to go. The boy on her left had relaxed his grip on her arm slightly, and she reckoned she could spin out of his hold if she was quick enough. As for the shank on her right, if she timed the manoeuvre just right, she would be able to knock it away as she spun, and end up with the first goon in front of her like a human shield.

But even if it worked, what then? She would still be outnumbered, even with her two friends' help, and there would also be Kitty herself to deal with. And after it was over, they would all still be trapped in this godforsaken prison.

'I said, *is that understood?*' Kitty repeated, showing the first sign of losing her temper. She looked at Aya, who nodded. Ember's arm was wrenched high behind her back, and even though her eyes were screwed tight, tears were running down her cheeks.

'I'll take that as a yes,' said Kitty, before turning to Lily. 'What about you, newbie? Have I made myself clear?'

Lily winced as one of the goons bent back her wrist. 'Crystal,' she replied, making her decision. Whether her friends agreed to come with her or not, she was getting out of this place the first chance she got.

16 PRISON BREAK

Now that she knew what she was searching for, it didn't take Lily long to identify the main ventilation duct drawing air into the prison. And once she'd found it, she was also able to locate a maintenance panel at the base of the shaft. It was only small, maybe fifty centimetres square, but it was large enough that she reckoned she would be able to post herself through. The difficulty would be loosening the screws that secured it in the limited time she would no doubt have available to her.

'Guys?' she whispered to Aya and Ember over dinner in the mess hall, on the tenth day of her incarceration. 'I'm going to need your help.'

Despite Lily's repeated attempts to persuade them, neither girl was prepared to risk trying to break out with her. Aya was committed to remaining in the prison on the chance she would at some point be reunited with her parents. Ember maintained she had nothing worth breaking out *for*, although Lily suspected the truth was the younger girl was afraid – and Lily could hardly blame her. But both Ember and Aya had promised to do anything they could to aid Lily's escape.

'I need you to create a diversion,' Lily told them, and she proceeded to outline her plan.

The next evening, as they were being marched along the walkway back to their respective cells, Lily waited until they could see the ventilation shaft ahead of them, and then tipped Ember the nod. For a moment Lily was worried the younger girl's nerve would fail her. But with a glance at the guards looking down at them from the walkway above, Ember summoned her courage. '*Braveheart*,' Lily heard the younger girl mutter to herself. 'You're Mel Gibson in *Braveheart*.' And then Ember gave a yell, and then pushed Aya in the back. Having known what was coming, Aya reacted as they'd discussed, and pretended to stumble into the girl beside her, forcing her to collide with a much bigger girl next to her.

As Lily had predicted, a shoving match ensued. The bigger girl retaliated, and then others waded in to protect the girl Aya had forced into her.

'Fight!' yelled Ember, throwing herself at Aya. The two girls grappled, as though locked in combat, but in reality bundling out of the way as a scuffle broke out all around them. From where Lily was standing, it was like watching dominoes fall, as first one of the inmates became involved, and then whoever was standing beside them. Over the yells and shouts, the alarm went off, triggered presumably by one of the guards watching from above, and in moments the entire walkway was consumed by a whirlwind of fists.

Hoping her friends would be able to extricate themselves before the guards began wading in with their cattle prods, Lily edged away from the centre of the brawl and towards the ventilation shaft. All eyes were on the fight, so nobody noticed her. When she ducked down to address the access panel, she found herself concealed by a forest of orange legs, exactly as she'd hoped.

She pulled a strip of metal she'd swiped from the workshop that morning from her sleeve, and frowned at the screws holding the access panel in place. Really she could have done with a screwdriver, but all the tools in the workshop were chained to the benches, to prevent prisoners stealing them and using them as weapons. So the best Lily could manage was a piece of old computer casing from the machine she'd been working on. She just had to pray that it was up to the job, and that the screws weren't rusted tight.

As it happened, she needn't have worried. The screws came loose easily, and Lily untightened them just enough that she would be able to free them with her fingers when she needed to.

She slipped the piece of computer casing into her sock and stood up among the press of prisoners. Raising herself on tiptoe, she searched for Aya and Ember, and was relieved to see them off to one side, trapped against a barrier, but away from the main clash of inmates.

Her primary goal accomplished, Lily found herself with time to spare, and an opportunity she knew she wouldn't get again. She looked up, around, and noticed a door open on the walkway above them. Prisoners weren't allowed up there, and usually the top level was lined with guards. Now, though, it was deserted, because all the guards were caught up trying to quell the fight that was in danger of turning into another riot. And that open door Lily had spotted was like an invitation. Maybe it was a control room of some kind. Lily knew that bypassing the electronic lock on her cell door wouldn't be easy, but perhaps there was some way of overriding it, or of altering the automatic timer so that it unlocked itself ahead of its usual schedule.

From nowhere, her brother's voice echoed in her mind. *In the midst of chaos*, Lily heard him saying, *there is also opportunity*. It was another Sun Tzu quote he'd pinched from Wikipedia, and one of several he'd regurgitated constantly in the days leading up to their disastrous mission to the detention centre. At the time, Lily had begged Flea to shut up, but now she found herself smiling, picturing her brother folding his arms and intoning the words sagely – completely unaware that he sounded like an idiot.

Still smiling, and thinking about how hard she would hug her brother when she got back to him, Lily turned, and started shoving her way past the other inmates towards the stairs that would lead her to that open door.

Near the top of the stairwell, she froze, having spotted two guards rushing towards her on the walkway above. She'd spied them through the gaps in the metal floor, and had just enough time to swing herself over the banister before the guards appeared at the top of the staircase. Hanging from the handrail, with her legs dangling in thin air, Lily felt like bait on a hook. But the guards were evidently in too much of a rush to notice her fingers around the banister, and they sped past without so much as a glance.

As Lily pulled herself back over on to the stairs, she realised she was coming close to actually *enjoying* herself. Maybe that was putting it too strongly, but she felt a definite buzz from the physical exertion, as well as the excitement. She had been imprisoned for less than two weeks, but already it felt like a lifetime, and this was the first occasion Lily had been able to do anything where it felt as if *she* was the one in control.

At the top of the staircase, she paused, cautioning herself about getting so caught up in the moment that she became overly reckless. She made sure the coast was clear before darting along the upper walkway towards the door that she hoped would lead her to the control room – and realised when she reached the threshold that she'd risked everything for a peek into what turned out to be a guards' break room.

Lily cursed. There was nothing in the room but a few chairs and some basic creature comforts: a kettle to make tea, a table bearing an ashtray and an open packet of cigarettes, and a vending machine in one corner that dispensed junk food.

There was no sense lingering. So her little foray had been a waste of time, but at least she hadn't been caught. If someone spotted her now, it would be solitary confinement for her, for sure. Would she be beaten and starved, the way suspected Haven sympathisers were? Or might she be made to suffer even *worse*?

She turned, meaning to head back out on to the walkway, but as she spun something caught her eye. A bottle, poking from one of the pockets of a jacket that had been slung over the back of a chair. Lily moved closer, and saw it was a half bottle of vodka. The hard stuff: at 120 proof, it was 60 per cent pure alcohol.

Lily paused, an idea fermenting in her mind. She swiped the bottle of vodka and tucked it behind the inner waistband of her jumpsuit. Then she turned back towards the table she'd spotted when she'd first entered the room. There was the ashtray, and the packet of cigarettes, and . . . *yes*: a cigarette lighter protruding from the open packet. She snatched it up, then hurried back through the break-room door. She looked over the barrier to see what was happening down below her, and saw that the guards were close to regaining control.

She made a dash for the top of the stairwell, trusting to luck that there were no guards watching. She half expected to hear a shout, the crackle of a cattle prod behind her, but she made it without anyone trying to stop her. She started down the staircase, but realised she was already out of time. The fight was over, and in seconds everyone on the walkway below would turn towards her, and see her halfway down the off-limits staircase. She had no choice, she realised: she had to jump.

Before she could allow herself to change her mind, she vaulted the banister the way she had before, but this time made no effort to grab the handrail. Instead she allowed herself to fall the full five metres to the walkway below. There was every chance she would break her leg, or at the very least turn an ankle, but as she landed, she rolled – using the break-fall Song had taught Lily and the others in the dojo – and other than a few shaken bones, she was able to get to her feet unscathed. She got ready to rejoin the crowd, parting her lips to disguise the fact she was out of breath, but smiling even so – until she turned, and came face to face with Connor Ward: Kitty Xu's sidekick and *consigliere*.

'What are you up to?' the boy asked Lily, his sly eyes arrowed. Unusually for Connor, he was alone. He and Lily were standing apart from the main group of inmates, the closest of which were beginning to trudge in their direction, shepherded by a phalanx of guards with their cattle prods raised just behind them.

Lily swallowed. Connor by himself was no physical threat. Lily didn't doubt she could have dispatched him with a single palm strike if she needed to. But with the guards closing in, a stand-up fight was out of the question. Besides, it wasn't Connor's hand-to-hand combat skills that Lily feared. Her worry was what he might have seen – and who he might tell.

'Get out of my way,' Lily blustered, making to push past him.

Connor didn't even attempt to stop her. 'Nice move, by the way,' he said. 'Getting your friends to pretend to fight to create a distraction.'

Lily stopped walking and turned to face him. Connor's lips made the shape of a smile, and Lily saw his eyes fix on the bulge formed by the vodka bottle beneath her jumpsuit. His reputation was well earned. He really *did* see everything.

'What I'm wondering, though,' Connor said, 'is whether you're stupid enough to be planning what I think you're planning. There's no getting out of this place, you know. And if you try, and fail, Kitty will make sure your life in here isn't worth living. She doesn't take kindly to little girls who jeopardise her relationship with the warden.'

'Who are you calling a little girl?' Lily snarled, looming over Connor now, and as the main group of inmates drew closer.

Connor's smile broadened. 'You are a feisty one, aren't you? Resourceful, too,' he added, nodding at the bulge in Lily's jumpsuit. 'Particularly for a *civilian*.' There was a note of admiration in his tone, but Lily didn't allow herself to be lulled.

What was Connor implying? Had he worked out that Lily was from the Haven?

'You two! Get moving!'

The closest guard yelled at them through her mask. She jabbed Lily with her cattle prod, the charge set low enough that it felt like little more than a bee sting, but even so, Lily riled. The guard had a smoker's rasp, and Lily took some small satisfaction from the likelihood the guard would be forced to spend the entirety of her next break hunting for her cigarette lighter.

Connor faded into the crowd, and Lily led the procession of prisoners back towards the cells. As she walked she contemplated Connor's warning. *If you try, and fail, Kitty will make sure your life in here isn't worth living.* Well, Lily thought, there was only one answer to that. She wouldn't fail. She *mustn't*.

'Tonight,' Lily told her friends. 'It has to be.'

It was the following day, and having enjoyed a dinner of congealed pasta topped with a thin, grey sauce containing the occasional lump of meat, Aya, Ember and Lily were hunched together in a corner of what was laughingly referred to as the recreation room. The single nod to actual 'recreation' was the television that blared in one corner, which was permanently tuned to UK Gold. Other than that, there was a bookcase filled mainly with novels by Charles Dickens – which of course all the prisoners ignored – and a stack of board games with most of their pieces missing. Again, nobody ever touched them. The kids who came in here only did so to gawp at the TV. The majority of prisoners opted to spend their rec time in the cell block, hanging around in one another's cells, or doing endless numbers of press-ups.

'Did you bring it?' Lily asked Ember eagerly. Lily herself had the vodka bottle, her bed sheet and the rubber seal from the sink in her cell all stuffed inside her jumpsuit. She planned to set a fire in the corner behind the bookcase, using the vodka and the bed sheet as fuel, and the black rubber seal to generate smoke. But without something to use as a fuse, the fire would be discovered before they'd even been locked back in their cells.

'Ye of little faith,' said Ember, beaming, and she reached below the table to pull the length of cord she'd promised Lily from her trouser leg. Ember had spent the past few days doing shifts in the laundry, and the cord was the drawstring from one of the laundry bags. It was thin but tightly woven, and just under two metres in length. It was hard to be certain, but Lily reckoned that, once lit, it would burn for about an hour before the flame reached the main, vodka-soaked pyre. And after that, the fire and the smoke would most likely be enough to buy her a twenty-minute window.

Lily checked around. The only guard in the rec room was facing in the opposite direction, and all the other kids were glued to the TV. She accepted the rope from Ember with a grin.

'Cover me,' Lily said, even though she knew this part would be easy. She ducked behind the bookcase and set up her little distraction, and less than four minutes later was back in her seat. Neither the guard nor any of the other children appeared to have moved.

'Now I just need to light the fuse before we leave, and the clock will start ticking,' Lily told the others. She was grinning again, but Aya in particular didn't appear to share her excitement.

Are you sure you've thought this through? she signed. *What if they catch you?*

Lily reached across the table, taking hold of her friends' hands. 'It will all work out,' she told them. 'And I'll come back for you. I *promise*.'

Rather than appearing reassured, Lily's friends gazed back at her anxiously.

'It's not us we're worried about,' said Ember, with uncharacteristic gloom.

Nobody spoke much after that. They sat around the table pretending to play cards, with a deck that was missing most of the hearts. In no time at all, it felt like to Lily, a buzzer sounded, indicating it was time for lockdown. Her confidence had dipped over the course of the evening, but she did her best to snap herself out of it. As the rest of the children began to file out of the rec room, she ducked back down behind the bookcase and used the lighter she had stolen to light the fuse – and immediately felt a steely resolution. There was no turning back now.

She would have liked to have hugged her friends to say goodbye, but there was no chance of that with the guards watching. Instead when Lily reached her cell, she gave both Aya's and Ember's hands a quick squeeze. With terrified eyes, they nodded back at her, and then Lily had no choice but to step into her cell and watch the door slide shut behind her.

As soon as the electronic lock engaged, Lily set to work. The clock was ticking, and there was no time for indecision. And actually, once she'd focused on the task in front of her – removing the panel that housed the circuitry of the lock, and then overriding the signal that sealed the door – she felt that familiar buzz of adrenaline, and a resurgence of the optimism she'd experienced before. She was getting out of here. Out of her cell, and along the hopefully deserted corridor, and then up the ventilation shaft – and eventually, somehow, back to her friends.

After so many days and nights being stuck inside a cage, it made Lily almost giddy to think that she would soon be *free*.

17 SCHOOL TRIP

Less than thirty-six hours after meeting with Montgomery Ross in St James's Park, Ollie and his friends were back in central London. Or *beneath* it, rather, and for once they were surrounded by other people. They were in the Churchill War Rooms, the underground bunker below Whitehall that Prime Minister Winston Churchill and his cabinet had used as their emergency headquarters during World War Two, and which was now a public museum.

They'd arrived in pairs to avoid arousing any suspicion: first Ollie and Sol, then Flea and Jack, and finally Song and Erik. Once they were inside, they were able to draw closer together, although Ollie for one remained conscious of the cameras tucked high against the ceilings, and the beady eyes of the resident security guards. But with so many other kids down here – families of tourists, schoolchildren visiting with their teachers – it was relatively easy for the Haven kids to blend in. And surely the Rat Catchers couldn't get to them *everywhere*.

'Whoa, check it out,' Sol enthused, and he disappeared around a corner in one of the narrow stone tunnels.

The War Rooms were a specially constructed network of passageways and chambers, with enough space to allow an entire government to function while being protected from the hailstorm of Nazi bombs. There were meeting rooms, offices, even bedrooms, all sheltered beneath an umbrella of concrete and steel. And most importantly as far as Ollie was concerned, the entire complex was right in the heart of Westminster, a stone's throw from the Houses of Parliament themselves.

Sol was peering through a doorway at a small room containing a bed, a rug and a desk bearing a microphone. 'This was Winston Churchill's bedroom. And he sat *right there*,' he said, pointing to the desk. 'It's where he made his speeches!' He cleared his throat, and tucked his chin against his chest. ' "I have a dream . . ." ' he intoned, in what was evidently his best Churchill voice.

Jack tutted. 'That was Martin Luther King, you idiot,' she said. 'Churchill said stuff like – ' Jack lowered her voice and began pumping her fist – ' "We shall fight on the beaches . . ." and "I have nothing to offer but blood, toil, tears and sweat." '

'Um, guys . . .' said Song, and she motioned with her eyes to indicate that their performances were attracting the attention of other visitors funnelling past them in the narrow tunnels.

'Well, anyway, it's pretty cool whatever he said,' Sol responded. 'To think, while Aunt Fay and her mates were setting up the Haven, mapping all the tunnels below the streets of London, the entire British government was underground, too. In its own haven, basically.'

Flea sniffed derisively. 'I don't see what's so impressive about it.' He cast around, ducking slightly to avoid the low hanging ceiling. 'I mean, talk about pokey. You'd think that, with all the resources at the government's disposal, it could have done a better job than a bunch of penniless, homeless kids. I'd take the ghost station over this place any day of the week.'

For once Ollie agreed with Flea. As impressive as the War Rooms were, and for all their historical significance, there was barely space down here to spread your arms. The ghost station may have felt crammed when a hundred and fifty Haven kids had been living there, and the air might not exactly have smelt of daisies, but at least the tunnels had been spacious enough that there was rarely any danger of banging your head. And apparently in Churchill's day, pretty much everyone had smoked, even in the underground bunker. Ollie tried to imagine what it must have been like for all the people who'd had to live and work down here. He felt claustrophobic enough from just the press of other visitors, but if you added in the cigarette smoke, and the rumble of bombs detonating on the surface above . . .

'Come on,' he said to the others. 'Best keep moving. And maybe we shouldn't all gather so closely together. You never know who might be watching.' He eyed one of the security cameras, which seemed to be tracking Ollie and his friends along the passageway.

He led off, heading deeper into the complex. It would have been easy to become disorientated down here, but Ollie had studied a map of the place before they'd set out, and anyway his sense of direction had improved a hundredfold since he'd joined the Haven. When it came to navigating through labyrinths of underground passageways, they'd all had plenty of practice.

'I've just realised,' said Sol, who was walking at Ollie's shoulder. 'This is, like, the Haven's first ever proper school trip.'

Ollie smiled. He was trying hard not to worry about the dangers that lay ahead of them, and he took heart, as he always did, from his best friend's presence at his side. 'Let's just hope nobody asks to see our permission slips,' he responded.

They veered right, bypassing a group of American tourists, and past a chamber that had apparently housed the world's first ever 'hotline' – between Churchill and the president of the United States.

'Is it just me,' said Erik, from somewhere towards the rear of the group, 'or does anyone else find it weird to be walking through tunnels and not have sewage sloshing around our feet?'

Ollie was concentrating on the mental map he was carrying with him in his head. 'I think we're just about . . . *there*,' he announced, and he gestured towards a doorway about twenty metres ahead.

'You mean we're supposed to go through that door?' said Sol. 'The big red one? With "Entry Strictly Forbidden" emblazoned across it?'

The door was down an offshoot of the passageway that was also closed to the general public.

'That's right,' Ollie answered. 'And without anybody seeing us.'

If anything, the crowd around them had thickened. None of the other visitors to the War Rooms gave any sign they'd noticed the doorway, however. They just continued shuffling in a messy huddle along the prescribed route around the museum.

'Jack,' Ollie said, 'can you do something about those CCTV cameras? And, Flea, do you think you can take care of the lock when we get close enough?'

'No problemo,' said Flea, twirling the key ring that held his lock-picks around a finger.

'Sure thing, Ollie,' said Jack, pulling out her phone and readying the app she'd developed. 'Just say the word.'

'But what about all these people?' said Erik. 'Even if we cut out the CCTV, how are the six of us going to slip away without anybody noticing?'

'Song?' Ollie prompted.

Song was looking at the watch on her wrist. 'Six, five, four,' she began, as she counted down the seconds. 'Three, two . . .'

'Ladies and gentlemen,' came a voice across the PA system, and Song looked up and smiled. 'The Churchill War Rooms will be closing in ten minutes. Please make your way to the exit. We hope you have enjoyed your visit.'

Almost immediately, the people who'd been studying the exhibits around them started hunting for the exit signs. After a moment, the Haven kids found themselves standing in the passageway all alone, except for one family of four who had continued staring at one of the displays and chatting away in what sounded to Ollie like Spanish. They either hadn't heard the PA announcement, or hadn't understood it.

'Erik,' hissed Ollie, 'it looks like you're up.' Now that they'd lost the cover of the crowd, Ollie realised they were dangerously exposed. Subtly, he eyed the CCTV camera that was right above them, and wondered who might be watching – and what whoever it was would make of the sight of six teenagers hanging around without an adult being present to supervise, in direct contravention of Sebastian Crowe's Emergency Action Plan. Would they already be reaching for the phone to summon the Rat Catchers?

Erik nodded at Ollie, and then marched up to the family of tourists.

'*Perdóneneme*,' he said, in what Ollie knew would be perfect Spanish. Erik spoke six languages fluently, and a handful of others well enough to hold a conversation. '*El museo está cerrando*,' he informed the stragglers. Then, when they simply stared back at him, '*Tienen que irse,*' he added more forcibly. Still the family didn't move, clearly confused by the fact they were being told what to do by a kid. Losing patience, Erik clapped his hands and jerked his head towards the exit. '*¡Rápido! ¡Vamos, vamos!*'

Startled, the family started backing away, and then turned and hurried towards the exit. The mother threw a worried look at Erik over her shoulder, as though fearful he might be about to pursue them.

'Nice work,' said Ollie, with a wry smile. 'Your turn, Jack.'

Jack gave a single tap on the screen of her phone. 'Done. I've disabled those cameras for the next sixty seconds. Any longer than that, and the people watching will start to wonder whether it isn't something more than just a technical glitch. Reckon that gives you enough time, *el Fleabag*?'

'Probably not,' Flea responded cheerily. 'But I do like a challenge.' He swung a leg across the rope that was blocking off the passageway, and led the way towards the door. After spending a good ten seconds or so looking at the lock, he selected one of the tools on his key ring and set to work.

'Flea . . .' Song warned, twenty seconds later, and with her eyes on her watch once more.

'Almost there,' Flea muttered, but to Ollie his voice sounded strained, as though he was trying to convince himself as much as anyone.

Ollie looked at Jack, and saw she was already primed to give the CCTV system another jolt – although he'd noted her earlier warning, too, that if the system was out for much longer than a minute, an alarm would almost certainly be raised.

Flea continued wriggling his pick in the keyhole. 'Damn, this lock is proving – ' there was a click – '*way* easier than I thought,' he finished, beaming. He stood up and opened the door. 'I'd wait for a round of applause, but I realise we're in a bit of a hurry. Shall we?'

They bundled through. Ollie dragged the door closed behind them, and just as the latch clicked back into place, Song's watch emitted a beep, signalling the sixty seconds was up.

Jack powered on the torch beam on her phone and looked around. 'Is this . . . ?'

'A broom cupboard,' finished Erik. He looked up, down, left, right. 'We went through all of that to break into a *broom cupboard*?'

Ollie cast around doubtfully. It did indeed appear as though they'd achieved nothing more than managing to lock themselves inside a storage cupboard. The room was maybe two metres square, with the door they'd just negotiated the only way in and out. In fact it was the only noticeable feature in the room at all. Beneath them was a stone floor, and the walls were bare concrete.

'Ollie?' Sol said questioningly.

Ollie closed his eyes, and ran through the map in his head, retracing their steps since they'd entered the War Rooms. 'This is definitely where we're supposed to be,' he said, with more conviction than he felt.

'So what now?' said Song.

The six of them were pressed so close together, there wasn't even space to sit down.

'Now . . .' said Ollie, checking about him once more. He shrugged. 'Now I guess we wait.'

Deadfall. The word had been running around and around Ollie's head since Montgomery Ross had first mentioned it. Now, as Ollie and his friends waited in the darkness for something to happen, he found his thoughts returning to it.

Deadfall. It sounded like . . . like the headquarters of some comic-book supervillain. Why was it the word on the lips of Crowe's allies in the Houses of Parliament? What did it mean? And would it really lead them to Lily? It had been almost two weeks now since Lily had been taken, and not a word had reached the Haven about her whereabouts. Was Deadfall the place she was being held? Or was it a red herring – a clue to another mystery entirely?

All of a sudden, after more than four hours waiting – a period that felt like an eternity – there was a click, and Ollie and the others were immediately alert, ready for whatever was coming. Instinctively, Ollie focused on the door. But rather than through the doorway, the shaft of light that appeared came from behind them.

Ollie spun, shielding his eyes against the brightness – and saw, once they'd adjusted to the light, that the wall had slid almost noiselessly to one side. It wasn't a wall at all, but a secret entrance, so well disguised it had fooled even Ollie and his friends.

'Ollie?' came a voice. 'Are you . . .'

'Mr Ross,' said Ollie, wriggling his way to the front. Or the rear. Or whatever it was. 'We were beginning to give up hope.'

'Well, I . . .' Ross bridled slightly. 'I had to wait for night to fall, obviously. And this wasn't the most straightforward of operations, I can assure you.' He cast around the faces in front of him. 'And I must say I wasn't expecting so *many* of you.'

'In for a penny,' said Flea, 'in for a pound. We figured if we were going to get arrested, we may as well get arrested together.' He shoved his way past Ross and into the space beyond him. Flea stretched, cat-like, as he took in their new surroundings. 'Now *this* I can appreciate. They should make all sewers like this.'

Ollie and the others emerged, too. The 'broom cupboard', it turned out, was an access point, like an airlock, into the tunnel that they were standing in now. And it wasn't like any other underground tunnel Ollie had ever been in. The walls were made of lime-washed stone, and there were strip lights on the ceiling above them, leading off into the distance. Below their feet, covering the flagstones, there was even a stretch of *carpet*.

'This isn't a sewer, young man,' said Ross, as though personally offended. 'This is one of the tunnels that was specially constructed to allow top-level government officials to evacuate the Houses of Parliament should they ever come under direct attack. As far as the outside world knows, this tunnel doesn't even *exist*.'

'Q Whitehall,' muttered Jack, looking around with obvious awe. 'So the rumours were true.'

'Q Whitehall?' echoed Sol.

'It's what they call this place,' Jack explained. 'I mean, it's not the official name. Nobody knows what it's really called. It's classified, naturally. But people have been speculating on the existence of a secret network of tunnels below Westminster for years.'

'Q Whitehall is just *one* of the tunnels that are down here,' said Ross, almost dismissively. 'There are entire underground citadels, scattered right across the city. Even the prime minister hasn't been told about them all.' He cast around the tunnel and added, 'It *is* quite impressive, though, isn't it? A remarkable feat of engineering.' He seemed to catch himself, and turned back to Ollie. 'Anyway, this is what you asked me to find for you. *A way in.*'

Ollie moved towards the front of the group, peering to try to make out the far end of the tunnel.

Ross moved aside and held out an arm. 'If you really want to break into the Houses of Parliament,' he said, 'this is how you do it. *This* is how you gain access to Sebastian Crowe's private office.'

18 HIGH TREASON

Ross led the way along the tunnel.

'Personally,' said Flea, 'I hope Crowe's there to greet us when we kick down the door to his office. I'll teach *him* to kidnap my sister. To blame *us* for the murder of those two guards.'

Ross looked over his shoulder, eyes wide. '*Kick* down the door to Crowe's office? No, no, no. That wouldn't do at all! You do realise what will happen to you if you're discovered? To me, if *I'm* discovered?'

'Sure,' said Flea. 'They'll try to arrest us. Well, let them try, I say. The Flea won't go without a fight.'

Ross stopped walking and spun. 'Young man,' he said, as the entire group was forced to a halt. 'Once we're inside the Houses of Parliament, it won't be a bunch of Rat Catchers we'll be dealing with. The guards in the Palace of Westminster are some of the most highly trained police officers in the land. And they have licence to shoot first and ask questions later. At the slightest provocation, they'll—'

'Relax,' Sol told him, patting his arm. 'Old Fleabag is just mouthing off. It's how he deals with tension. You'll get used to him. Or not,' he added, with a shrug.

'*Tension*,' muttered Flea, as they resumed walking. 'Pah. What tension? The Flea doesn't *do* tense. This, right here – it's what the Flea was *born* to do. As Sun Tzu said, "He who knows when he can fight and when he cannot will be victorious."'

'Oh,' Sol added, leaning into Ross conspiratorially, 'and he also has a tendency to start spouting random quotes he picked up on the internet. And to talk about himself in the third person. His sister is usually the one to shut him up, which is why it's *doubly* important we rescue her.'

Ross seemed unsure whether Sol was joking.

'Remember, everyone,' said Ollie, as the end of the tunnel came into sight, 'we'll only get one shot at this. We get in, get what we need and then get out again. Clean and quick. Agreed?'

Flea made a grumbling noise, but didn't object. For all his bluster about kicking down the door to Crowe's office, he was clearly doing his best to curb his most reckless instincts. Ollie knew Flea blamed himself for what had happened to Lily, because he was the one who'd led the charge into the detention centre. That was nonsense, as far as Ollie was concerned. *Maddy Sikes* was the person most responsible, for everything that was happening – but even so, Ollie knew exactly how Flea felt. It was hard not to blame yourself, when Lily was the only person who'd been on the team who'd argued against going to the detention centre in the first place.

But at least now they had a chance to make things right.

'That door at the end of this tunnel will take us into a basement directly below Westminster Hall,' said Ross. 'From there, we'll be able to access a stairwell that will take us to the top floor, which is where Crowe has his office. The tightest security is focused on the various entry points to the building, so we'll have bypassed all of that, but there will still be armed security officers patrolling the corridors.'

Who will open fire at the slightest provocation, Ollie reminded himself, recalling what Ross had said before.

'What about the people who actually work here?' said Erik. 'Won't they be wandering around, too?'

'It's – ' Ross checked his watch – 'twenty to midnight. At this time on a Friday night, everyone will already have gone home. Back to their constituencies, in the case of the MPs. And once *they* leave, the building fairly rapidly empties out. On the other hand, there are CCTV cameras *everywhere*,' he went on. 'Not down here, or else it would become common knowledge that this tunnel actually exists, and not in Crowe's office itself, obviously, but as soon as we get level with the main hall, there will be somebody watching.'

'We've got that covered,' said Ollie. 'Right, Jack?'

'Right,' Jack agreed. 'I've set up a rolling wave of interference, so that the coverage will cut out as we approach. We'll effectively be walking in our own personal cloud of static. With any luck, the people watching will assume it's an electrical fault flowing around the circuitry. It happens occasionally, particularly in a building as old as this one. We'll need to move quickly, though,' she warned, 'or else we run the same risk we faced in the War Rooms. If a camera cuts out for more than twenty or thirty seconds, someone will be dispatched to investigate. This isn't just a tourist attraction, remember. This is the most important building in the country. With security already on high alert, nobody will be taking any chances.'

They'd reached the door. Ollie took a deep breath. 'Ready?' he asked, looking around.

Ross visibly gulped. But Flea, Erik, Song, Jack and Sol each responded with a swift, determined nod.

The first thing Ollie noticed when they passed through the doorway was the smell. Somehow the insides of the Houses of Parliament *smelt* important: old and musty, with the scents of wood and leather and polished brass all mingling together in the weighty air.

As Ross had promised, they were able to bypass Westminster Hall, the huge open space that Ross informed them was the oldest part of the Palace of Westminster. Through a window on the stairwell as they climbed, Ollie caught a glimpse of vast stone walls, and an enormous oak-beamed roof. He also saw at least half a dozen armed security guards clustered at the end of the hall nearest the doors that led outside. If Ollie and his friends had attempted to enter the building that way, they would have been apprehended for sure.

'How much further?' puffed Erik, who was helping Song with Jack's wheelchair. Flea was carrying Jack herself, and he didn't even appear out of breath.

'Just another four flights,' Ross replied, as he led the way up the narrow stairwell.

'*Four?*' Erik echoed, horrified. He adjusted his grip on the wheelchair.

'At least you're getting some exercise,' said Song. 'Half an hour ago, when we were crammed in that antechamber, you were complaining about not being able to move.'

'Yeah, well,' huffed Erik, 'you would have been complaining, too, if it had been *your* nose wedged in Flea's armpit.'

Just as Ross had predicted, there were security cameras everywhere. Ollie had spotted three, so far, on the stairwell alone.

'Whatever you do,' he said, 'keep moving. You heard what Jack said about those cameras. And keep your eyes and ears open for any guards.'

But they saw and heard none. By the time they'd reached the top floor and Jack was back in her wheelchair, Ollie had started to wonder whether security was really as tight as Ross had feared it would be, or whether the security guards weren't clustered solely around the entry points to the building. Either way, their luck appeared to be holding. It made a change, Ollie thought to himself grimly. Since their battle with Maddy Sikes had begun, the odds seemed to have been stacked against them.

'Crowe's office is at the end of this corridor,' said Ross, as they huddled in a camera's blind spot at the top of the stairwell. 'You can't miss it. Look for the big, gold plaque on the door. He's the only person in the cabinet who has one. And his office is three times as big as anyone else's. When he was appointed home secretary, he had three junior MPs kicked out of the building, and the rooms they'd occupied knocked through into one.'

Ross moved towards a doorway opposite.

'Now if you'll forgive me, I have an appointment with the prime minister. I'm supposed to be briefing her on Crowe's proposed new security measures, in – ' he checked his watch again – 'fifteen minutes' time, in a meeting room on the opposite side of the building.'

'At this time of night?' said Sol. 'I thought you said everyone who worked here had already gone home?'

'The prime minister is *always* working,' Ross replied. 'Which means *I* am always working. Lately, and since Crowe initiated his little power grab, neither the prime minister nor I have had more than two or three hours' sleep at a time. Fighting to save democracy really is quite exhausting.' He ran a hand across his face, and Ollie realised that Ross *did* look exhausted. Having barely slept lately himself, he recognised the signs.

'We can take it from here, Mr Ross,' Ollie said. 'And we know our way out now once we're done. Thank you. For everything.' He extended his hand, and Ross took it.

'Good luck to you, Ollie Turner,' said Ross. And then, seemingly at a loss for what else to say, he nodded, turned and was gone – with evident relief, Ollie would have said.

'Well,' said Jack. 'I guess we're on our own again.'

'That's just the way I like it,' Flea growled, and he started forwards. Ollie and the others fell in behind him.

Unlike in the stairwell, there were no lights on in the corridor, but there was enough of a glow from the emergency exit signs that they were able to see. Halfway to Crowe's office, they noticed the flash of a security guard's torch from around a corner up ahead. Flea raised a fist to bring the others to a halt, and then edged forwards to make sure the guard had passed on.

'All clear,' he hissed, gesturing them forwards.

Once they'd reached the door to Crowe's office, Flea wasted no time in picking the lock. He spared Ollie and the others the showboating, too – a sure sign, Ollie felt, that even Flea recognised the gravity of what they were about to do. This wasn't just *anyone's* office they were breaking into. It was Sir Sebastian Crowe's, the most powerful politician in the country. And attempting to steal state secrets would surely count as treason, a crime that, even before Crowe's Emergency Action Plan, would have been punishable with life imprisonment.

'Whoa,' whispered Erik, as the door swung open, 'check out that view!'

Crowe had requisitioned his office from three junior MPs, Ross had said, and Ollie could see why he'd been so eager to have it. The windows offered a panoramic view of Westminster Abbey, which was perhaps all the more impressive at night. The abbey was lit up by powerful spotlights, and its golden glow extended into every corner of Crowe's office. Ollie saw a huge chandelier hanging from the office's ludicrously high ceiling, and the portcullis symbol of parliament embossed on everything from the mantle over the enormous fireplace to the rich, green wallpaper. There were ornately framed oil paintings on the walls, almost all of which were portraits of old, important-looking white men, and rows and rows of leather-bound books. Spread across the floor was a thick, intricately woven rug, in the centre of which was an emblem of the Tudor rose.

'And I thought Professor Strain's decor was over the top,' said Sol. 'This place makes the headmaster's old office look like the insides of a coal shed.'

'Spread out,' Ollie instructed, as he noiselessly closed the office door behind them. 'Song, see if you can locate a safe. If there's one in here, it will probably be hidden by one of those paintings. Sol, you search Crowe's desk. And, Jack, try to work your magic on Crowe's computer. The rest of us will look everywhere else, starting with those bookshelves.'

Everyone immediately set to work.

'Remember,' Ollie reminded them, 'we're looking for anything at all that will give us a clue about where Lily and the other people who've been arrested have been taken. A location, a building, an address on a piece of correspondence that seems unusual. And Deadfall. Keep an eye out for anything that mentions Deadfall. If Ross was right, it's some kind of code word, the name Crowe's given to his operation.'

'I've found the safe, Ollie,' said Song, seconds later, and when Ollie turned to her she was already taking down an oil painting from one of the walls. She put her hands on her hips and studied the electronic keypad that would open the safe's door. 'Although I get a feeling *finding* it will prove to be the easy part.'

'I'm going to struggle to access the files on Crowe's computer, too, Ollie,' Jack put in. She was frowning into the glow from the computer screen on Crowe's desk. She tapped away at the keyboard and her frown deepened. 'There are at least four levels of encryption here, including facial recognition and a random computer-generated PIN code. Even if I could work on this thing back at the Haven, it would take me a week just to bypass the login.'

Ollie cursed. They'd reckoned on Crowe's computer being their best chance of finding what they were looking for, and they'd been banking on Jack's ability to hack her way in. And if she couldn't do it in the time available to them, no one could.

'Anyone want a Percy Pig?' said Sol. He'd been crouched beside Jack as he searched the desk drawers, and he rose at her shoulder holding a half-full bag of sweets. 'From what I can tell from the contents of Crowe's desk,' he went on, 'the man's a sugar-addicted neat freak. There's nothing in here but posh sweets and even posher stationery.'

'I'll take one,' said Erik, cupping his hands, and Sol frisbeed a Percy Pig across the room.

Flea clicked his fingers, and held out a palm. Sol stole a sweet himself, then tossed Flea the rest of the packet.

'Damn it,' said Ollie. 'That just leaves the bookshelves and the safe. Erik, Flea, have you found anything?' As he spoke, Ollie continued to rifle through the bookshelves himself. He'd so far found nothing either inside or behind the books apart from several layers of dust. The leather-bound tomes were clearly only in Crowe's office for show.

'Nothing over here,' said Erik, through a mouthful of sweet.

Flea had already reached the end of the section he'd been searching. 'Not a sausage,' he said, before stuffing three Percy Pigs into his mouth in one go.

Ollie moved from the bookshelves to stand at Song's shoulder. He sensed the others fall in behind him. 'It looks like the safe's our last hope, Song. How are you getting on?'

'About as well as the rest of you, from the sound of it,' Song said. She was punching six-figure codes into the keypad on the safe, and cross-referencing the numbers she entered with a list she'd brought with her on her phone. As well as being the Haven's martial-arts expert, Song was a whizz at mathematics. Knowing that any safe they found in Crowe's office would have a combination code, Song had spent the past twenty-four hours researching possible PINs Crowe might have used: from typical defaults such as 1-2-3-4-5-6, to notable dates in the home secretary's personal history. Starting with those combinations Song had calculated to be the most likely, she was now working her way down the list she'd compiled. But each time she keyed a sequence of figures into the keypad, she was greeted with a scrolling ERROR message, glowing red like a traffic stop light.

'I'm running out of guesses, Ollie,' Song told him. 'If none of the codes I've written down work, we may as well resort to guessing, and the chances of us stumbling on the correct combination in the time we have are literally a million to—'

There was a beep, and the safe door sprung open.

'One,' Song finished, sounding as surprised as Ollie felt. For a moment, they only gawped at the open safe door.

'Well, what do you know,' said Song, recovering her smile. 'It turns out Crowe's PIN code of choice is 230616. The date he was appointed home secretary.'

'It's a shame we haven't got his bank card,' said Sol. 'I'm sure he wouldn't have objected to us making a few charitable donations in his name.'

Song was already pulling out the contents of Crowe's safe: a stack of manila folders, each of which was labelled 'Top Secret'. She passed them to Jack, who was opening them and dismissing them with worrying speed.

'No,' she said, dropping a folder into her lap. 'No,' she repeated, having opened the next one. 'No, no, no.'

'That's it,' said Song. She was sweeping her hand around the empty safe. 'That's everything that was in here.'

Ollie cast a glance towards the office door, then focused nervously on Jack. She'd already discarded half a dozen of the folders, leaving only two she hadn't yet checked. Was it really possible that they had come this far only to have to walk away with *nothing*?

'No,' Jack said, tossing the penultimate folder to one side. 'These are all just boring procedural documents, stuff that every other cabinet minister would have received copies of, too.' She opened the last folder, and Ollie found himself holding his breath. Jack opened her mouth, ready to dismiss the final document as well . . . but then she paused. Her eyes narrowed. The folder slipped from her grip, leaving her clutching a single piece of paper.

'No,' said Jack. 'Surely not . . .' Slowly she started shaking her head. She was staring at the piece of paper in her hands, as though struggling to decipher its meaning.

'What is it?' said Ollie. 'What does it say? Does it mention Deadfall?'

Jack closed her eyes. To Ollie's horror, a tear appeared and ran down her cheek. 'We've lost her,' she said, in a voice that was barely above a whisper. 'Lily, she . . . she's gone. There's no way we can get to her now.'

'What are you talking about?' growled Flea, shoving his way to the front of the group. 'Why not?'

Opening her eyes, Jack turned the piece of paper towards them. Ollie found himself staring at a photograph. And there, in one corner, was the single word they'd been hunting for.

'Because *Deadfall* is an *oil rig*,' said a voice from behind them, and Ollie spun to see Sebastian Crowe leering at them from the doorway. 'And it's three hundred miles from land,' the home secretary went on, 'right in the middle of the North Sea.'

19 HOPE FAILS

'No, no, *no!*'

Lily's hands fell uselessly to her sides. And then the tears came. She couldn't stop them. It was all she could do to stand there weeping, as a shadow fell on her from the side and behind her came the unmistakeable sound of laughter.

'What's the matter?' said a voice Lily recognised at once. 'Not a fan of sea views?'

Lily swiped the tears from her cheeks. Having made it so far – beating the lock on her cell door, then inching up the ventilation shaft and eluding the guards with their cattle prods – she could barely comprehend what she was looking at; what had been waiting for her all along. The prison was in the belly of a huge, abandoned oil rig, and all around it there was nothing but the churning sea. All of a sudden everything made perfect sense: the metallic walkways and the lack of windows, the complete absence of contraband among the prisoners, even the constant groaning sound Lily had noticed on her very first day: it was the sound of the vast metal structure straining against the wind and the waves. And it explained the brutish behaviour of the guards, too. Out here in the middle of the ocean, with no public scrutiny to contend with, the people in charge could treat the prisoners any way they liked. Probably as far as the general public was concerned, the prison didn't even *exist*.

As Lily surveyed the rolling greyness all around her, a cold, white sun dipping below the endless horizon, she felt her despair turn into anger: at Maddy Sikes, at Sebastian Crowe, at his cruel, heartless Emergency Action Plan, which had torn people like Aya from her parents. And what about all the other kids who were trapped down below, in cells no bigger than cupboards? Kids like Ember, for example. What had *they* done to deserve this punishment, other than not being lucky enough to have a home, or a family to help keep them out of trouble? It wasn't *right*. It wasn't *fair*. You couldn't hold people like this, not when they hadn't done anything wrong!

Lily spun, ready to hurl herself at the warden, whose voice Lily had heard behind her, and who, as Crowe's lackey, had made all of this possible.

'Now, now,' said the warden pleasantly, when she found herself confronted by Lily's fury. 'It wouldn't do to lose your temper, young lady. Not given your current . . . predicament.' She turned a hand palm up, towards a sky as iron grey as the sea below it – a loose, careless gesture that somehow managed to convey how desperate Lily's situation really was.

Lily was aware of guards all around her. There were six of them, converging in a circle. They had their cattle prods pointed and primed, like gamekeepers trying to contain a lion. Their mistake was expecting Lily not to try anything. They had her trapped, they would have figured – surely she must have realised resistance was futile.

But Lily had other ideas.

She skipped backwards, in the direction the guards would have been least expecting, and unleashed a devastating *ushiro geri*, the same technique she'd used to break down the door that had led to the rig's main deck. The back kick caught the prison guard at Lily's six in the groin, and although the guard's features were covered by a mask, Lily could tell from the way the guard crumpled that he was a man.

The guard to Lily's right reacted quickest, driving at her with his cattle prod. Lily swerved, dodging the guard's thrust. She caught the cattle prod with her left hand and used her right arm to deliver an *empi* strike. The guard was moving forwards so rapidly, Lily barely had to move. She just set her hips and pointed her elbow, and allowed the guard to drive himself into it. It struck him on the bridge of the nose, and he too doubled over in pain.

Not counting the warden, who'd backed away in alarm, it was now four against one. Still not exactly even, but now Lily had a cattle prod of her own.

She swung it, bringing it down like a baseball bat on to the arm of a guard who'd moved to grab hold of her. From the shriek, this guard seemed to be a woman. She dropped her own cattle prod and clutched her damaged elbow, rolling away from the fight in her agony.

Three against one.

But Lily was no longer interested in the guards around her, who seemed to be having second thoughts of their own. She set her sights on the warden, who had pressed herself against a nearby wall, shrinking from the confrontation like the coward she clearly was. Worse than that: Warden Bricknell was nothing more than a common bully. Lily had known plenty in her time, and the only difference between the warden and all the others was that Warden Bricknell had been given a uniform, as well as a playground to call her own.

Cattle prod in hand, Lily flew at her, determined to give the warden a taste of her own medicine. Lily knew it would probably be the last thing she ever did, that she would be overpowered eventually, but she didn't care. She just wanted Warden Bricknell to feel the same sting Lily had experienced so many times, which was itself nothing compared to the bitter throb she felt at the knowledge she would never again see her friends. Her brother, Flea. Casper. *Ollie*.

Lily pressed the trigger on her cattle prod and the prongs crackled, ready to deliver their shock. Too late the warden tried to run, but Lily was faster. Using her shoulder, she barged the guard who'd been protecting the warden out of the way, so that there was nothing between Lily and Warden Bricknell but empty air. She lunged . . .

And felt her body explode with agony as the three guards who'd remained on their feet jabbed their cattle prods simultaneously into Lily's back. Her body went rigid, and her scream of pain lodged like a physical object in the back of her throat. It was as if she were choking on it, unable to swallow or breathe. And then, once the devastating shock had been delivered, Lily collapsed forwards, on to the salt-stained deck.

'Oh dear,' came the warden's voice. It sounded dim, far away, as though Lily were at the bottom of a hole. 'Oh dear, oh dear.'

Half paralysed from the voltage that had been delivered into her body, Lily was just about able to crane her neck. Gradually the warden came into focus.

'That *was* foolish,' Warden Bricknell continued, her voice clearer now, closer. 'And now I'm afraid you're going to have to pay.'

She extended an arm, reaching for something beyond Lily's field of vision. Lily tried to move her head to see, but like with the scream that had lodged in her throat, her muscles had cramped tight, and she found herself unable to move.

'I wouldn't normally turn one of these up to maximum,' said the warden, and Lily saw she'd taken a cattle prod from one of the guards. There was a dial beside the handle, and the warden

231

turned it until it clicked. 'I'm told that a shock of this magnitude could prove fatal.'

She lowered the cattle prod until the prongs were resting against Lily's neck. 'Which means,' said the warden, 'that it should also be excruciatingly painful. If you survive, perhaps you can tell me all about it.' She snarled, and before Lily could react, or even work out whether she would be able to, the warden depressed the trigger.

The pain was like nothing Lily had ever known. Greater even than the combined shock she'd received from the guards, this was like a thousand needles being machine-gunned into her body, coursing around her veins and ripping through her organs. She felt it in every part of her, from the tips of her hair to the cores of her bones. And there was nothing she could do to stop it. She couldn't move, couldn't yell, couldn't wail, not until the warden had decided she'd had enough.

The worst part was, Lily could hear the warden laughing. The sound cut through the pain as though it were being carried on the electricity itself, as though it were fuelling it somehow – as though the warden's laughter *was* the electricity. And it wasn't just that the warden was enjoying herself, Lily knew. She was laughing because she'd *won*.

After it was over – seconds, minutes, hours later; Lily had no way of telling – they hauled her to her feet. It took two of them to hold her upright, because Lily's legs were like ribbons dangling beneath her. Even her brain seemed to be only half functioning, to the extent she barely noticed when they took her inside. From lying on the sea-sprayed deck, she was all at once back in the gloom of the prison, her feet dragging on one of the metal walkways. They descended a set of steps, and here the guards had to carry her, draping Lily's arms around their shoulders, and hooking their wrists under each of her legs.

They passed doors, an endless parade of them, and dimly Lily realised the doors led to the prisoners' cells. She could hear some of the inmates calling out, hurling obscenities and threats – not at the guards, but to inmates in rival gangs who were locked up across from them. Through her pain Lily couldn't help but laugh. Not because it was funny, but because it was so futile. And because she finally understood how desperate the situation of the inmates here really was. All the fighting, the rioting, the petty squabbling – how the warden must have been enjoying it all. How easy it would have made her job! Not only were Lily and the others on an oil rig, in the middle of the ocean, where nobody would ever find them, they'd also become their own worst enemies, fighting each other rather than the people who'd locked them up in the first place.

They dragged Lily along walkway after walkway, and eventually left the cells behind them. Lily had no idea where they were taking her, and she found she no longer cared. Her cell, another one, what did it matter? She was trapped here, and she would probably die here, just like everybody else.

They reached another stairwell and went down, down, so far into the substructure of the rig that Lily imagined they must soon hit the seabed itself.

Finally the stairs ended in another corridor. A dead end this time, and once again there were narrow doorways lined up along either side. The doors looked exactly like the cell doors on the higher deck, except these were smaller, and instead of electronic locks, they were sealed from the outside with steel bolts as thick as Lily's wrists.

The air down here was dank and fetid. To Lily's mind, it stank of sweat and fear. She thought she could smell blood, too, although that may have been the tang of rusted metal.

The guards came to a halt, and Lily had no choice but to stop beside them. They let go of her, and Lily had to throw her hands against the dank, slime-covered wall to prevent herself falling.

There was a creak, like a floorboard in a haunted house, and Lily realised the guards had opened one of the doors. She found herself laughing again as she looked inside. She knew this place. The box they were about to throw her in was one she'd occupied before, the day she'd first woken up on the oil rig. The cells in the basement of the prison must have been where they put all new arrivals before they were transferred to the general population, meaning Lily was right back where she'd started.

'Enjoy your time in solitary confinement,' one of the guards said as he shoved Lily inside. 'You've earned it.'

Lily stumbled forwards, and there was so little space inside the metal box that she immediately collided with the wall opposite. Her fingernails scraped the metal surface as she slid gracelessly to the floor. Then the door slammed shut with a *clang*, and the bolt was driven across, leaving Lily crumpled on the floor.

As she surveyed the familiar surroundings – the ceiling that was barely head height, the walls too close together for her to extend her arms, and a lone light bulb that was only half aglow – it occurred to Lily that she'd been wrong in what she'd told herself before. This was worse than being back where she'd started, because at least back then she'd still had some fight left. Now, she'd lost the one thing that had been keeping her going.

She had finally lost all hope.

20 SIR SEBASTIAN

Sebastian Crowe took a step into the room, two armed police officers at his shoulder. Then a third appeared, this one with stripes on his arm, and he seemed to be dragging someone behind him. The sergeant moved into the room behind Crowe, and Ollie realised who it was he'd taken prisoner.

'Mr Ross!'

The police sergeant gave Montgomery Ross a shove in the back, and the former Haven member stumbled into the room.

'I'm sorry, Ollie!' Ross blurted. 'They knew! Somehow they knew!'

'Stop your snivelling, man,' said Crowe, looking disgusted. 'Is it really such a surprise that we've been watching you all along? Everyone knows you're a PM loyalist. And now it's clear that you're a traitor to the country, too. You led this Haven scum into the Palace of Westminster itself. Into my very office!'

His shirt tails loose and his tie askew from where he'd been manhandled, Ross reddened. '*Me?* If anyone's the traitor here, it's you! A traitor to democracy! To the freedoms in this country it was your task as home secretary to protect!'

'Sergeant,' said Crowe dismissively, 'level your weapon. If this man says another word, shoot him.'

Ollie had no idea whether the sergeant would actually squeeze the trigger of his automatic rifle, but he pointed the barrel at Ross's chest.

'As for *you*,' said Crowe, turning to Ollie and the others, 'I ought to have you executed on the spot. If the laws in this lily-livered country permitted it, I wouldn't hesitate in giving the order.'

'That sounds about right,' Flea snarled. 'Why bother getting your own hands dirty, when you can get some lackey to do it for you?' The officers with guns twitched, as Flea took a step forwards. 'Give me back my sister, you pompous, self-important son of a—'

'Flea,' Jack warned, touching his arm. 'Don't.'

'I would urge you to listen to your cripple friend, *boy*,' Crowe said. He swung his gaze across the faces of the kids in front of him, and – perhaps because Ollie had positioned himself at the front of the group – settled it on Ollie. 'You think you're so clever, don't you? So *street-smart*. Do you really think it would have been possible for you to break into the Houses of Parliament if I hadn't decided to *let* you in? To use Ross to lead you exactly where I wanted you?'

Ross was caught in the no man's land between the Haven kids and Crowe. He let out a despairing moan.

'Oh, I admit, you didn't come in the way we were expecting,' Crowe continued. 'And you got deeper into the building than I'd intended . . .' His eyes fixed on his open safe, then on the picture of the oil rig that was still in Jack's hand. 'But no matter. You clearly wanted to find out all about *Deadfall*. Now you'll be able to experience it for yourselves.' Crowe moved his chin to his shoulder. 'Officers,' he instructed to the policemen behind him, 'seize them!'

'*What on earth is going on here?*'

Before anyone could move, a figure appeared between the two police officers in the doorway. Ollie felt his eyes widen, as Crowe continued to turn.

'Prime Minister!' the home secretary blurted, clearly as surprised as Ollie was to see the prime minister herself at the threshold of the room. But Crowe recovered himself quickly. 'You're just in time, Prime Minister. Now that you're here, you'll be able to witness for yourself the apprehension of these young *terrorists*. As you can see, they broke into my safe, and as far as we know, they were on their way to deal with *you* next – to finish the job they came so close to completing in September.'

There was an outburst of indignation among Ollie's friends.

'That's *rubbish*!' said Sol. 'We're not here to *kill* anyone. We're here to save people! The way we saved the prime minister at Forest Mount!'

239

The prime minister had stepped past the police officers, so that she was level with Crowe. She kept her distance from him, however, Ollie noted. She was surveying the scene before her, and when her eyes settled on Ollie, they snagged.

'*You*,' she declared, in recognition.

Crowe's eyes creased in confusion. 'You know this boy?'

The PM blinked. 'This is Ollie Turner. He was the one who saved my life.' She turned to Crowe, her eyes tightening. 'It was Ollie Turner who saved me from *your son*.'

Crowe bridled at the accusation in the prime minister's tone. He did everything but sneer back at her, and it became obvious to Ollie that, more than simply being rivals, the two politicians positively loathed each other. 'You've got things back to front,' Crowe told the PM. 'Not for the first time, I might add. It was these fanatics who tricked my son into attempting to assassinate you in the first place. Each and every one of them is a member of the Haven.'

Now it was the prime minister's turn to look surprised. Was there also a hint of fear in her reaction, too? 'The *Haven*?' she repeated, still staring at Ollie.

'Ask them yourself if you don't believe me,' said Crowe. And then, to Ollie and the others, 'Go on, deny it, I dare you!'

Ollie opened his mouth to answer, but hesitated when he noted the look of betrayal on the prime minister's face. Ollie recalled the last time he and the PM had spoken, in St Thomas' hospital, after they'd both been treated for exposure to the nerve agent that had claimed Sebastian Crowe's son's life. At the time, Ollie hadn't lied to the PM about who he was, but he hadn't exactly told her the truth either. The prime minister, in contrast, had been nothing but kind to him. Now, though, she'd clearly come to believe everything the country had been told about the Haven, all the lies Crowe had been peddling. And why wouldn't she? She had no proof to the contrary, and here Ollie and his friends were, standing in front of an open safe in the home secretary's private office.

Flea stepped until he was level with Ollie's shoulder. 'We don't deny it,' he said. 'Why should we? What we deny is all the garbage you've been spouting about us!'

'The Haven isn't a terrorist organisation,' put in Erik. 'We help kids in trouble. That's *it*. We give them a home, an education, a family. The only terrorist in this room is standing right *there*!' He levelled a finger at Crowe, and Ollie could see it shaking – with anger or fear, he couldn't tell.

'Erik's right,' said Ollie, finally finding his voice. 'It's Sebastian Crowe who's trying to undermine democracy, Prime Minister. He's been deceiving everyone, inventing threats, all to get the public feeling scared, and to give him cover for his draconian new laws, and for building his private army. If Crowe gets his way, it won't be the police patrolling the Palace of Westminster, or anywhere else. It will be his army of brownshirts, whose only loyalty is to *him*.'

Ollie noticed the sergeant and the two police officers by the door share a look, though the sergeant didn't lower his weapon. It was still pointed at Montgomery Ross's chest.

Tentatively, Ross cleared his throat, and winced as though expecting the sound to trigger a bullet. 'Ollie's . . . Ollie's telling the truth, Prime Minister. Your home secretary is the only traitor here.'

The prime minister turned Ross's way, and seemed to notice for the first time where the police sergeant was aiming his gun. 'Lower your weapon, sergeant!' she commanded. 'This man is my personal secretary!'

The police sergeant looked from the PM to Sebastian Crowe. Hesitantly, he dipped his weapon until it was pointing at the floor.

'Monty?' the PM continued. 'What are *you* doing caught up in all of this? We were supposed to be meeting twenty minutes ago. That's why I came looking for you.'

'He's a Haven sympathiser, Prime Minister,' Crowe answered before Ross could. 'It was your personal secretary who brought this *filth* into the building.'

The prime minister looked back at Crowe, appalled. 'What on earth are you talking about?' She turned to Ross. 'Monty? Is this true?'

'It . . . it is, but . . . but I had good reason, Prime Minister! The Haven is a peaceful organisation. Its mission is to help people, just as young Erik said. It—'

'You see!' bleated Crowe, victorious. 'The Haven has penetrated even to your inner circle, Prime Minister. From day one you have been opposing my legislative agenda, and now it turns out your own faction is part of the rot. How much more evidence do you need that the country is under direct attack? Can you see now why my Emergency Action Plan was necessary? Why the Civil Defence League is so crucial to the protection of freedom in this country? It is time you stood aside, Prime Minister, and made way for someone who is prepared to make the tough decisions you are not.'

'Don't listen to him, Prime Minister, *please*,' said Jack. 'You can still stop this! Ask Crowe who he's working for. Ask him about Maddy Sikes, about what secrets she's using to blackmail him into doing what she tells him to!'

Now Crowe was the one to shift slightly.

'Sikes?' said the PM. 'Maddy Sikes *died*. Didn't she? In the terrorist attacks that started all of this.' She was clearly beginning to question everything she thought she knew, and her eyes fell on Ollie as she cast around for answers.

'Maddy Sikes is alive, Prime Minister,' Ollie said. 'Those terrorist attacks were down to her, and now she's using Crowe as her puppet, manipulating events until *she* is the one who can assume power. It wasn't the Haven who duped Colton Crowe into trying to kill you. That was her, too. It was all her. The detention centre, the murder of those two guards . . . Sikes and

Crowe are using the Haven as a scapegoat, because she wants us out of the way as well. That's why we're here,' he added, gesturing to the safe. 'To get proof. And to find out what Crowe is doing with all the people who are going missing. People like our friend!'

Crowe snorted, as though at the ridiculousness of Ollie's story.

'Here,' said Jack, passing the photograph she was holding to the prime minister. 'This is *Deadfall*. We thought it was a code word for something, but actually it's the name of an oil rig in the middle of the North Sea. A secret prison. This is where Crowe is sending all of his political enemies. Asylum seekers, too. People from the streets. Everyone he wants out of the way, or whose absence will help him get the public on his side. And needless to say, it's totally illegal. He's violating pretty much every human-rights law in existence, but he's getting away with it because nobody knows it's happening.'

The PM stared down at the picture in horror. After a moment she turned to Ross. 'Monty?' she said almost pleadingly.

'It's true, Prime Minister. Every word. You trust me, don't you? And you've never trusted *him*.' Ross levelled a finger at Crowe. 'I urge you to follow your instincts!'

The prime minister looked again at the picture. Ollie saw it crumple slightly in her grip as her fingers tightened. 'I always knew you were a snake, Sebastian,' she finally said, the tension carrying into her voice. She raised her head. 'I didn't realise you were also a traitor and a *fascist*. You lock up innocent people and call it freedom? You have your thugs drag people from the streets and claim you're doing it for the good of *democracy*?' The PM shook her head. 'I hope you've enjoyed your time in office, Home Secretary, because it ends here. You're *done*.'

Ollie shared a glance with Sol, who was doing nothing to conceal his grin. But Ollie couldn't share his friend's delight. Crowe had been found out, the prime minister herself believed what Ollie and his friends had told her, and yet Crowe was the one standing there looking victorious.

'You really don't realise when you're beaten, do you, Miriam?' said Crowe, using the PM's name for the first time. 'So maybe the Haven isn't exactly what I said it was. Maybe I exaggerated the threat to the country *ever so slightly*.'

Crowe raised his hand, holding his thumb and forefinger a centimetre apart. He sneered at the prime minister's evident dismay.

'But whose name do you think is on the order to convert *Deadfall* into a prison?' the home secretary went on. 'Who do you think carries the responsibility for everything this government is doing? *Your* government, *Prime Minister*,' he added mockingly. 'Maybe you opposed my policies in private, but you did nothing to stop them. True, there wasn't much you *could* have done – we all know you're a dead woman walking, that the MPs and party members owe their loyalty to *me*. But as far as the public knows, as far as the *courts* will know – ' Crowe gave a contemptuous glance at Jack – 'it has been your signature on every piece of policy we have enacted.' He tilted his head, and watched what he was saying sink in. 'You're culpable, Miriam. For everything. Not least, for the security lapse that allowed a group of young terrorists to waltz into one of your cabinet ministers' private offices. And as for *Deadfall* . . .' Crowe *tsked* and shook his head theatrically.

Ollie saw the prime minister tense her jaw. So that was why Crowe had let Ollie and his friends break into the Houses of Parliament – so he could prove to the country how incompetent the prime minister was when he decided it was time to depose her, and so he had further proof, as though he needed it, of the threat the Haven presented. He clearly had the prime minister exactly where he wanted her. Or Sikes did, rather: she'd engineered it so that the prime minister would be held accountable for everything if the truth about *Deadfall* and the rest were to ever come out. At best, the prime minister would lose her job. At worst, she would face going to prison herself, for crimes she hadn't even known were happening.

It was all pure Maddy Sikes, Ollie thought bitterly. She was like a chess master, always thinking eight moves ahead. And Ollie walked into her traps *every time*.

'Where is she, Crowe?' he said. 'Maddy Sikes. Your *master*. Where is she hiding? Why doesn't she show herself?'

Slowly Crowe turned his head. He fixed his gaze on Ollie, and smiled. 'Patience, little boy. Patience.' He took a moment to register Ollie's helplessness, then raised a hand and gestured across his shoulder. 'Now, enough of this. Officers, arrest these thugs. You are authorised to discharge your weapons if they resist.'

The three police officers started forwards. As if released from a spell, the prime minister stepped across their path.

'No, Sebastian, I can't let you do this . . .'

'*Get back!*' Crowe roared, spinning in the prime minister's direction. Startled, the PM pressed herself against the wall. Ollie recalled what Ross has told them before: *She's afraid. She knows exactly what will happen to her if she crosses Crowe.*

'Don't make this worse for yourself, Miriam,' Crowe said, pointing a finger. 'You're beaten. You were beaten before it even occurred to you that you were playing. Now stand aside and let me finish the job I started, and maybe I'll allow you to retire gracefully when the time comes. Otherwise, it won't just be these children who get to experience *Deadfall* first-hand.'

The prime minister looked from Crowe to Ollie and his friends. She opened her mouth, but floundered for something to say. One way or another, Crowe had her cornered.

'Prime Minister!' Ollie pleaded. 'You can't just stand by and let this happen!'

'I . . . I'm sorry, Ollie. I . . .' She shook her head uselessly. 'I just . . . I don't know what I can . . .' She let her sentence trail into silence, and Ollie stared at her, dumbfounded.

'Mr Ross,' he said, turning to the PM's assistant instead. 'Tell her! Tell her she needs to *do* something! If *she* doesn't stop Maddy Sikes, it will be too late! *No one* will be able to stop her!'

'Prime Minister,' Ross begged, moving to the prime minister's side. 'Did you not hear? Do you not see what's happening?'

'Of course I heard!' the prime minister snapped. 'And I can see perfectly well! But what would you *have* me do, Monty? Crowe's won, and you and I both know it!'

Crowe smiled and folded his arms. Beside him, the three police officers converged on Ollie and his friends, their weapons raised and ready to fire.

21 HEAVY METAL

'I suggest you leave, Prime Minister,' Crowe said. 'And to show I'm not completely without mercy, I'll let you take your little lapdog with you.' He flicked a hand towards Ross. 'I dare say neither of you has the stomach to witness what's about to happen. Perhaps instead you could make a start on writing your memoirs.'

But rather than the prime minister, Jack was the first one to move. As she approached the line of police officers, one of the men produced a set of handcuffs.

'Really?' said Jack. 'You're going to put a poor *cripple* girl in cuffs?' She shot a glance towards Crowe as she echoed what he'd called her before. 'How do you suggest I move my chair with my hands bound together? Unless one of you intends to put your gun down and push me?'

The two more junior police officers shared a glance. 'Sorry, miss,' said one, in a tone that suggested he didn't have a choice.

Jack sighed theatrically. 'Fine. Go ahead.' She placed her forearms on the armrests of her chair, hooking her fingers around the ends. The police officer who'd spoken swung his weapon across his shoulder and readied one of the bracelets of the handcuffs.

Suddenly, there was a click, and the armrests of Jack's chair appeared to detach themselves. From sitting meekly waiting to be cuffed, Jack was all at once holding what looked like a steel truncheon in each hand. Her fingers around the ends of the armrests must have triggered a hidden release catch on each side, and the armrests themselves had converted into two fearsome-looking nightsticks.

Ollie heard Erik sound his surprise. 'So that's why that thing was so bloody heavy!'

Before the police officers either side of her could have known what was happening, Jack swung the steel bars in an arc. She brought the first down on the weapon of the man closest, and the barrel crumpled with a crunch. At the same time the butt of the gun jerked upwards, and there was a clatter of teeth as it hit the police officer under the chin. He howled in pain, and staggered backwards, clutching his hands across his face. The police officer who'd been holding the handcuffs had in the meantime recovered his weapon, but his movements were cut short as Jack struck the rear of his knee. The man's leg immediately buckled, and he arced backwards. His gun went off, the bullets hammering into the ceiling.

Someone – the prime minister? – screamed, and through the falling plaster Ollie spotted Crowe cowering into a corner. But he didn't have time to take in any more than that, because Flea had made a grab for the police sergeant's weapon, and he was in danger of losing the resulting tussle.

'Sol!' Ollie called. 'With me!'

With Sol at his side, Ollie dipped his shoulder, aiming a rugby tackle at the sergeant's midriff. All four of them collided with an armchair and toppled into a messy heap on the floor. But the police sergeant had clearly taken the brunt of the fall, and he lay in a daze as Ollie and his friends scrambled to their feet.

Song and Erik had moved to help Jack, but it was clear she had things under control. The two police officers were lying moaning either side of her, and Jack was already urging the others towards the door.

Ollie sidestepped the police sergeant, who was slowly coming to his senses, and attempted to drag Sol with him.

'But . . . Flea!' Sol blurted.

Rather than running for the door like the rest of them, Flea had made a lunge for Crowe. He was gripping the man by his lapels and pinning him up against the wall.

'No, please, don't hurt me!' Crowe begged.

Flea appeared ready to tear Crowe limb from limb. 'Did you show my sister any mercy?' he growled. 'Would you have let her go if she'd been cowardly enough to beg?'

'Flea!' Ollie yelled. 'Come *on*!'

Flea ignored him. He tightened his grip on Crowe's jacket.

'Flea, leave him! We need to go! Right *now*!'

With a snarl of frustration, Flea slammed Crowe against the wall, then released him and darted to join the others.

Ollie waited until Flea was past him, then spun to catch up with his friends. As he turned, he locked eyes with the prime minister. She was standing beside Ross, clearly in shock at the scene that was playing out in front of her. When she looked at Ollie, she closed her open mouth, and dropped her eyes towards the floor.

Ollie darted for the exit, trying not to think about the despair that was welling inside him. With the PM afraid to act, what hope did they have of stopping Sikes now? How would they ever rescue Lily?

'Which way?' said Jack, when they were all in the corridor outside.

'Back the way we came in,' said Ollie. 'It's the most direct route out of the building we know.'

But as they dashed towards the end of the corridor, they heard an angry scurry of boot steps in the stairwell. One of the police officers in Crowe's office must have called for backup.

'There!' said Song, pointing to another door midway along the corridor.

They bundled through the doorway, and emerged straight into what appeared to be a building site. In contrast to the opulence of Crowe's office, the room they'd stumbled into had been completely stripped bare, right down to the ancient floorboards. There was plastic sheeting everywhere, and tools scattered in every corner.

'Looks like they've got the decorators in,' said Erik.

'This whole building is supposed to be falling to pieces,' said Jack. 'I guess this is part of the renovations.'

'So what now?' said Flea, as the sound of voices filtered through from the corridor outside.

Ollie cast around. The glass panes in the windows across from them had been removed, and in their place were metal security shutters. There was no way they would be able to break through those. But the wall separating the room from the office next door appeared to have been demolished. It was in the process of being rebuilt, but so far it was little more than a wooden frame, and there were clear gaps behind the plastic sheeting that covered it.

'Anyone ever wanted to walk through walls?' said Ollie, hauling the plastic sheeting aside. Through the space beyond it, he could see another room – this one with scaffolding outside the window, which appeared to lead down into the courtyard below.

After helping Jack manoeuvre her wheelchair through one of the gaps in the wooden frame, Ollie and Sol led the charge towards the window.

'Ollie, look,' said Erik. 'How about we take the express route?'

Beside the window, there was a hole: the opening of a giant plastic rubbish chute.

Ollie pressed his nose to the window. From what he could see through the darkness outside, the chute offered a near vertical drop to the courtyard below. It appeared to kink at the bottom, which would slow their descent, though it was impossible to make out where they would land. He thought of Keya, and the glass from the skip that had sliced into her thigh.

'Sir? In here! I heard voices!'

Through the half wall and opaque plastic sheeting, the policewoman's voice sounded disconcertingly near. The reinforcements had obviously arrived.

'I'll go first to make sure it's safe,' Ollie said. 'Jack, you'll have to ditch your chair, but Flea will be able to carry you when we reach the bottom.'

Ollie swung his legs into the rubbish chute. With the gaping blackness directly below him, he was suddenly unsure whether this was such a good idea. But they were out of options. *It will be just like riding a slide in a water park*, he told himself, while trying to ignore another voice that reminded him it wouldn't be a swimming pool waiting for him at the bottom.

'If you die horribly,' said Sol, 'try to scream or something as you go. That way the rest of us will know to use the scaffolding instead.'

Ollie readied himself to take the plunge. *One . . . two . . .*

'Ollie, wait!'

He felt a hand on his shoulder, and turned to see Jack staring back at him apprehensively.

'We have to do this, Jack,' Ollie told her. 'It will be fine, I – ' *promise*, he'd been about to say, but stopped himself – 'I'm almost certain.'

'No,' said Jack, 'it's not that.'

Across Jack's shoulder and through the plastic sheeting, Ollie could make out torch beams sweeping the room they'd just come from. It would be a matter of seconds before one of the police officers turned their way. 'What then?' Ollie asked.

'We need to give ourselves up,' Jack said, and the expression on his friends' faces mirrored the astonishment Ollie felt.

'Are you *crazy*?' said Erik.

'Give ourselves up?' echoed Flea. '*Why?*'

Jack focused on Ollie. 'All this running, all this fighting, it's not going to get us anywhere. Say we make it down the rubbish chute, and then somehow get over the fence into Parliament Square. What are we supposed to do next?'

For a moment it was all Ollie could do to stare back at her.

'You heard what Crowe said,' Jack persisted. 'Think about it!'

Ollie did. And he thought he understood what Jack was suggesting. It made sense, sort of, but it would also be a leap into the unknown. They'd gone to Foulness Island without any real plan, and look how *that* had turned out.

He peered down the rubbish chute, then through the window into the London night. When he looked back at the others, Sol and Song were frowning deeply, and Flea and Erik appeared aghast. But Ollie knew that Jack was right. Giving themselves up was the only option left open to them, irrespective of how things might end.

He pulled his legs from the rubbish chute. Realising he was shaking, he planted his feet on the dusty floor.

'PJ . . .' Flea warned.

Ollie swallowed. He looked at Jack again, who nodded.

'Hey!' he called. 'We're in here!'

22 SECOND THOUGHTS

The helicopter skimmed the rolling sea. Every so often a wave would rear up at them, like a great beast trying to paw the chopper from the sky. Ollie watched forlornly through one of the small, oval-shaped windows. Salty, steel-grey water splattered the glass, obscuring his view, but it hardly mattered. The outlook didn't change. They were being flown further and further away from land, deep into international waters.

After giving themselves up in the Houses of Parliament, Ollie and his friends had been treated by the police officers like the terrorists Crowe claimed they were. Officers with guns had surrounded them, and had barked at them to lie face down on the floor.

From the top level of the building, they'd been jostled downstairs, and locked all together in a room that had been little more than a concrete box. Ollie had lost track of how long they'd been kept there, but when somebody had finally come for them, it wasn't the police officers who'd arrested them. Rather, it was a squad of brown-shirted Rat Catchers, and they'd dragged Ollie and his friends through the bowels of the building, and into the back of a waiting van.

The van had driven for hours, and when it had finally come to a halt and the rear doors opened, the sun had been coming up over a distant horizon. They'd seemingly arrived in the middle of nowhere, with nothing but a single, anonymous building to greet them. It had taken a few moments for Ollie's eyes to get used to the daylight, but when he'd looked around, the flat, featureless landscape had reminded him of Foulness Island. Other than the plain concrete building, there was nothing but empty fields and a pale grey sky. From the marked drop in temperature compared to London, however, he'd guessed they were somewhere much further north. The only other clue to their location had been the tang of sea salt in the air.

With barely enough time for a comfort break, they'd been shepherded through the building, and out on to a helicopter pad at the rear. Soon they'd heard the sound of an approaching rotor blade, and a helicopter had appeared in the sky, before coming in to settle on the helipad. The chopper had been painted black, with no markings of any kind. It had made Ollie think of the mercenaries who'd stormed the detention centre – and, sure enough, just as though he'd summoned them himself, two men in black had emerged from the rear of the helicopter, ducking to avoid the rotor blades. One of the mercenaries had spoken to the Rat Catchers – an exchange that had been drowned out by the noise of the chopper – and then the Haven kids had been shoved forwards, into the passenger hold of the helicopter.

Seconds later, the chopper had risen back into the air, and immediately the ocean Ollie had smelt earlier had come into view. The helicopter had dipped its nose and headed straight for it, and within minutes the land beneath them had disappeared. From that point on, there had been nothing outside the windows but an endless expanse of water.

Now, hours later it felt like, the view remained unchanged. Given that they appeared to be flying east, Ollie had concluded that it was indeed the North Sea beneath them, just as Crowe had said. But so far there was no sign of their destination.

'There,' said Sol. 'I see it.' He had to shout to make himself heard, and it was the first time anyone had spoken since they'd boarded the chopper.

In his seat beside Sol, Ollie craned his neck to look where his friend was pointing. After a moment scouring the sea, he saw it, too.

Deadfall.

Even from this distance, Ollie could tell the oil rig was enormous. And as it gradually came into closer view, he got a sense of how big it really was. It rose from the sea like a vast metal island, replete with a small cityscape of cranes, drilling rigs and buildings. But it also looked very much like a ghost town, because there was no movement that Ollie could see, either on deck or in the equipment, and everything was the colour of rust. The main deck was suspended above the sea by four huge pillars, one on each corner of the square structure. Between the deck and the pillars there was a fat underbelly that Ollie guessed must once have housed both the crew and the oil rig's machinery – but that he knew was now serving an entirely different purpose.

After a moment, the helicopter began to bank. Ollie lost sight of *Deadfall* then, and only glimpsed it again when the helicopter was hovering directly over the oil rig's helipad, which jutted from one corner of the structure's main deck. He looked at Sol, and both boys braced themselves as the pilot brought the chopper in to land.

There was nobody to greet them when they touched down. Not that Ollie had expected a welcome committee, but even so he was surprised when it was the mercenaries themselves who escorted them beneath the whirling blades of the helicopter and towards the main building.

But then it occurred to Ollie why there was nobody there to meet them. *Deadfall* was playing the part of an abandoned oil rig, left to rust and rot in the middle of the ocean. If there had been guards stationed on the rig's surface, they might have been spotted by passing vessels, or even by satellites above. As it was, there was nothing about the oil rig's dilapidated appearance that betrayed its new purpose. It truly was the perfect camouflage for an off-grid, maximum-security prison.

They had to brace themselves against a vicious crosswind as the men in black hurried them towards the building. A door opened as they approached, and Ollie took the opportunity to steal one last glance at the sky. He had a feeling he might never see it again.

Three prison guards were waiting for them inside. They wore masks, which were oddly terrifying in their bland, featureless appearance. Ollie for one was so transfixed, he didn't notice when the mercenaries who'd handed them over disappeared. He only thought to look behind him when the door into the building slammed shut. By then, the mercenaries must already have been back in the chopper, because seconds later Ollie heard the helicopter lift into the air. Rapidly the sound of the rotor blades began to fade, and Ollie felt his heart sink further. Somehow the chopper leaving made their presence here feel a lot more permanent.

But it was too late now for second thoughts.

The only thing that gave Ollie any encouragement was the hope that he might soon see Lily. That was why they were here, after all. As Jack had said, giving themselves up had been the only course of action left open to them. The prime minister had refused to act, and there would have been no way they'd have been able to locate *Deadfall* themselves, let alone get to it if they had. But this way, Crowe's lackeys had taken Ollie and his friends exactly where they needed to go. Ollie and the others had needed a bit of time to cotton on to what Jack had been trying to tell them, but they'd got there in the end. Now that it was too late to change course, they just had to hope that they could come up with some way of breaking Lily out from the *inside*. And not just their friend, of course. If they failed to find a way to escape the prison, Ollie and the others would be permanently trapped here, too.

'The prisoners must all be below deck,' Ollie whispered to Sol. Once the door had been sealed behind them, the guards had moved to another doorway at the opposite end of the room. Jack, Flea, Song and Erik had pulled slightly ahead, leaving Ollie and Sol just out of earshot. 'They must have converted the old drilling structure into cells.'

To Ollie's utter surprise, Sol turned to him and grinned.

'What on earth are you smiling about?' said Ollie.

'You're thinking about Lily. About how pleased she's going to be to see you.'

'What?' objected Ollie. 'No, I'm not!'

'Yes, you are. I can tell. And hey, I'm not judging. Things are looking pretty grim for us all right now. A love story is just what we need to cheer things up.'

'A *love story*?' Ollie spluttered.

'Form a line!' one of the guards boomed. 'If anyone steps out of formation, you'll get a blast from my cattle prod!' The guard who'd spoken held the stick he'd been carrying slightly aloft, and the end crackled threateningly.

The Haven kids had been walking pretty much in a line anyway, but they shuffled until it was straighter, then stood waiting for the door ahead of them to open. A red light was showing on a control panel next to it, suggesting they were waiting for it to be unlocked.

'What do you mean, a *love story*?' hissed Ollie, when the guard had turned back to face the door.

Sol shrugged, with maddening indifference. 'Just, you know. You and Lily. It's been on the cards since the two of you first met.'

On the cards. What the hell did that mean? That Ollie had failed to hide how he felt? But how was that possible, when he didn't even *know* how he felt? And did *everyone* think the same way Sol did? Was it obvious even to Lily? Ollie grew warm just at the thought.

'Lily was with Dodge when we first met,' Ollie said, low. 'And now she's with Casper.'

Once again Sol rolled a shoulder. 'Maybe. And Casper's nice and everything. But even Errol would be able to tell you he's just a rebound boyfriend.'

'A *rebound* boyfriend?'

'You know, someone to help her get over Dodge, before she moves on to something more serious.'

'I know what it means,' said Ollie. 'What I don't know is how you can be so sure.'

Sol was standing ahead of Ollie in the line. He glanced back at Ollie across his shoulder. 'Mate. It's pretty obvious. They're friends, aren't they? I mean, they were friends even before they got together.'

'So?'

'So he was the ideal candidate. Someone to make her feel safe. To get her trusting people again, before she opens herself up to someone else.'

For a moment Ollie was lost for words.

'Besides,' Sol went on, 'he even looks like you. It's obvious who Lily *really* fancies.'

Ollie's mouth dropped open. 'Casper doesn't look anything like me! I *wish* I was as good looking as him!'

'I didn't say you were as good looking. Casper's like . . . like a Photoshopped version of you. You know, taller. And more talented. With better hair and stuff.'

Now Ollie couldn't help but snort. 'Gee, thanks. That makes me feel a whole lot better.'

'What? It should. Lily's not the kind of person to care how handsome you are.'

'Seriously,' said Ollie. 'Stop talking.'

Sol grinned at Ollie's despair. 'There's no need to get upset,' he whispered. 'I mean, look on the bright side. We're probably all going to die here anyway. So it doesn't really matter if I'm right or not. None of us are going to get a chance to find out.'

There was a beep from up ahead, and the red light Ollie had noticed turned green. One of the guards pulled the door at the head of the line open, and Ollie realised they'd been waiting for a lift.

'Inside!' commanded the guard who seemed to be in charge. 'Face the wall! One twitch and . . .'

'Yeah, yeah,' muttered Sol, so that only Ollie could hear. 'You'll blast us with your toy lightsaber. I'm telling you, we'd better get out of here sharpish, or this is going to get boring very quickly.'

One by one they filed into the lift, eyes to the walls as the guard had instructed. The door closed and they began their descent. The lift juddered as it moved, and Ollie had to press a hand to the wall to steady himself. Without warning, he felt a sensation like a nail being hammered into his spine. He tried to cry out in pain, but all his muscles had gone rigid.

'Hands by your sides!' yelled the prison guard in charge, and Ollie realised the guard had shocked him with his cattle prod, merely for trying to stop himself falling over.

After a moment the lift stopped moving, and the doors behind Ollie slid open.

'Out. All of you,' the guard said. 'Follow the yellow line, then stop when you're told.'

Ollie trailed after the others, out of the lift and into a room with a sodden floor, and walls that appeared to be made of rusting steel. There was a faded yellow line beneath Ollie's feet, and he shuffled along it until the guard issued the order to stop.

'Now turn. Drop to your knees and put your hands behind your heads.'

'What do you suggest I do?' said Jack, glaring up at the guard from her wheelchair.

'I suggest you keep your smart mouth shut,' said the guard, and he jabbed his cattle prod into Jack's stomach and depressed the trigger. Ollie caught sight of Flea at the head of the line, his teeth bared in fury, and his hands twitching as though he meant to try something. Desperately Ollie shook his head at him. *Save it*, he silently broadcast, hoping Flea would get the message – and knowing that the time to fight back would come soon enough.

The other two guards who'd been in the lift had moved to the wall opposite, and each of them picked up one of several buckets that were lined up waiting for them.

'I think we can dispense with the usual welcome ceremony,' said a voice, and Ollie turned to see a small, round woman in a grey jumpsuit emerge from a shadowy corner. She had a hand raised, and the guards seemed to take this as a signal to put the buckets back down. 'From what I've been led to understand,' the woman went on, 'these aren't our usual breed of guests.'

She stepped forwards, and it struck Ollie that she was the only person they'd so far encountered on *Deadfall* who wasn't wearing a mask.

'So,' she said, moving along the line, '*this* is what Haven members look like. After all the stories I've heard, I was expecting something slightly more impressive.'

She stopped at Ollie, and raised his chin with her fingernail. 'Even accounting for the fact that you're on your knees, you seem awfully *short*.'

She was one to talk, Ollie thought. If he'd been standing, the woman's eyes would barely have been level with his.

She withdrew her finger, letting her nail scrape along Ollie's skin as it curled. 'Still, perhaps appearances will prove deceptive. After all, you and I have a lot to talk about. And I would hate for our conversations to be over too quickly.' Abruptly, she turned to the guards. 'Take them down below. Keep them separate from the general population. A cell in solitary confinement for each of them, I think. We don't want them telling the other inmates what they know. And once we start our interrogations, it wouldn't do for the rest of the prisoners to hear their screams.'

Ollie felt his eyes widen, though it wasn't the threat of interrogation that troubled him. It was the fact that they were going to be kept apart, away from the other prisoners. How were they going to rescue Lily if they weren't even able to let her know that they were here?

'On your feet!' ordered the head of the guards. 'All of you! And there are no lifts where we're going now, so unless your friend can wheel that chair of hers down stairs, you're going to have to carry her.'

With the woman who presumably ran the prison watching on, Ollie and the others were herded from the room and along a metal walkway. At first Jack was able to wheel herself, but when they reached the first flight of stairs, Flea and Song were forced to help her. The steel armrests had been taken away from her in the Houses of Parliament, so the wheelchair would have been lighter than it was before, but even Flea appeared to be struggling by the time they reached the lowest level of the prison. And Jack herself was visibly fuming. It wasn't that her friends were carrying her, Ollie guessed, which they'd done plenty of times before. It was the fact that none of them had any choice in the matter, and that the guard was using Jack's disability to deliberately try to humiliate her.

At the bottom of the final set of stairs, Jack was able to take control once again. They found themselves in a narrow corridor with a seemingly endless parade of steel doors. The solitary confinement cells, Ollie assumed.

'You, Wheelchair,' said the guard who was leading. He opened one of the cell doors and pointed his cattle prod at Jack. 'In here. You'll have to crawl, I'm afraid,' he added sneeringly. 'There isn't room for that contraption if you want space to lie down at night.'

'I'll manage somehow,' Jack spat, and she wheeled her chair into the cell.

The guard turned his cattle prod on Flea. 'You're next. And don't even think about trying anything. One little twitch and I'll put enough volts in your belly that it'll be your friends next time who have to carry *you*.'

Snarling, Flea allowed himself to be herded into the cell next door to Jack's. As soon as the door was sealed, there was a *thump*, as though Flea had hurled himself against it. But the bolt on the outside of the cell door was thicker than Ollie's arm. Even Flea would have found it impossible to break.

They continued along the corridor, and one by one Ollie's friends were thrown into their cells. Soon it was just Sol and Ollie, with only one more empty cell in the passageway.

'What are you waiting for, a red carpet?' said the guard, as he grabbed hold of Sol's arm. He tossed Ollie's friend into the darkness, and then bolted the door behind him before Sol could so much as meet Ollie's eye.

'Looks like you get a wing all to yourself, pipsqueak.' With his colleagues bringing up the rear, the guard in front dragged Ollie around the corner. The next cell was some distance away, and when they reached it, the guard tossed Ollie inside without another word. The door slammed and darkness descended, and Ollie found himself in a room not much bigger than a wardrobe. There was a single bulb, barely alight, and a stench that was even worse than one of London's sewers.

As his eyes adjusted, Ollie pressed his ear to the door, and dimly he heard the guards' retreating footsteps. He waited until they'd faded completely.

'Sol!' he yelled, aiming his voice at the edge of the door. 'Can you hear me?'

He turned his head, so that his ear was touching cold steel, and waited for his friend to respond. But if Sol could hear him, no sound carried back to Ollie. It was hardly surprising. There must have been fifty metres of metal between them.

'Sol! Are you there?'

Once again Ollie pressed his ear to the door. But there was nothing, not even—

'*Ollie?*'

He tensed. He'd heard something, he was sure of it: his name echoing back at him. But unless it was a trick of the metal passageway, the sound seemed to be coming from behind him. And it wasn't Sol's voice that he'd heard.

23 REBEL ALLIANCE

'She's back!'

The guards dragged Lily past her friends, and tossed her broken body on to the bunk in her cell. She collapsed like a rag doll, too weak from lack of food to hold herself up. And every inch of her ached after the days she'd spent crammed in the tiny cell in the solitary-confinement wing.

It was rec time, so the cell doors were open, and as soon as the guards were gone, Ember and Aya rushed into her cell. It wasn't quite the reunion Lily had hoped for when she'd embarked on her escape attempt, but even so she was happy to see them, even if her eyes struggled to find focus. She smiled up at them weakly.

'Holy hamburgers,' exclaimed Ember. 'You look as bad as Han Solo in *Return of the Jedi* after Princess Leia frees him from the carbonite! What did they do to you?'

Lily shook her head. 'It's what they didn't do that hurts the most. I haven't eaten in . . .' Lily gave another headshake. She couldn't tell how long it had been since she'd last had a proper meal, and it had been almost a day since she'd had anything to drink.

'Are you hungry? Thirsty? What can we get you?' said Ember.

'That hamburger you mentioned would be nice,' Lily croaked. 'But I'd settle for a glass of water.'

'Wait right there!' There was a water fountain at the end of the passageway, and Ember made a dash towards it. When she returned, she was carrying a plastic beaker she must have pinched from the refectory, full to the brim.

With Aya's help, Lily struggled upright. Every instinct told her to down the water in one long swallow, but knowing she would only throw it back up again, she made herself take small, intermittent sips.

Aya was signing something at her, but Lily was too dazed to make out what she was saying.

'Sorry, I . . .'

'She's asking you what happened,' Ember interpreted for her. 'I mean, we know you got caught. Everyone does. One of the guards must have let it slip, and it's all anyone's been talking about. But Aya's asking how far you got. What stopped you from getting away.'

'You understand sign language now?' said Lily. The last time she'd seen her friends, it was Lily who'd had to interpret for Ember. 'How long have I been gone?'

'Just over a week,' Ember told her, and Lily half choked on a mouthful of water. She'd assumed she'd been gone for two or three days, maximum.

'As for the sign language,' Ember went on, 'Aya's been teaching me the basics. With you not around, we had to be able to talk to each other somehow. And as there isn't much else to do in here anyway . . .' She shrugged, and then peered at Lily eagerly, waiting for her to supply her own answers.

Lily finished the water. It made her stomach ache, but at least she could swallow now without feeling as if she was ingesting crushed glass.

'I'll tell you all about it,' she told her friends. 'I promise. But there's something I need to do first.'

She made to rise from the edge of the bunk. She wobbled, and Aya and Ember caught an arm each.

'You need to rest, Lily,' said Ember. 'You can barely stand, let alone walk.'

'I'll manage,' said Lily, finding her balance. 'I have to. But I could do with some moral support. I don't imagine the person I need to speak to is going to be particularly pleased to see me.'

Kitty Xu was leaning against the wall outside her cell.

The cell itself was no bigger than anyone else's, Lily knew, but it was the last in the row, and the walkway came to a dead end just beyond it. No guards bothered patrolling this far down – in deference to Kitty's relationship with the warden, Lily assumed – and the cells leading up to Kitty's were all occupied by Kitty's cronies, with Connor Ward's cell right next door. The upshot was that Kitty had a corner of the prison she could call her own, and though Lily could see Kitty in the distance, she couldn't get to her. There were at least a dozen members of Kitty's gang on the walkway between them, and as Lily and her friends approached, two of them stepped directly across Lily's path.

'I need to speak to Kitty,' Lily told the two goons, doing her best to hold herself upright. She was aware she should have given herself time to recover her strength before confronting Kitty, but time was pressing, and she knew she had to act *now*.

The two boys confronting Lily laughed. 'Maybe you do,' one said. 'But what makes you think Kitty wants to speak to *you*?'

If she'd been feeling stronger, Lily might have dispatched the two boys with a shin to the groin and a *nukite* strike – finger jab – into the eye. Not to injure them permanently, just to prevent them wasting any more time.

'Listen,' she said, 'I don't want to hurt you. But if you don't let me through *right now*, I'm going to have to do something you'll regret.'

There was a pause, and then both boys broke into laughter. They each had two years and twenty centimetres on Lily at least, and they seemed to be under the impression that someone younger and smaller wouldn't be able to hurt them. Sighing inwardly, and summoning her strength, Lily got ready to prove them wrong.

But before she was obliged to act, Connor Ward appeared. 'What's going on here?'

The two boys were still chuckling to each other. Lily was half tempted to knock them on to their backsides anyway, just to teach them a lesson.

'This little girl says she wants to speak to Kitty. Said if we didn't let her through, she'd do something to us that we'd regret.'

The boy who'd spoken to Connor beamed his amusement. Connor looked back at him impassively, then turned his gaze on Lily. To Lily's surprise, he didn't join in with the two boys' mocking laughter. 'Yes,' he said. 'I imagine she was about to do just that. Consider yourselves lucky. And stop giggling. You sound like a pair of drunk chickens.'

The grins fell from the two boys' faces. Gormlessly, they moved to one side, as Connor gestured Lily and her two friends through.

'You've got a nerve,' he said to Lily, as he led her along the walkway towards Kitty. 'I hope you're not anticipating a friendly reception.'

'It's going pretty much as I expected so far,' Lily answered.

Kitty had spotted Lily approaching, and she pushed herself away from the wall.

'Look who it is,' she said. She was showing her sharpened teeth, and she wasn't smiling. 'If the first words out of your mouth aren't to beg for mercy, this is going to be a very short conversation.'

'We need to talk,' Lily answered. She noted the other kids hanging around outside Kitty's cell getting to their feet and drawing back their shoulders. 'In private,' Lily added.

Kitty sneered in response. 'Give me one good reason why I shouldn't have you thrown over this handrail right now.'

Lily moved only her eyes. The handrail was at the edge of the walkway, and beyond it there was a twenty metre drop to a jagged array of pipes and ducts. Lily sensed Ember and Aya at her shoulders, doing their best not to appear intimidated.

'Because if you do that,' Lily said, 'you'll never know what I do. And you'll want to hear this, I promise you.' She raised her chin, confident that Kitty's curiosity would get the better of her anger.

But the older girl just flicked a hand. 'Throw them over. All three of them. And nobody can claim I didn't warn them.'

Hands seized Lily from both sides, and she found herself being dragged towards the handrail. This time she didn't hesitate. She stamped her heel on the toes of the girl who'd seized her from the right, and the girl yelped and immediately let go. The boy on Lily's other side had her left arm wrenched behind her back, but Lily simply stepped forwards, breaking the hold, then cupped a palm and struck the boy's ear. He staggered, and Lily knew that his skull would be ringing like a bell.

Lily was left standing on her own. The scuffle had been over in seconds, but she was panting nonetheless. There were a dozen more potential opponents surrounding her, and Lily knew that, in her weakened state, she wouldn't be able to fight them all off. Aya and Ember were unlikely to be able to help, either. They'd been seized by kids almost double their size.

'Didn't you hear what I said?' Lily growled at Kitty. 'I've got something to tell you! This place, the prison, it's . . .'

But she got no further. Kitty lunged for her. Lily tried to sidestep, but Kitty's first move had been a feint, and at the last moment she swerved, catching Lily off balance. Lily recovered, and tried to turn, but Kitty had managed to get behind her, and the next thing Lily knew, she felt a shank being pressed into her kidneys.

'Shut your mouth,' Kitty hissed into Lily's ear. 'Do you hear me? Just *shut your mouth*.'

Lily felt her eyes crease in confusion. Why was Kitty so determined not to hear what Lily had to tell her?

And then it dawned on her.

'You already know,' she said. Kitty's arm was a bar around her neck, and she had to strain to get out the words. 'Don't you? That's why you don't need me to tell you.'

'That we're on an *oil rig*?' hissed Kitty, so that only Lily could have heard. 'Of course I know! Which doesn't mean anybody else needs to. And I know something else, as well. I know why they let you out of solitary confinement. What, did you think the warden had decided to go easy on you?' Kitty laughed. 'She would have let you rot down there, but I convinced her to let me dispose of you for her. As a personal favour, let's say. Didn't I warn you not to cross me?' Kitty drove Lily closer to the barrier, and forced her head over the side. Lily was caught between the blade in her back and a fall that would prove just as deadly.

She tried to wriggle free, but Kitty was bigger, and stronger, and hadn't been left weakened by more than a week spent sweltering in a dungeon. The hope Lily had felt when she'd been released back into general population had been a mirage, she realised. A cruel illusion. One way or another, her fight was over.

'*Wait.*'

Lily felt Kitty tense.

'Let's hear her out.'

Kitty slackened her hold on Lily just enough that Lily was able to turn her head. Connor was staring at them both, his sharp eyes arrowed. And in his hand there was a shank of his own.

Kitty had clearly seen it, too. She smiled at Connor icily. 'I'm disappointed, Connor,' she said to him. 'You of all people

278

should know better than to question my decisions. Now, once I've finished with her, I'm going to have to deal with *you*.'

'I want to hear what she has to say,' Connor answered, with quiet authority. 'If it turns out she's wasting our time, I'll help you shove her over the railing myself.'

'It doesn't matter what she's got to say! You follow *my* orders, and *I* say she dies. Right *now*.'

'We're on an oil rig!' Lily blurted, before Kitty could shut her up permanently. 'This whole prison is in the middle of the ocean. Which means there's no way out, not unless we all work *together*!'

Lily felt herself being lifted over the railing, and there was nothing she could do to stop it.

'No!'

Out of the corner of her eye, Lily saw Ember and Aya dashing forwards. The kids holding them must have slackened their grip as they'd watched Connor and Kitty argue, just enough that Lily's friends had been able to squirm free.

Ember threw herself at Kitty, and Aya made a grab for the shank. It was three against one, but with Lily so weak, and Kitty a hardened fighter, the odds were pretty much even. It was all Aya could do to stop Kitty slicing at the air with her blade, as Lily and Ember sought to drive her back from the edge of the walkway.

They tripped, and toppled over, and Lily heard a scream of agony. Kitty's arm was still wrapped around Lily's neck, but she slipped free and rose on to her knees. Somehow the shank had slashed Kitty across the stomach. Her orange jumpsuit was blooming red.

'Quick!' said Lily to Connor, who was standing beside her. 'Get some bed sheets! A towel! Anything we can use to stop the bleeding!'

Connor didn't move. 'An oil rig?' he said. 'We're on an *oil rig*. And she *knew*?' He raised his own blade, pointing it at Kitty where she lay on the floor.

Kitty heard him talking and snarled up at him. Her hands were clutching her bleeding stomach. 'Yes, I knew! So what? Would it have made any difference if I'd—' She winced in agony. 'Would it have made any difference if I'd told you?'

'But you were talking about us escaping!' Connor said. 'About how you were using your relationship with the warden to find us a way out! How were we supposed to get away if, all this time, we were in the middle of the ocean?'

Lily had never seen Connor looking so furious. His features, usually so in control, were twisted in rage.

'I got us the best deal that was available!' spat Kitty. 'You and I virtually run this place! That's more than either of us had where we came from. Out there, my old man wouldn't have let me run for a bus! In here, *we* make the rules!'

'Big deal!' Connor bellowed. 'We're still in prison! I *trusted* you to get us *out* of here!'

Kitty sneered through her pain. 'Oh, please. We were never really getting out of here. Deep down, you knew that as well as I did!'

Connor took a step towards her, raising his shank. Lily caught hold of his arm.

'Connor, listen to me! We can still break out. There's still a chance!'

Connor was snarling at Kitty, and he turned his rage on Lily. '*How?* Weren't you listening to what you just told us? We're on an oil rig in the middle of the ocean. With more than a hundred prison guards to keep us here!'

'That's true. But there are more of *us* than there are of *them*. And so far they've been content to let us fight among ourselves. It's like I said, if we work together for a change, there's no reason we can't *all* get out of here.'

Aya appeared with a pile of bed sheets she'd grabbed from the nearest cell. Lily ripped one of them in half, and bent to attend to Kitty's stomach. Kitty reared as Lily pressed down, and Lily got her first proper look at the wound. It was bad, but not fatal – not if they got Kitty medical attention quickly. Which made the situation even more urgent than it was before, because the prison staff wouldn't do anything to help her. Under Warden Bricknell's regime, if you got hurt, or ill, you were on your own.

Connor was shaking his head. 'The inmates in here, they're a rabble. How do you propose we get them to co-operate?'

'We tell them what we found out. And we let them know *you're* giving the orders.' Lily had been looking at Connor, and she turned to Kitty. '*Both* of you. It's like you said,' she told Kitty, 'the two of you virtually run this place. The rest of the inmates will do whatever you tell them to. Particularly when they find out it's their only chance of ever getting out of here.'

Kitty grimaced, and Lily couldn't tell whether it was in scorn or pain. 'You're involving me in this?' she said. 'Even after I tried to kill you?'

Lily looked back at her steadily. 'Trust me, I wouldn't be asking if I had a choice. Of course, we can always let you bleed to death. Then Connor will be number one, and it wouldn't matter if you'd agreed to help or not.'

Kitty's eyes flicked to Connor, who glared down at her. It was clear they'd lost all trust for each other, but their silence suggested they realised that any score they had to settle would have to wait.

'Oh, and one other thing,' Lily told them. 'I'm from the Haven. And if you help me get back down to solitary and free my friends, I'll be able to show you exactly what we can do.'

24 SHOCK TACTICS

The buzz in the refectory was nothing like the noise Lily had become used to. It was tense, expectant, as though from a crowd in an auditorium who were reluctant to be there, but at the same time were impatient for the main event to start.

Unless that was just Lily projecting her own feelings on those around her. Since the point she'd been captured up on deck, her emotions had swung from despair to elation and back again. Despair that she'd been caught, and that her escape attempt had failed; elation when, in the bowels of the prison, she'd heard Ollie's voice carrying through the darkness. He'd come for her; they all had! Flea and Jack and Sol and Song and Erik.

But the joy she'd initially experienced as she and Ollie had begun to speak hadn't lasted long. They'd shared their stories, and gradually it had become obvious that, with all seven of them locked in *Deadfall*'s dungeon (for *Deadfall*, Ollie had told her, was the oil rig's name), their fate was surely sealed. They were trapped here for ever, and Warden Bricknell would torture Lily's friends until they gave up the Haven. Worst of all,

Sebastian Crowe would succeed in his mission to take over as the prime minister, and Maddy Sikes would be able to claim the victory she'd always craved: total domination, with a puppet politician at her command, and a population governed through fear and intimidation.

Now, though, and against all odds, Lily had a chance to stop it. A *final* chance, she was sure. And it all depended on what happened in the next few minutes.

She looked around the refectory, and caught sight of Connor at his and Kitty's usual table in the choicest corner of the room – away from the entrance, but near the food, and in a section ignored by the guards. Kitty herself was back in her cell. She'd followed through on what Lily had asked of her, spreading the word to the other gang leaders, and telling them what needed to be done, but Lily had insisted she sit out the next phase. Kitty's wound was deeper than Lily had originally thought, and though they'd patched her up as best they could, she remained dangerously weak. It was important she rested until they could get her medical attention.

Lily, too, should probably have kept out of sight. If the warden spotted her, she would want to know from Kitty why Lily hadn't already been disposed of, as per their agreement. But Lily had been careful to keep her head down, and anyway Warden Bricknell was nowhere to be seen. Plus, this was Lily's fight, and there was no way she was going to miss it.

She checked to see if the guards had noticed the shift in atmosphere. But they were arrayed in their usual places around the circumference of the room, looking alert but not unduly on edge. The queue at the food counter was down to the last few inmates, and the tables in the room were almost full. Lily nodded at Aya and Ember, across from her.

It was time.

Right on cue, there was a yell in the middle of the room – from the table right in the centre. A chair was tipped over, a tray upended, and all at once the scene in the refectory became one that was all too familiar: the kids fighting among themselves, as the masked prison guards stood watching on.

The guards reacted the way they always did. There were around forty stationed in the room – almost half of the guards in the prison, according to Connor's and Lily's best guess. At least twenty of them began shoving their way towards the brawl. The other inmates in the refectory had immediately got to their feet, and the guards who were closing in on the central table shoved them ruthlessly to one side, firing their cattle prods indiscriminately.

'*Now!*' Lily yelled.

On her command, and as the bulk of the guards allowed themselves to be sucked into the middle of the room, the kids around the central table turned. Abandoning the fight with each other, they launched themselves at the phalanx of guards. Simultaneously, the inmates on the periphery of the room

– including Lily and Connor – spun the other way, to deal with the guards who'd remained at their posts. It was a classic divide-and-conquer manoeuvre. Sun Tzu – and Flea – would have been proud.

Except it didn't take the guards long to realise what was happening. Lily had hoped the element of surprise might give them a few extra seconds to exert their control on the situation, but the alarm started sounding immediately, and even as Lily and the others charged, the masked prison guards levelled their cattle prods. They looked like spearmen braced against an infantry charge – the difference being, none of the infantry troops had weapons of their own.

As the opposing sides clashed, the room was filled with a maelstrom of noise. The combatants roared, the alarm continued to shriek, and all around there was a crackle of electricity as the guards discharged their cattle prods.

Lily drove herself at the nearest guard. He'd seen her coming, and was ready with his cattle prod, but at the last minute Lily dropped to the ground. The floor was slippery from the dozens of overturned food trays, and she was able to slide the last couple of metres. She trapped the guard by scissoring her legs around his knees, and he toppled forwards at the same time as he pressed the trigger on his weapon. He landed as the cattle prod released its charge, inadvertently smothering the live end and catching the full voltage in his chest.

'Lily! Here!'

Lily raised her head, and saw Ember holding a cattle prod in each hand. Who knew where she'd got *two* of them from, but Lily was delighted to see that her friend was unhurt. She searched for Aya, and caught sight of her just as she dispatched one of the guards with a kick to the groin. Lily winced as the guard crumpled.

Ember tossed Lily one of the cattle prods she'd scavenged, and Lily caught it one-handed. It was the first time she'd held one, and it was strangely light considering the damage it could do. She checked the setting, and wasn't surprised to see it dialled to ten. She adjusted it to eight, and started to look around for anyone who might be able to use her help. Then she stopped, imagining herself running into Warden Bricknell, and nudged the cattle prod up to nine.

All around her the battle was continuing, but Lily could tell immediately that the inmates were winning. The guards in the centre of the room had been completely overwhelmed, and were being penned in a forlorn circle by prisoners who'd relieved them of their weapons, as well as their masks. Without anything to hide behind, the guards looked like regular men and women, the kind of people you would pass on the street. Lily couldn't decide whether this made them less frightening, or the opposite.

Just as Lily was about to join her friends, someone bumped into her from behind. She spun, ready to discharge the cattle prod in her hands, and found herself face to face with Connor, who had a cattle prod of his own.

They let their weapons fall, and Connor grinned.

'There'll be more guards coming,' Lily warned him. 'We need to secure the refectory and get the rest of these guards contained.'

There were only a handful of guards still on their feet, and even they were trapped in a corner. But it wasn't over. Lily saw another squad of prison guards had arrived from elsewhere in the prison. They were outside the main doors, battling to get inside the refectory.

'We'll take care of it,' Connor told her. 'You go. Get to solitary. If your friends are as good as you say they are, we're going to need their help.'

Lily checked again towards the doors. There would be another sixty or so guards for Connor and the others to deal with, but now they could fight fire with fire, there was every chance the inmates would prevail.

'Aya!' Lily shouted as she waved. 'Ember! Let's go!'

Aya and Ember rushed over to join her, and Lily made to lead them towards the main doors, hoping there would be an opportunity to slip through amid the confusion. But a hand on her shoulder pulled her round. 'Not that way,' Connor told her. 'Head through the kitchens. There's a door at the back that will take you into the main walkway. The stairs that lead down to solitary are off to the right, all the way at the end. Watch out though – more guards will be coming that way, too.'

Lily nodded, grateful. 'Good luck,' she said.

Connor nodded back at her, and then Lily was off.

Aya and Ember were right on her heels as Lily vaulted the food counter. When she entered the kitchens, the absence of people was strangely disconcerting after the chaos in the refectory. It was like stepping outside a dream.

The door at the back of the room opened on to the main walkway through the prison, just as Connor had said. They turned right, alert for the sound of approaching guards, and it wasn't long before they heard a clatter of feet pounding towards them on the metal walkway, close enough that the entire structure began to vibrate.

'Quick!' said Lily. 'Down here!'

There was a narrow offshoot of the passageway ahead of them, and Lily shoved her friends out of sight. She followed, and all three girls pressed themselves against the metal wall. The thunder of footsteps rolled towards them, and seconds later an entire squad of prison guards was streaming past. If they'd turned their heads, they would have spotted Lily and the others instantly, but they were evidently too intent on reaching the refectory.

Lily tried to keep a tally of the number of guards as they passed, but they were moving too quickly, and she lost count when she hit twenty. She just had to hope Connor and the others were ready for the trouble that was heading their way.

They found the stairs, and Lily dimly recalled being hauled down the stairwell herself. It was just as far to the lowest level as she remembered. For most of the time she'd been incarcerated, Lily had assumed the prison was arranged solely over two floors, and it was true that the kids' cells were all on the same level, with the guards looking down on them from above. But piecing together what she knew now, and remembering the vastness of the oil rig when she'd seen it from the surface, there was clearly much more to the structure than she'd realised. There was surely space for *thousands* of prisoners on *Deadfall*. The kids' prison must have taken up only a fraction of the rig's vast underbelly.

Something about the realisation prompted a moment of dread, but Lily didn't have time to stop and think about why. And anyway the mounting excitement she was feeling overrode it. She'd spoken to Ollie, but the others had been locked in cells too far away for them to be able to hear her. Soon enough, however, they would be reunited.

Ignoring the stench of the dank passageway, she pressed on. There were no guards this far down. By now they'd surely all been drawn into the battle that was raging in the refectory. Unless the fight was over already? Could it be that victory was already in their grasp?

'There!' Ember said, pointing. Lily had spotted the first of the solitary-confinement cells at the same time as the younger girl had. Immediately she started calling the names of her friends.

'Flea! Jack! Sol! Where are you? Song? Erik? Shout if you can hear me!'

'In here!' came a voice back.

Lily darted towards the nearest of the cell doors and started undoing the lock. In the damp air, the bolts had rusted, and it took all of Lily's strength to try to work it free.

'Aya, Ember, make a start on the other doors!'

The two girls were several steps ahead of her, already dashing towards the other cells along the passageway.

Lily returned her attention to the door in front of her. In a rush, the bolt slid free and the door sprang open. Lily barely had time to raise her head when she was bowled from her feet, and she found herself wrapped in her brother's arms.

'Lily! You're alive!'

'Keep . . . squeezing me . . . like this . . . and I soon won't be.'

Her brother released his hold and Lily dropped back on to her toes. She grinned at her idiot younger brother, and then wrapped him in a hug of her own.

'We came to rescue you,' Flea told her, as she squeezed.

'So I heard,' Lily responded, finally letting her brother go. 'And I'm glad someone thought to tell me. Otherwise I might not have guessed.'

Flea's grin turned sheepish. 'Yeah, well. We didn't figure on being tossed into a dungeon.'

'It shouldn't have come as such a surprise,' said Lily, still beaming. 'We're beginning to make a habit of it, after all.'

'Lily!'

Lily spun, and saw Aya and Ember had already freed the rest of her friends. 'Jack! Sol! Erik! Song! You have no idea how pleased I am to see you!'

'And us you,' said Sol, as they hugged. 'Seriously, what's with this place? I was promised a sea view, but the accommodation on this hunk of junk is tighter than Flea's wallet. And I called for room service *hours* ago. I'm thinking of complaining to the manager.'

'Where's Ollie?' said Jack, as she checked around.

'This way,' said Lily, pushing her way through the group. She led the others towards the end of the passage. 'His cell ended up being next to mine. I heard him calling for you, and we were able to communicate through the wall. He caught me up on what's been happening,' she added bleakly.

'You were locked up down here, too?' said Erik. 'The whole time we were?'

'Some of the time. They put me down here after I tried to escape. It's a long story, and it's probably best if I save it till later. For the moment we need to concentrate on—'

They'd reached Ollie's cell door. It was open, and there was no one inside.

'He should be in here,' Lily said.

'Guys, look,' said Jack. She'd moved inside the cell, and was staring at something on the end of her fingers. She rubbed them together, and then pointed to a dark patch on one of the walls. 'It's blood,' she said. 'And it's still wet.'

'Lily? *Lily!*'

Connor appeared around the corner, and Lily laid a hand on Flea's arm. 'It's OK, he's with us.'

Connor was alone, and it was clear he'd seen his fair share of action in the time since he and Lily had parted. His orange jumpsuit was ripped, and there was a bruise forming around his left eye.

'We're in trouble,' he panted. '*Serious* trouble. I thought it was over, but somehow they've summoned reinforcements.'

'I know,' said Lily. 'We passed them on the way down. But there can't have been more than thirty of them.'

'*Thirty?*' said Connor, scrunching his eyes. 'No,' he said, 'you don't understand. We dealt with the guards we knew about. We had them trapped in a circle in the refectory. But then more arrived. *Hundreds* more. We need help up there and we need it *now.*'

All at once Lily realised what had been nagging at her before. She thought about the computer equipment that was somehow being reassembled, after Lily and the others had taken it apart: an endless loop of futile work. And Aya's parents; her insistence that they were being held somewhere, too. Because the reality was that *Deadfall* was *huge*, meaning there was space for another prison, too. And if there were other prisoners aboard the oil rig – *adult* prisoners – it stood to reason there'd be more guards.

Lily looked from the blood on the wall of Ollie's cell, and back into Connor's desperate eyes. And then, from up ahead, there was a scream.

25 TRUTH SERUM

Ollie was aware of a shrill, piercing noise in the distance, like a car alarm going off on a neighbouring street. But just as though he were hearing it in the middle of the night, his grogginess convinced him to ignore it, and he found himself drifting into unconsciousness. He might almost have been asleep in his old bedroom, back in his and Nancy's flat, before he'd even heard of the Haven, or Maddy Sikes, or Dodge, or Sol, or Lily . . .

A slap across his cheek brought him round.

The hand that had hit him had felt large and calloused, but the face looking down on him when Ollie opened his eyes was soft and round. The face of a school nurse, or a woman behind the counter in an old-fashioned sweet shop. All except for her eyes, which were hard like coal, and blazing with eager intensity.

'You remember me, don't you, young man? My name is Warden Bricknell.'

It was the woman who'd been waiting for them on their arrival, who Ollie had presumed to be in charge.

'I see my men here have had some fun with you already,' she said. She touched Ollie's head and he flinched at the pain.

He tried desperately to get his bearings. He was on *Deadfall*, he remembered that much, and he recalled being in his cell when the door had opened, and two huge prison guards had been standing there in the passageway. Ominously, the guards hadn't been wearing masks. Ollie presumed the other guards did so to maintain their anonymity, because they knew that what they were doing here was wrong, and they wanted to be sure no prisoners – and no other guards, perhaps – would be able to identify them if the secret of *Deadfall* ever got out.

But these two guards hadn't cared about Ollie seeing their faces. Meaning they weren't worried about any repercussions. Or, more likely, they knew that Ollie would soon no longer be a concern.

One of the guards had grabbed him, and Ollie had fought back. He'd struck the man on his bicep, using a technique he recalled instinctively from one of his *katas* – *ippon ken*, or knuckle fist – and the man had howled and let him go. But then he'd come raging forwards, his good arm reaching, and the last thing Ollie remembered was being slammed against the wall of his cell.

He guessed he must have hit his head, hard enough to knock him unconscious. And now . . . now he was in a different room altogether. It smelt just as bad as his cell had. Worse, if that were possible: as well as the damp and a stink like the drains in the boys' toilets in Ollie's old school, there was the tang of something sharper, like bodily fluids gone bad.

He tried to sit up, and found he couldn't. His thoughts remained sluggish, and there was a fog around the edge of his vision, but he realised he was sitting in something like a dentist's chair, stripped of any padding, and with leather straps binding his wrists to the armrests. He couldn't see past his bent knees, but it was obvious that his ankles were shackled, too.

The room itself was a metal box, like all the chambers on *Deadfall*, it seemed. It was only the contents of the room that distinguished it from the rest. As well as the dentist's chair, which was right in the centre of the floor, there was what Ollie could only have described as a tool bench along one of the walls. But there were no hammers, no screwdrivers or anything like that. The tools that were on display looked sharper, more precise than the kind you might expect to find in a workshop or a garage, and they were all made of polished metal. Setting aside the obvious lack of hygiene, they wouldn't have looked out of place in a surgeon's operating theatre.

'You're admiring my toys, I see,' said the warden, noticing Ollie taking in his surroundings. 'Most, I have to admit, are purely for my own interest and entertainment. Over my years of extensive practice, I have discovered that there are far simpler means of eliciting answers from a subject who is minded to withhold them.'

A syringe appeared at the edge of Ollie's vision. One of the guards was passing it to the warden. Ollie hadn't noticed the man standing at his shoulder. It must have been the guard who'd slapped him awake. Now, the guard moved to the warden's side and folded his massive arms. He glared at Ollie, and Ollie noticed with some grim satisfaction that he was surreptitiously rubbing at his bicep.

The other guard was stationed beside the door, eagerly watching on.

The warden held the syringe up to the dim bulb that was hanging from the dripping ceiling. She flicked the needle, then lowered it towards Ollie's arm.

Ollie tried to buck. The leather loop around his left wrist felt slightly loose, to the extent he might have been able to slip his hand free if he'd had enough time. But before he could do more than test its resistance, the needle in the warden's hand pierced his skin and the liquid in the syringe flowed into his veins.

'What . . . what is that?'

'Just a little concoction I helped to develop myself, in . . . a previous role, shall we call it? Working for a different government from the one that employs me now. I suppose I could tell you all about it, seeing as you're not going to be with us much longer anyway, but I was sworn to secrecy and, well . . . old habits die hard.'

She smiled – perfectly pleasantly, Ollie might have said.

'But to answer your question, the mix of chemicals currently flowing through your system is designed to help you focus on the answers to the questions I'm about to ask you. The *real* answers.'

'You mean a . . . a truth serum?'

The warden chuckled. 'Oh, dear boy. I'm afraid you have been reading too many comic books. There is unfortunately no such thing. But certain chemicals, in the appropriate mix, do indeed reduce the ability of a subject to relay falsehoods. Sodium thiopental is the main component, together with a few secret ingredients of my own.' The warden passed the needle back to the guard, and folded her hands in her lap. 'Now we just need to wait a few moments for your blood to deliver the message to your brain.' She gazed at Ollie amiably.

'I'm sorry it took me so long to come and talk to you, by the way,' she said, as though making conversation to fill the time. 'Keeping this operation . . . afloat requires a considerable proportion of my attention. And, as you may have gathered, we are currently dealing with a minor disturbance.'

The car alarm. It was still going on. As Ollie attempted to tune in to the distant siren, however, he found it harder and harder to pinpoint the noise. Even the warden's words were beginning to swim away from him. Whatever had been in that syringe was clearly beginning to take effect.

'But there is nothing for you to worry about, I can assure you,' the warden said. 'Everything is under control.'

Ollie's thoughts came briefly into focus, just as though he'd been slapped again. *Under control.* What did that mean? After Lily had been removed from her cell – Ollie had heard it happen – he'd feared the worst for her, but he'd managed to convince himself that maybe it meant she was being taken back to general population. They evidently didn't know *she* was a member of the Haven, after all. And when the alarm had begun to sound, Ollie had started to hope that maybe Lily was somehow responsible.

But whatever was happening, the warden was clearly unconcerned enough that she was leaving others to deal with it. It was *nothing to worry about*, she'd said. *Everything is under . . . under . . .*

Ollie shook his head to try to clear it.

Under . . . what? Water? Ground?

He'd lost track of what he'd been thinking about. For some reason he had an image of Lily in his head, but when his eyes focused he saw the warden's face. She was leaning forwards eagerly.

'That *was* quick,' she declared. Her hand appeared out of nowhere, and Ollie felt one of his eyelids being prised apart. The warden tilted her head as she studied the state of his pupils. 'I suppose, given the situation, your pulse must be substantially elevated. And perhaps that bump to your head helped things along.'

She allowed Ollie to blink, and clasped her hands together excitedly. 'So,' she said. 'Why don't we make a start? Let's begin with an easy one, shall we? What is your name?'

'My . . . my name?'

'I know it already, of course. You were singled out to me before you arrived, which is why you and I are having this opportunity to speak before I move on to your friends. But I want to check that my little cocktail hasn't affected your memory.'

For some reason it suddenly felt vitally important that Ollie refuse to tell the warden what he was called. And yet . . . and yet he couldn't quite remember *why* it was important. How could it hurt, after all?

'I'm . . . I'm Ollie,' he heard himself saying.

'That's correct! Ollie Turner. And your parents' names? Do you recall those?'

This time the question was like a pinprick. Even through his grogginess, Ollie could tell that the warden was goading him. Another name floated to the front of his consciousness. Sikes. Maddy Sikes had put the warden up to this.

This time Ollie managed to shake his head. He wouldn't talk about his parents in front of this woman. He *wouldn't*, no matter how many drugs she pumped into him.

'Now, Ollie,' the warden responded, warningly, 'I would remind you what I told you before. If you don't give me the answers I require, I shall have to ask your friends. And perhaps with them I shall employ less . . . *compassionate* methods.'

Ollie's vision came into focus, and he found himself gazing at the sinister-looking instruments arrayed on the counter beside him. He screwed his eyes shut and shook his head again.

The warden gave a dissatisfied sniff. 'Well,' she said. 'No matter. As it happens I know the answer to that question as well. So let's move on, shall we?' Once again the warden checked Ollie's pupils, and was evidently content with what she saw. 'The Haven,' she said. 'Where is it? Tell me now and I will let you rest. Wouldn't that be nice, Ollie? To be able to rest. To *sleep*?'

Ollie felt himself being lulled. It *would* be nice to be able to rest. Fully. *Finally*. With no more hiding, no more worrying. No excitement or danger or responsibility. He could simply float away, allow himself to be carried into unconsciousness on the soft, warm memories he had of his parents, of Nancy, of his life before Maddy Sikes. And all he had to do was tell the warden what she wanted to know . . .

Ollie raised his head. His eyes were closed, but he felt his lips parting. He couldn't see the warden, but he could picture her, bending towards him in anticipation, her ear turned to the sound of his voice.

'The Haven,' she crooned. 'Tell me, Ollie. Tell me where it is.'

With a burst of effort, Ollie drove his head back against the chair. He hit his skull in the same spot it had struck the cell wall earlier, and the pain was like a bucket of cold water. He even gasped, as though he were coming up for breath. And this time when he looked at the warden, he saw her with perfect clarity. 'I'll never tell you where the Haven is. *Never.*'

The warden lashed out, slapping Ollie across his cheek. She glowered at him, then turned to the guard beside her, and nodded. The guard produced another syringe. The warden didn't take it from him. Instead she watched, as the guard stepped forwards to administer the injection himself.

'It seems we will have to up the dosage,' the warden said.

The guard lowered the needle towards Ollie's arm.

'I should warn you, however,' the warden went on, 'that there is a limit to how much of this particular mix of drugs your body will be able to process. It is not my intention to kill you. Not yet, anyway. But I feel it only fair to warn you what the consequences of your refusal to co-operate might be.'

'No, wait . . .'

The guard touched the needle to Ollie's skin.

'Please! Don't! I'll . . . I'll tell you. I'll tell you everything! The Haven, it's . . . it's . . .'

Ollie felt a stabbing pain as the needle punctured his vein. But when the warden touched the guard's shoulder, the man paused – and just that moment's delay was enough. Even through his daze, Ollie had been working to slip his left wrist from the strap he'd realised was loose. Now, his arm finally free, he whipped his hand across his body and grabbed for the syringe that was protruding from his vein. In one swift movement, he brought the needle down on the back of the guard's hand.

The guard screamed in agony, and stumbled away, flailing to pull the needle from his skin before the warden's toxic chemical could find its way into his bloodstream.

Ollie didn't pause to savour his victory. Three of his limbs were still strapped to the chair, and he immediately started working at the buckle that was constraining his other arm.

The warden had staggered backwards in shock, but now she came at him, her fingers set like claws. Ollie abandoned his attempts to loosen the strap and flailed for one of the tools on the workbench instead, wrapping his fingers around the first thing they touched. He slashed at the air in front of him just as the warden came within range. Whatever he was holding, it was sharp, and it left a bloody score across the warden's forearm. Just as the guard had, she screamed, and fell backwards, colliding with the second guard as he rushed forwards from the door.

Ollie looked at what he was holding, and realised it was something like a scalpel, but with a wickedly curving blade. He sliced at the shackle around his arm, and the blade went through the leather as though the strap were made of melting butter. He freed his ankles next, but when he attempted to stand, he felt unsteady, either from the bump to his head or the remnants of the warden's truth serum. He toppled to the floor, and the blade he'd been holding clattered from his grip.

Ollie found his feet again, but when he spun he saw that he'd been cornered. There was a guard to his left, and another to his right, while the warden blocked his path towards the door. The guard Ollie had stabbed with the needle had picked up a weapon of his own – a steel spike, twenty centimetres long – and steadily he began to close in.

It was over, Ollie realised. He was trapped.

Except that was when the door flew open, and Lily burst into the room.

26 SINKING FEELING

Lily had only a second or two to take in the scene before her. A chair in the centre of the room, with straps on the arms and footrests; a collection of vicious-looking instruments on the counter beside it; the warden and two unmasked guards; and Ollie, trapped in one corner. There was blood caked to one side of his head and he was clearly struggling to stay on his feet. And yet, incredibly, he was smiling.

'What took you so long?' he said.

'By the look of it we got here just in time,' Lily answered, grinning back. And then everything seemed to happen at once.

The guards spun away from Ollie and charged towards Lily and her friends. One of the men had a long skewer in his hand, and as he drove towards Lily, he brought it down in an arc above his head. Lily leapt to one side, and then watched as her brother steamed forwards, meeting the guard with a diving tackle around his middle. Song was right on Flea's heels, and as the second guard bore down on her, she simply veered and stuck out a foot. The guard went sprawling, and there was a sound like a broken bell as the man's skull collided with the metal wall.

From the centre of the room there was a crash. Flea was lying on top of the first guard, who'd somehow become entangled with the chair. He tried to wriggle free, but Erik popped up behind him, and brought one of the metal trays that had been bearing the spikes and scalpels down on top of the man's head.

'Lily! The warden!'

Ollie had been knocked back against the wall, but he was pointing to a second door that had opened up behind the head end of the chair. The guards may have been out cold, but Warden Bricknell was getting away.

Lily rushed over to Ollie. 'Are you OK?' she asked him. 'What did they do to you?'

'I'm fine,' Ollie reassured her. 'I promise.' He let Lily help him to his feet. 'It's . . . it's good to see you. In the flesh, I mean.'

Lily smiled. 'It's good to see you, too.'

'Sis?' came a voice at Lily's shoulder. Lily broke her attention away from Ollie to see Flea looking at her urgently. 'This is your show and everything, but don't you think we should save the reunions for later?' He pointed towards the ceiling, to indicate the alarm that was resounding through the air.

'Right,' said Lily. She cast around, and saw everyone in the room was looking at her. 'Guys,' she said, 'this is Aya, Ember and Connor. Aya, Ember, Connor – this is everybody. We'll make proper introductions later. In the meantime, we've got a situation on our hands. We've disarmed the guards we knew about, but it turns out there's another wing to the prison. All I can think is, it's where the adults are being held. Including your parents, Aya.'

Aya's eyes grew wide: in hope or fear, Lily couldn't tell.

'According to Connor,' Lily went on, 'there are more guards now than we can cope with. The kids up there are in danger of being overwhelmed. Which, the way I figure it, means we need reinforcements of our own.'

'From *where* exactly?' said Connor.

Ollie answered before Lily could. 'The same place those guards are coming from,' he said. 'The other wing.'

Lily nodded. 'Exactly. We need to free the adults and get them to help us take over the prison. Connor, you need to show my friends where to go.'

'Wait,' said Flea. 'What about you? Aren't you coming with us?'

Lily looked at the doorway Warden Bricknell had escaped through. 'I'll meet you up there,' she said. 'In the meantime, I've got a score to settle.'

The warden was already out of sight. But the doorway led directly to a stairwell, so there was no questioning in which direction she'd fled. And though Lily couldn't see Warden Bricknell, she could hear her footsteps reverberating on the metal steps above.

Still clutching her cattle prod, Lily began to bound up the spiral staircase in pursuit. She took the steps two at a time, ignoring her clamouring lungs, and the fire that began to build in her legs. It wasn't just the thought of the warden getting away that drove her on. For some reason she couldn't identify, it felt vital to Lily that she stop Warden Bricknell before she got wherever she was heading. They hadn't known about the second wing to the prison. What other surprises might the warden have up her sleeve?

The staircase seemed to run right through the core of the oil rig. There were doors to the various levels every twenty steps or so, and at one point Lily heard the sounds of the conflict that was raging in the prison between the kids and new influx of guards. The noise seemed to be all around her, suggesting the fighting had spilled from the refectory, and that the entire prison had now become a battleground. It sounded as if the inmates needed all the help they could get. Lily just had to hope that Ollie and the others would be able to free the adult prisoners in time.

The warden ignored it all. She was clearly heading for the very top of the staircase, and though Lily appeared to be gaining on her, it was becoming clear she wasn't going to catch her before they ran out of steps.

A door burst open up above, and the stairwell turned into a wind tunnel. Lily had to grab the handrail to stop herself being blown from her feet. The cattle prod slipped from her grip, and went clattering to the base of the steps. Lily watched it fall. Then, cursing, she looked up, and for a second saw the warden framed by daylight. She had reached the oil rig's main deck.

With a final despairing glance after her cattle prod, Lily doubled her pace. Her legs were screaming now, but adrenaline powered her on. When she reached the doorway herself, she once again had to brace herself against the wind. The sun was dipping towards the horizon, shining directly into Lily's face.

She cast around, and saw only the vastness of *Deadfall* spread before her. The main deck was enormous, with a helipad off to one side, and an enormous metal derrick, a bit like a pylon, right in the centre. Before *Deadfall* had been decommissioned, it would have been the pipeline running through the derrick that had sucked the oil from the sea bed, countless metres below the waves. Now the derrick was just a rusting hulk, much like the rest of the enormous metal island.

Lily turned, and realised the main building was looming over her. It was three storeys high, judging by the rows of windows, making it about the size a large house. The spiral staircase had led Lily through a doorway at the structure's base, and there was another staircase, like scaffolding, at its side. It led all the way to the top row of windows, and the warden was already halfway up.

Lily set off after her. The warden disappeared through a door at the top of the stairs. There was a brief commotion, the sound of voices being raised, and then three men in the same grey uniforms as the guards bundled through the doorway in the opposite direction.

At first Lily assumed the warden had sent them to deal with her, and she readied herself for a fight. But none of the men carried cattle prods – they weren't even wearing masks – and they flew past Lily with barely a glance. They must have been technicians of some kind, Lily realised, and the room at the top of the stairs the oil rig's control room. She watched the men for a moment, confused, and saw one of them raise an arm, gesturing towards a lifeboat on the side of the main deck. It appeared to be the only one, at least on this side of the building, and it was attached to some kind of winch.

But why on earth would *Deadfall*'s control crew be heading for a lifeboat? Surely the lifeboats would only be used if the oil rig was sinking, and what could possibly cause a structure of *Deadfall*'s size to topple into the sea, short of a deliberate—

Lily felt her stomach drop. She looked up, towards the control room, feeling sure that she knew now what the warden intended to do.

She took the remaining steps in a series of leaps. She reached the door to the control room and threw it open – then dived behind one of the panels of instruments when a gunshot ricocheted against the metal doorframe beside her.

'You stupid girl!' came the warden's voice. 'You don't even realise what you've done. You've killed yourself. Your friends, too. You've killed them all!'

Lily raised her head, and there was another gunshot. This time the bullet hit the control panel next to her. There was a shower of sparks, and Lily ducked. In the brief glance she'd had, she'd seen the warden beside a computer screen on the far side of the room, frantically keying commands into the interface. And now Lily was beyond all doubt: the warden was attempting to scuttle the oil rig – to initiate whatever self-destruct process had been installed on *Deadfall* as a safeguard against its secrets ever getting out.

Lily dived for another point of cover, but the next bank of screens was barely a metre closer to the warden, and there was nothing now but open space between them. Lily couldn't see what type of gun the warden had, but knew that she'd only fired two bullets. She surely had more than enough left to stop Lily in her tracks if she attempted to get any closer.

But what choice did Lily have? If she didn't act now, the warden would trigger the explosives that were no doubt strapped to the four huge pillars that held the oil rig above the surface of the sea. If that happened they would all be dead soon anyway.

Her only chance was to attempt to close the gap as quickly as possible – to rush across the open floor and hope she could avoid getting shot. The warden would have time to fire at least once, but perhaps not enough time to aim.

Feeling like a soldier in a trench, Lily peered across the bank of computer screens in front of her, then threw herself to the floor again when one of the monitors exploded under the impact of another gunshot. The warden had been waiting for Lily to show herself, and had missed her head by centimetres.

But Lily had spotted an open metal case on the surface above her – the box that had presumably contained the gun that was now in the warden's hand – and she silently curled her fingers around the handle, preparing to hurl it at the warden the instant before she sprang into action. She rose on to the balls of her feet, readying herself to make the leap forwards, and silently gave herself a countdown. Three . . . two . . .

'Hey! Over here, you rancid piece of fish guts!'

'*Kitty!*' Lily didn't know where Kitty had come from, but she'd appeared in the middle of the doorway. And just her presence was enough. Lily rose and swung the metal box. The warden fired her gun, but she'd been just as surprised as Lily had been by Kitty's sudden appearance, and the shot went wild as she raised her free hand to defend herself. The bullet hit a window midway between the two girls, and even before the final shards of glass had landed, Lily had crossed the open floor.

She made a grab for the gun, catching hold of the warden's wrist, but failing to prise her fingers from the handle. In her panic, the warden squeezed the trigger once more, and a bullet hit the ceiling. At some point Kitty had joined the fray, and the three of them became locked in a tussle.

The warden shrieked – a sound of pure rage and frustration – and lashed out with an elbow. It struck Lily on the jaw, but she clung on, and yet another gunshot went off. This time Lily was sure she'd felt the bullet rush past her cheek. Was that the fifth bullet? Or the sixth? And how many bullets had been in the clip in the first place?

An elbow struck Lily again, and this time she went sprawling, cracking her head on one of the computer desks on her way down. She tried to get immediately to her feet, knowing it was now just Kitty against the warden, and that Kitty was in no state to fight *anyone*. But before Lily could come fully to her senses, she heard another shriek. The warden was clutching her shoulder, and the shank Kitty had threatened to use on Lily earlier was jutting from her flesh. The gun, meanwhile, had fallen to the floor, and Kitty leapt for it. Then she rose, triumphant, and levelled the weapon at the warden.

'Kitty, no!' Lily shouted. She'd read the intent in Kitty's eyes.

'Stay out of this, newbie,' Kitty said. 'Don't you realise what this mad cow was trying to do? If she'd got her way she would have murdered us all!'

As if to prove what Kitty was saying, there was a message displayed on the screen where the warden had been working.

'Are you sure you want to initiate SELF-DESTRUCT?' it read. 'Hit any key to TRIGGER DETONATION.'

With blood dripping from her shoulder, the warden was backed against the counter. Slowly she began edging towards the keyboard.

'Don't you move!' Kitty yelled. But just raising her voice seemed to take all her remaining strength, and Lily noticed Kitty's wound had started to bleed profusely. It wasn't just her jumpsuit that had become sodden. She had her free hand pressed against her stomach, and there was red filling the gaps between her fingers.

Lily was still on all fours. She pulled herself to her feet using a nearby chair.

'Kitty? Put down the gun, Kitty. She's not worth it. We can lock her up in one of the cells or something. The important thing now is to help the others. And we need to get you some attention for that wound!'

Kitty visibly wobbled on her feet. 'No!' she yelled, raising the gun after the barrel had dipped. 'She . . . she deserves to be punished. To be made to suffer the way she's made *us* suffer.'

The blood from Kitty's stomach was dripping on to her shoes. The warden was still clutching at her shoulder, but Lily could see she'd noticed it, too. Her eyes darted towards the computer screen. 'Hit any key . . .' it implored. And the warden was closer to the keyboard than Lily was.

All at once Kitty toppled forwards. Whether or not she was aware that she was doing it, her finger tightened on the trigger of the gun. But the only sound was an empty click – and the noise was like the firing of a starter's pistol.

As Kitty hit the floor, the warden darted for the computer. Lily did, too. But she was always going to be half a second too late. She had time to register the warden's grin, and then to watch in horror as her fist hammered down on to the keyboard.

27 MASKED INTRUDERS

Ollie and the others didn't waste any time. They'd watched Lily dart after the warden, and now they were heading towards the upper levels themselves, back the way Aya, Ember and Connor had come. Flea and Song were helping Jack, while Erik and Sol brought up the rear. Struggling to overcome his grogginess, Ollie was doing his best to keep pace with Connor.

'Did you see where the new guards came from?' Ollie asked him. 'Are the two wings of the prisons directly connected?'

'They must be. There's a door in the main passageway, at the opposite end from the stairs we're climbing now. It's sealed electronically, like the cells in the main block, with cameras to monitor who goes in and out. I always assumed it led to the guards' quarters or something. I've never actually seen it used before, but the guards were streaming in from there.'

The higher they climbed, the louder the sound of the fighting became. Ollie heard shouts, and wails of agony, and an angry crackle as though an electrical storm were raging above their heads.

As soon as they reached the last flight of stairs, they saw evidence the battle was going exactly as they had feared. There was a guard sprawled across the top three steps, but of the casualties in the area, she was the only adult, and one of her colleagues was already helping her to her feet. Just beyond them, there were kids dressed in orange lying prone on the floor, as a squad of masked prison guards bound their hands behind their backs, and then dragged them up on to their knees. Further along the walkway, the scene was much the same. The inmates had been overwhelmed, and steadily the guards were reasserting control.

Ollie and the others ducked out of sight, crouching around the corner beneath the final flight of stairs.

'The *other* end of the passageway, did you say?' Ollie asked Connor. 'Is there another way around?'

'Not that I know of,' Connor answered.

Ollie stood up to peer once again over the topmost step. 'There must be at least twenty guards blocking our way.'

Connor made a face. 'It could be worse. The battle must have spread all over the prison.'

'What are we waiting for?' growled Flea, popping up at Ollie's shoulder. 'We just need to get ourselves a bunch of those cattle prod thingies, and then the odds will be pretty much even.'

'Here,' said Ember, passing the one she was holding to Flea, 'have mine. I've decided I don't really like them.' She was cringing at the sound of the conflict, and looked almost on the verge of tears. For the first time it occurred to Ollie how young she was.

Flea tested the weight of the cattle prod in his hands. 'You and me then,' he said to Connor. 'We'll forge a path, and the rest of you can follow.'

Connor readied his cattle prod, but as the two boys made to move up the stairs, Ollie hauled them back.

'Wait. We can't just go charging along the walkway. Even if we make it to the door at the other end, what then? Whoever's controlling it isn't just going to let us through.'

Flea seemed to realise Ollie had a point. He started to frown – and then his face lit up. 'Wait,' he said. 'Sun Tzu!'

There were groans from Erik and Sol.

'No, seriously,' Flea insisted. 'Know your enemy. Right? That's what Sun Tzu said. Well, how about *be* your enemy instead?'

Ollie and the others frowned their confusion, but by the time Flea had finished explaining what he had in mind, their expressions had changed. Sol, for one, looked impressed.

'That could just work, you know,' he conceded.

Ollie was peering once more over the edge of the steps. 'We still need to get past all these guards,' he pointed out. 'And at the moment we're outnumbered two to one.'

'We need a distraction,' said Song. 'Something to draw the guards away.'

From looking pensive, Ember broke into a grin. 'Leave that to me.'

Aya prodded Ember's arm. She signed something frantically,

too fast for Ollie to catch what she was saying. But he worked out the gist from Ember's response.

'Don't worry,' Ember told her. 'I'll be fine.' She turned to Ollie. 'Those masks they wear are all very frightening and everything, but they're also a disadvantage. I've worked out that if you get the angle right, you can show the guards two fingers, and they don't even notice. It's as though they can only see what's right in front of them.' She winked mischievously, and before Ollie could stop her, she was off.

'Hey, losers!' she yelled, when she reached the top of the stairs. 'Bet you can't catch me!'

She waited for the guards to turn and see her, then darted off along the walkway, swerving as the guards dived for her, and sticking as best she could to their blind spots. She kicked one guard on the backside, then ducked through his legs when he turned. Within seconds, she had half the prison guards in the passageway rushing after her, like clumsy cats chasing after a bee.

'She's leading them towards the cells,' marvelled Connor, as he and the others watched on.

Sure enough, Ember disappeared through an opening midway along the walkway, and the guards in pursuit thundered after her. The numbers were suddenly a lot more even.

'Ready?' said Ollie to the others. 'Let's go!'

They charged, Ollie, Flea and Connor leading the way. They overran the first pair of guards before they would have realised what was coming, stopping just long enough to kick the guards' weapons away, and free the inmates who'd been shackled. Song, Jack and Erik had continued past, to deal with the next set of guards, and were soon joined by Sol and Aya. Aya wielded her cattle prod ruthlessly, Ollie noted, and he recalled what Lily had said about the girl's parents. If she was battling to be reunited with her family, it was no wonder she was fighting with such ferocity.

As Ollie and his friends progressed along the walkway, their numbers were swelled by the inmates they'd freed, and it wasn't long before the remaining few guards turned tail and fled, leaving the passageway completely undefended.

It was time to put Flea's plan into action.

'Flea, you're up!' Ollie told him. 'Song, you're the next tallest. You stand alongside him. And Connor,' Ollie added, picking up an abandoned set of shackles, 'you probably ought to wear these.'

As Connor reluctantly wrapped the shackles around his wrist – loosely enough that he would be able to slip his hands free when he needed to – Flea and Song stripped two of the guards they'd overpowered of their uniforms, and slipped into the grey boiler suits themselves. And then, as a finishing touch, they put on their masks.

'How do I look?' Flea asked, his voice muffled.

'Like a psycho killer in a horror movie,' said Sol, making a circle with his thumb and forefinger.

More guards appeared from another passageway, but the inmates Ollie and the others had freed rushed forwards to hold them off. Flea and Song moved either side of their 'prisoner' and pretended to drag him towards the electronically sealed door at the end of the walkway. The rest of them hung back, beyond the field of the cameras.

Flea waved his arm at whoever was watching. 'We've caught one of the ringleaders!' he declared, deepening his voice. 'We need to isolate him from the rest. Open the door!'

'I've just had a thought,' whispered Sol to Ollie. 'Who's to say all the guards from the other wing already came through? How do we know there's not a hundred more of them waiting for us on the other side of that door?'

'It's too late to worry about that now,' put in Jack. '*Look.*'

The light beside the door had changed colour from red to green, and it was beginning to slide open.

'It worked!' said Ollie, breaking cover. As Flea and Song ripped off their masks, Connor slipped his hands from the shackles and grabbed the cattle prod he'd discarded earlier from the floor. And then all eight of them were bundling through the doorway, to be met by at least a dozen more guards. But it appeared to be a skeleton crew, the last handful of guards on this side of the prison. And they were totally unprepared to ward off a full frontal assault. One managed to jab Erik with his cattle prod, but paid the price for his attack when Aya knocked his weapon from his grip and shocked him in the belly with her own. The rest of the guards flew into a panic, and Ollie and his friends overcame them easily. Song and Sol had a cattle prod in each hand, and they pinned the defeated guards against the wall.

'What now?' said Flea, casting round. They appeared to be in an extension of the passageway they'd just come from, and there was no clear pathway to the cells.

Aya signed something. Once again Ollie struggled to catch what she'd said.

'She says it's like a mirror image,' said Erik, looking pained and rubbing at the place he'd been shocked. 'Like two houses next to each other on a street.'

Connor looked up and around. 'She's right,' he said. 'The door we just came through must be in the exact centre of the complex – the dividing point between two identical prisons. Which means the cells will be off to the left.'

He led the way, as Song, Erik and Sol stayed behind to keep an eye on the guards.

Ollie, Flea, Jack, Aya and Connor reached the junction up ahead without encountering any further resistance. The sound of the fighting continued to filter through the doorway behind them, but it seemed to be becoming more sporadic, as though the guards had already quelled the worst of the revolt.

'We need to hurry,' Ollie said.

'There, look.' Connor was pointing to the first of the doors in what appeared to be an endless row up ahead. Aya immediately rushed past him, casting aside her cattle prod, and hammering on the first door she reached. But unlike in solitary confinement, there were no bolts on these doors, nor even any handles. The locks were sealed electronically.

'There must be a computer terminal somewhere,' said Jack. 'A button to override the locks.'

'It's probably on the next level up,' said Connor, pointing to another walkway above them. 'That's where the guards are usually stationed.'

Voices were beginning to call out from behind the cell doors, as the inmates locked inside started to realise that something was up. Some shouted in English, others in languages Ollie didn't recognise, but there was no doubt that the prisoners on this side of the complex were all adults.

'Up there,' said Jack, pointing to a stairwell. 'Flea, I need a lift.'

Flea carried Jack to the next level, and they spread out to try to find what Jack needed.

'Over here, Jack!' called Ollie. He'd found a room with a single computer terminal on a desk, with little else inside but an empty coffee mug, and a cigarette smouldering in an ashtray.

'This seat's still warm,' said Connor, as he rolled it aside to make way for Jack's wheelchair. 'The operator must have scarpered when he heard us coming.'

Ollie and the others moved aside to allow Jack to enter the room. She frowned at the computer screen, but not for long. 'If only Sebastian Crowe's computer had been this straightforward,' she said, breaking into a wry smile, and she hit a single button on the keyboard. Immediately a buzzer sounded, and there was a clang that resounded along the walkway below them.

'That's done it!' called Sol.

Ollie and the others rushed back outside. The walkway below them was filling with the inmates who'd been released from their cells. Aya was leaning precariously over the railing, clearly desperate to catch sight of her parents. Then she frantically began waving her hands.

'Aya!' came a woman's voice from down below them, and Ollie saw a man and a woman shoving their way through the throng of prisoners. Aya thundered down the metal steps, and threw herself into the woman's arms. The man, who was presumably Aya's father, buried his head in his daughter's hair, then wrapped both his wife and Aya in a huge embrace. He turned his head towards the ceiling, seeming to utter a prayer of thanks. His smile stretched across his face, but his cheeks were streaked with tears.

When Ollie and the others reached the bottom of the stairs, Flea was yelling to try to make himself heard. 'You're on an oil rig in the middle of the sea!' he told the inmates. 'But we're taking over, and we need your help!'

Around a third of the prisoners in the corridor responded immediately, muttering to one another in anger and surprise. But the rest just stared at Flea in obvious confusion. If most were asylum seekers or refugees, swept up as part of Crowe's Emergency Action Plan, it was entirely possible they didn't speak English.

'Um, Erik?' said Flea, as he surveyed the blank faces. 'A little help here.'

Erik was shorter than most of the people around them, and he swung himself up on to the side of the stairs. He began to repeat what Flea had said in as many languages as he could. In the meantime, Aya had started signing to her parents, who were nodding to show they understood.

Aya's father laid a hand on Ollie's shoulder. 'We are with you,' he said, in faltering English. 'And . . . thank you. For bringing me my daughter.'

Ollie was about to respond, to tell Aya's father it wasn't him who deserved his thanks, but as he was about to speak, there was a deafening *boom*. The entire structure rocked, and then the floor seemed to fall from beneath Ollie's feet. He was thrown to the ground, even as the prisoners standing around him toppled, too. There were screams, and then another huge rumble – less like an explosion this time, more like the sound of a head-on collision. When Ollie looked up, he saw he'd landed beside Aya's father. They stared at each other, eyes wide.

And that was when Ollie heard the sound of rushing water.

28 EMERGENCY EXIT

It was as though the warden had plunged the handle of a detonator. As soon as her fist hit the keyboard, there was an explosion deep below them. Four simultaneous explosions, in fact, because Lily heard them all around her. It was like watching a movie in the cinema, with the detonation echoing in surround sound.

The shock was like a tremor from an earthquake. At first the floor juddered and tilted, knocking Lily from her feet. And then there was a sensation of falling, presumably as the legs of the oil rig collapsed and the rest of the structure dropped towards the sea. It crash-landed on the surface of the water, and once again Lily was thrown to one side. The warden had been braced for it, however, and she clung to the side of the computer terminal. Then she was moving, scurrying across the control room towards the door, and the lifeboat the technicians were no doubt getting ready on deck.

'No!'

Lily grabbed for her, swiping to try to hook the warden's ankle. She missed, and before she could regain her feet, the structure gave another lurch. Lily felt despair engulf her. She pictured the oil rig floating like a stricken vessel, and seawater greedily rushing in through the corridors in the prison down below her.

She pulled herself up, and for the briefest of instants considered running after the warden. But instead she rushed over to Kitty, and rolled the girl on to her back.

'Kitty! Can you hear me? We need to get out of here!'

Kitty groaned, and her eyelids fluttered.

Telling herself she had no choice, Lily slapped her. 'Kitty! Open your eyes! You need to try to walk. I can't carry you on my own!'

Kitty's eyes opened. 'What . . . what happened? Did we win?'

In spite of everything, Lily felt a smile flicker briefly on her lips. 'We're still working on it,' she answered. She ripped off one of the sleeves of her jumpsuit, and scrunched the material into a ball, before pressing it against Kitty's wounded stomach. 'Hold this here,' she instructed. 'Wrap your other arm around my shoulder. The oil rig's sinking. We need to find the others and get everybody up on deck.'

Ignoring Kitty's cry of agony, Lily hauled the older girl to her feet.

'What were you doing up here anyway?' Lily asked her, attempting to distract her from her pain.

'I came . . . I came to disable the radio, to stop anyone calling for help.' Kitty prodded her chin at a smouldering bank of computer equipment, destroyed by one of the bullets from Warden Bricknell's gun. 'But I guess the warden took care of that for us.'

Lily looked at the broken radio. 'Damn it. We could have done with a little help right now.' She struggled to bear Kitty towards the door. 'Do you know if the warden had any evacuation procedures in place?' she asked. 'I only saw one lifeboat, and by now it's already put out to sea. There may be another one on the other side of the building, but the one I saw would barely fit twenty people on board, let alone two thousand. How were the prisoners supposed to get off the rig if there was an emergency?'

Kitty shook her head. 'They weren't,' she said, with a grimace. 'But there are . . . life rafts. Inflatable ones. Somewhere on the main deck, I'm guessing. Not for the prisoners, but . . . for the guards. I . . . I heard the warden discussing it once. One of the guards had asked her the same question you just asked me. He . . . he laughed when the warden told him that the prisoners would have to swim.'

Lily did a quick calculation. Say there were three hundred guards on board, and that there were only just enough life rafts for them all, each raft would have to take at least four times its regular payload if everyone on *Deadfall* was to escape the sinking rig. And that was assuming they could locate the inflatable life rafts in the first place.

Kitty stumbled, and Lily almost dropped her.

'This . . . isn't going to work,' Kitty said. 'There's no way you'll be able to help me down those steps in time. Just go. Leave me here.' As if to prove Kitty's point, the rig lurched dangerously, as though it was already starting to list.

'Uh-uh,' said Lily. 'Not gonna happen.' From nowhere, she thought of Dodge, of the way he'd sacrificed himself aboard Maddy Sikes's plane. *Not this time*, she added silently.

She hoisted Kitty further on to her shoulder, and started once again towards the door. Then something caught her eye.

'Wait,' she said, stopping. She lowered Kitty into a nearby chair. There was a microphone on one of the desks, and the PA system it was attached to had mercifully escaped any errant bullets. Lily recalled the way the warden had spoken to the inmates over the loudspeakers that had been installed in the prison, and she had to hope the equipment in the control room was part of the same system. She took a moment to study the switches and dials, and then spotted what she'd been looking for. 'Prison-wide address' read one of the settings. Lily hit the switch, and heard a chirrup of electronic feedback as the microphone powered to life.

'Attention!' Lily said, her lips pressed against the microphone. '*Deadfall* is sinking! Repeat, *Deadfall* is sinking!

Head to the main deck, where life rafts . . .' She hesitated. 'Where life rafts will be waiting,' she finished. She stepped away, wondering what good the address would be, particularly if she and Kitty failed to locate the life rafts. Then she leant back towards the microphone. 'Ollie, Flea, the rest of you . . . if you can hear me, just . . . just get up here as soon as you can!'

The structure gave another lurch, and the microphone came loose in Lily's hand. The cable had ripped from its socket. She threw the microphone down on the surface, then rushed to help Kitty from the chair. 'Time to go,' Lily told her.

Below deck, the water was already around their ankles. Ollie was trying to work out the source of the explosion, when he heard Lily's voice across the PA system.

Ollie looked at the others as they listened, and saw the urgency of the situation dawn in their eyes.

'Let's go!' he yelled, when Lily had finished speaking. 'We need to get to the main deck!'

The oil rig rocked again, and somewhere a valve burst, or a door flew open, because the water that was flooding the walkway suddenly doubled in ferocity. In seconds the water was up to their knees.

Flea scooped Jack into his arms, kicking her wheelchair aside. Connor led the way, with the rest of them following behind. A man stumbled, and Ollie helped him back on to his feet. Behind them a woman screamed, but when Ollie looked, he saw other prisoners stopping to help her.

They reached the door leading back into the kids' prison, and astonishingly the battle they'd left behind them still appeared to be going on. A group of kids had been cornered by a squad of guards, but as soon as the adult prisoners saw what was happening, they surged forwards, and the guards threw down their cattle prods in alarm. The prisoners ripped off the guards' masks.

'Don't you understand what is happening?' one of the prisoners yelled at a guard, and Ollie realised it was Aya's father. 'The prison is sinking! Unless you want to die, you need to get to the life rafts!' He gave the guard a shove. 'Go!' Aya's father said. 'Tell your friends! Tell everyone!'

The guard looked at his colleagues in startled panic, and then he started running, presumably for the set of stairs that would lead him to the deck. His colleagues immediately began to rush after him.

'Follow those guards!' Ollie instructed the other prisoners. 'They'll lead you up on to the deck!'

Most of the prisoners did exactly as Ollie had suggested, and began streaming after the guards. But Aya's father and about thirty other prisoners remained with Ollie and the others.

'What can we do to help?' Aya's father asked.

'We need to clear the rest of the prison,' Ollie replied. 'Break up any more fighting, and make sure everyone else knows to get above deck.'

But as he spoke, Ollie found himself struggling to remain upright. The floor beneath his feet was tilting, and the water that had covered the walkway started rushing back towards the central door. The rig was beginning to list, as one side of the structure took on water faster than the other.

'If we're going to do this,' said Connor, 'we need to do it *now*.'

Following Connor's lead, they started their sweep of the prison, disarming any guards they came across, and sending everyone towards the stairs that led up to the deck. They cleared the cells, and then the refectory, and soon enough ended up back in the main passageway. But the structure had taken on so much water that the walkway was now a glistening slope, too steep and slippery to allow them to reach the stairs. If they wanted to escape *Deadfall* themselves, they would have to use the handrail as a ladder.

Aya's father helped the prisoners first, and soon the handrail came to resemble a human chain.

'You go next,' Ollie told Flea, when the last of the prisoners had started climbing towards the stairs. 'Get Jack to safety. Then you, Connor. Then the rest of us will—'

Ollie stopped talking at the sight of Aya waving one of her hands. Her father was carrying her on his back. They were already halfway to the stairs, but something was seriously wrong.

'Erik, what's Aya—'

But this time he didn't need an interpreter, because it suddenly struck Ollie what Aya was trying to tell them.

'Where's Ember?' he said, casting round. The main door was now almost completely submerged, meaning the adults' prison would already have been underwater. And Ollie was certain the rest of the prison was clear. They'd looked everywhere.

'Maybe she's already up top,' said Erik, but Song shook her head.

'We would have seen her. And given what she did to help us, I'm not sure she's the kind of person who would rush for safety if it meant abandoning her friends.'

There was a muffled cry, from somewhere beyond the refectory. It was a girl's voice, unmistakeably.

'The kitchen,' said Connor, wide-eyed.

'Show me,' Ollie answered. 'The rest of you, get up top. And start herding everyone into the life rafts! If they don't get clear before the rig goes down, they'll be in danger of getting sucked under.'

Before anyone could object, Ollie and Connor turned and ran. They splashed across the refectory floor, which already resembled a small lake. Here and there, a mask floated by, and Ollie shuddered at the sight of the empty eyeholes, like dead men staring sightless at the sky.

There was another desperate yell, and Ollie and Connor followed the sound. But when they reached the kitchens, they were empty, exactly as Ollie remembered from when they'd checked them before.

'Ember!' he shouted. '*Ember!*'

He stopped splashing, dragging Connor to a halt at his side. And then they heard it: a spluttering cry for help, coming from *inside* an upturned metal cupboard. The cupboard must have been knocked off balance, and it had landed door down on the floor. Somehow Ember was trapped inside, and judging by the rising water level all around it, she was rapidly running out of air.

'Quick,' said Ollie to Connor, 'help me turn it over!'

When they reached the cupboard, they each took an end, and Ollie hauled with all his might. The cupboard moved, but only a fraction. The suction of the water was holding it down.

'We need leverage,' Ollie said. 'Something like a broom handle, or . . .'

'Here!' said Connor, lunging for something that was floating by. 'How about this?' He held up a cattle prod, then felt below the water for a gap in which to lodge one end.

The two of them pushed down on the end of their makeshift crowbar. The cupboard shifted, breaking the vacuum that was holding it down, and they were able to roll the unit over. Ollie scrabbled at the door, flinging it open, and Ember sat up with a gasp, like a vampire springing from a coffin.

Ollie wiped the water from her face. 'Ember! Are you OK? What the hell were you doing in a cupboard?'

Ember coughed and spluttered. 'I was . . . hiding,' she managed to say. 'The guards, they . . . chased me, and . . .'

'Never mind,' said Ollie, getting the gist. He took Ember's hands and hauled her up. 'You did a great job. But now we need to go.'

Clasping Ember's hand, he dragged her towards the refectory. But when the three of them reached the threshold, they realised the oil rig had tilted further, and the water at the far end of the room was now almost level with the top of the doorway.

'Wow,' said Ember. 'This is just like watching *Titanic*.'

Ollie was surveying the scene before him. 'We're going to have to swim for it,' he said, wading into the water.

'Wait . . .' said Ember, when the water was up to Ollie's waist. 'I can't. No one ever taught me.'

There was a *crack* from above their heads, and then a shriek of metal scraping metal.

'Get down!' yelled Connor.

All at once the ceiling of the refectory split open, as the structure of the oil rig began to buckle. A steel strut broke loose, and one end dropped towards the water, dragging everything it was attached to with it.

When Ollie dared to raise his head, he saw their only escape route had been completely blocked off. The water level was continuing to rise, and the space above it was an impenetrable tangle of steel. Now, not only would they have to swim, but they were going to have to do so under water.

'Ember,' Ollie said, 'wrap your hands around my neck! And whatever happens, don't let go!'

Ember did as Ollie had instructed. Ollie could feel her shaking.

'Now, everyone take a deep breath!' Ollie sucked air into his lungs, and dived into the ice-cold water.

'There!' said Kitty, pointing. 'The life rafts have to be in that storage unit. It's the only thing on deck that looks out of place.'

They were almost at the bottom of the stairs that led down from the bridge. In the distance, Lily had spotted the crew's lifeboat already out to sea, and she could see the warden had made it aboard. She felt a surge of rage that Warden Bricknell had escaped, but at least they no longer had her to worry about. The priority now was to evacuate the oil rig. The main deck was already filling with people: kids who'd been locked up with Lily, men and women in the grey worn by the guards, and other grown-ups, too, in the same orange jumpsuits as the younger prisoners – meaning Ollie and the others must have succeeded in breaking in to the other wing. But there was no time to celebrate. It would all count for nothing if they couldn't get the people aboard to safety.

With Kitty's arm still wrapped around her shoulders, Lily surveyed the crowd below her. There was no sign of any of her friends. Even more alarmingly, it was clear *Deadfall* was beginning to sink. It was tilted to one side, and the main deck was already several metres closer to the surface of the sea than it had been before.

They needed to get to those life rafts.

When they finally reached the bottom of the stairwell, Lily could carry Kitty no further. 'Put me down here,' Kitty said, gesturing to the bottommost step. 'Come back for me if you insist when you've found a space for me on one of those life rafts. Now *go*!'

With a determined nod, Lily made a dash for the storage unit at the base of the main building that Kitty had indicated before. It was an anonymous white box, about the size of a horse trailer, and although it was devoid of all markings, it was clear it didn't really belong, just as Kitty had said. There was a hatch, and Lily opened it. Inside were rows and rows of what looked like yellow backpacks. 'Survival Systems Ltd', the writing on each of them read. 'Life raft. Rated capacity: 50 persons.' Lily felt a surge of relief, but when she tried to pick up one of the bundles, she found they were too heavy to lift.

'Need some help?' came a voice from across her shoulder.

'Sol!' exclaimed Lily when she turned. Her brother was there, too, and Jack was sitting beside Kitty, already attending to Kitty's wound. Song, Erik and Aya appeared next, with a man and a woman at Aya's shoulder.

'Are these . . .' Lily started to ask, but Aya was already beaming and nodding before Lily could finish the question. Seeing her friend reunited with her parents, Lily couldn't help but return her grin.

She turned to Flea. 'Is everyone on deck? Did you get everybody out?'

There was the merest of hesitations before her brother answered. 'Pretty much,' he said. 'And the rest of them are . . . on their way. Ollie included.'

Lily frowned, sensing there was something her brother wasn't telling her. But whatever it was, it would have to wait. 'We need to get things organised,' Lily instructed. 'Give me a hand lifting these things out.'

The Haven kids sprang into action. Flea moved to Lily's side, and helped her haul the life rafts from the container. Behind them, a group of younger inmates still clutching cattle prods had taken it upon themselves to round up the guards, to make sure they didn't cause any trouble. Sol, Erik and the others tried to instil some sense of order among everybody else. Within minutes, the adult prisoners had formed a chain, and were bearing the life rafts to the edge of the deck, which was getting perilously close to sea level.

The rafts self-inflated at the tug of a handle, and soon there was a small flotilla of them carrying figures in orange jumpsuits away from the rig. The older prisoners were making sure the kids got spaces on the life rafts first. The guards, someone had decided, would be last in line.

'Get as many people into one boat as you can!' Lily called. She looked at the remaining life rafts in the stack, and the huge number of people still on deck. It was going to be a close-run thing.

When the last of the life rafts had been passed out, Lily and the others gathered together and surveyed the deck.

By now at least three quarters of the people who'd been on *Deadfall* had been found a space on one of the rafts, and even the guards were being allowed on. Some of the inflatables – particularly those with more adults than kids – sat alarmingly low in the water. Rather than the fifty-person recommended capacity, there looked to be at least seventy souls aboard each vessel. But it was a good job Lily had insisted on overloading them. There were maybe ten life rafts yet to set off, and if everyone still on the rig was to get clear, every single one of the rafts would be full to the brim.

'Wait,' said Lily when she glanced around her. 'Where's Ollie? And Connor, and Ember?' She'd been looking out for them earlier, but had assumed they were masked by the crowds.

She looked at Flea, who struggled to meet her eye. 'Where are they?' she snapped. 'Tell me!'

'They'll be here, sis,' said Flea. 'I know they will. Ember got separated, and Ollie and Connor went back to find her.'

'To *find* her? You mean they didn't even know where to look? That means . . .' She shook her head in desperation. It meant the three of them could be *anywhere*. 'I'm going to look for them,' she announced. She made to run for the stairs, but Flea caught her wrist.

'They'll *be* here!' he insisted. 'And you can't go down there. It's too dangerous!'

For some reason Lily laughed. Not because what Flea had said was funny, more at the implication that Lily had experienced anything that *wasn't* dangerous since the day she'd got here.

But before she could respond, or break from her brother's grip, there was a shout from the side of the main deck. All of the life rafts had set off, apart from one. It was already almost full to capacity, but Aya's father was stopping it from leaving until Lily and the others were aboard.

'Hurry!' he yelled. 'Aya, come!' he added, signing at his daughter.

Aya looked at Lily with wide eyes, clearly torn between obeying her father's instruction, and wanting to help Lily find their friends. Then the oil rig gave a lurch, and seemed to drop another metre into the water.

'The rest of you get on that raft,' said Lily. 'Flea, go with Jack. Song, Erik, you'll need to help Kitty. I'm not leaving without Ollie and the others. I don't care if—'

'Hey! Wait for us!'

Lily spun.

'*Ollie!*'

He and Connor had popped up at the top of the stairwell that led below deck, looking like half-drowned rats. They seemed to simultaneously reach below them, and then Ember appeared, coughing and spluttering. Connor and Ollie were holding one of her arms each, and they manhandled her up on to the deck.

'Talking about cutting it fine, mate,' said Sol, as he rushed over to help them. Lily was rooted to the spot, paralysed by an emotion she didn't quite understand. It was relief. That was all. Pure relief. But when she met Ollie's eye and he smiled at her, she found her vision clouded by tears. She grinned at him, then had to cover her mouth to stop herself blubbing.

'See,' said her brother, beside her. 'I told you they'd make it.'

Lily turned to him, torn between wanting to hug him and hit him. She settled on shoving him towards the raft. 'Move it, meathead,' she said. 'And if there's only space for one of us, you can get out and swim.'

Water was already beginning to lap over the deck, and everyone hurried to board the final life raft. Aya's father waved his arms at the other occupants, insistent they move up to make space. Once Lily and the others were on board, he shoved the life raft clear of the oil rig, and then leapt on to the inflatable himself.

When Lily looked back at *Deadfall*, she saw how far it had already sunk. The rig had levelled off as it had taken on water, and only the derrick and the building containing the control room remained completely above the sea line. The prison would have been flooded entirely, meaning Ollie and the others had only just made it out of there on time.

Lily met Ollie's eye, and he smiled again – until his eyes caught sight of something across her shoulder.

'Um,' he said, which was enough to make Lily turn. She felt her own eyes widen. A Royal Navy destroyer had appeared on the horizon. Lily was caught for an instant between confusion and relief. And then there was a boom, like a rumble of thunder, and an explosion of water not fifty metres from where *Deadfall* lay stricken. The destroyer had opened fire.

29 FACE TIME

Seeing the vessel up close, Ollie knew it would have been dwarfed by *Deadfall*, which was still jutting from the water. But the destroyer was nonetheless huge, particularly when viewed from the life raft. And it was imposing in a different way. The weaponry that was on display was terrifying, and Ollie and the others had already been shown how devastating a single shot from the enormous, forward-mounted naval gun could be.

One by one, the life rafts were hooked in close, and the men, women and children either climbed or were winched aboard the ship.

'These *are* the good guys,' said Sol when it was their turn to board. 'Right?'

But Ollie wasn't so sure. At first he'd been relieved to see the white ensign on the destroyer's mast. After all, the flag – the red cross of St George on a white background, with a Union flag filling one corner – signalled the vessel was here under instruction of the British government. But then Ollie remembered that the government was effectively being run by Sebastian Crowe, the man who had commissioned *Deadfall* in the first place, on Maddy Sikes's orders. And if the destroyer was there to help, why had it opened fire, even if the shot had been deliberately aimed to miss?

Lily was looking at Kitty, and Ollie could tell she was as worried as he was. 'Maybe someone on *Deadfall* had time to make a distress call after all, before we got up to the control room.'

'If that's the case,' said Kitty, 'then we've all just taken a running jump straight from the frying pan into the fire.'

Ollie and the others were among the last people on their life raft to climb the net that had been thrown down from the destroyer. By the time they made it up, most of the other life rafts had already been pulled from the water, meaning the deck – to the aft of the ship – was crowded with *Deadfall*'s former occupants. Ollie was encouraged to see blankets being handed out, as well as bottles of water, but then he noticed the Royal Marines who were stationed around the deck, weapons at the ready. And it wasn't cattle prods they had in their hands; the marines were holding fully automatic assault rifles.

Ollie and his friends were shown to one of the last clear sections of the deck, and warily they hunched together on the floor. The former prison guards had gravitated together, too, Ollie noticed. It was hard to tell from the guards' expressions whether they seemed encouraged by the change in their situation, or if they were just as worried as Ollie was.

Eventually, a man in a peaked white cap and a navy blue uniform appeared, and started moving among the groups of people on deck. He looked significantly older than the two officers who flanked him, and there were thick gold bands stitched around his sleeves.

As he drew closer, Ollie could hear his words carrying against the wind.

'Ollie Turner,' the man boomed, in the manner of someone used to giving orders. 'I'm looking for Ollie Turner.'

Jack gave the barest shake of her head, and placed a hand on Ollie's arm, but slowly Ollie clambered to his feet. The officer saw him rise, and strode towards him.

'Ollie Turner?' he asked briskly, gazing down at Ollie with narrowed eyes.

Ollie's friends rose to stand at his shoulder.

'That's . . . that's right,' Ollie said. And then he flinched as the man whipped up a hand. Ollie had assumed he'd meant to strike him, but instead the officer was saluting.

'Welcome aboard HMS *Stalwart*. I'm Admiral Asquith.' The admiral lowered his salute, and to Ollie's astonishment broke into a smile. He held out his hand for Ollie to shake. 'It's an honour to meet you, young man. Your friends, too,' he added, casting around. 'I'm sorry we didn't reach you sooner, but from the look of things, it seems as though you had the situation just about in hand. And I'm sorry about that warning shot, by the way. At the time we couldn't be sure who was in control.'

'You're here to help us?' said Lily, at Ollie's side.

The admiral appeared taken aback. 'Of course,' he answered. 'Why else would the prime minister have sent us?'

'The *prime minister* sent you?' Ollie said. 'But she . . .' Ollie floundered. How was he supposed to put into words everything he knew? The fact that, the last time he'd seen the prime minister, she'd been cowering against a wall, powerless to intervene as Sebastian Crowe's men tried to take Ollie and his friends away?

'She did indeed,' Admiral Asquith told him. 'And she's waiting to talk to you.' He gestured with his arm towards the main structure of the ship.

'You mean she's here? Now?'

At this, the admiral smiled again. 'In a manner of speaking.'

'Admiral Asquith,' said Lily, before the man could lead Ollie off. 'There was another boat. A proper lifeboat. It put out to sea before the rest of us. There was a woman on board who—'

'Who currently resides in *Stalwart*'s brig,' the admiral finished for her. 'We ran across that lifeboat on our way here. Unfortunately there isn't space in the brig for everyone who was complicit in this atrocity, but rest assured they will all be isolated and treated accordingly.'

Behind them, there was movement on deck, and Ollie noticed that the Royal Marines had begun to separate the guards

348

in grey uniforms from the former inmates. Ollie looked at Lily, and noted his friend's grim satisfaction. There was a certain poetic justice to it, after all, Ollie noted. Warden Bricknell, who had been responsible for incarcerating over a thousand innocent men, women and children, was herself now locked in a prison cell on a vessel out at sea.

'Now,' said the admiral, turning back to Ollie, 'it wouldn't do to keep the prime minister waiting.' He held out a hand. 'Shall we?'

'Ollie Turner. I can't tell you how relieved I am to see you.'

The admiral had shown Ollie into a room with a large table at its centre, and chairs all around. The prime minister had apparently asked to speak to Ollie alone, so his friends were waiting outside. The admiral was with them, and Ollie could see through the door's frosted-glass panel that he was personally standing guard. At the far end of the room, there was an array of screens on the wall, though only the largest – the one in the centre – was currently switched on. It showed the prime minister sitting at a desk, and looking back at Ollie through a screen of her own.

Ollie moved to the end of the table and faced her.

'You're surprised to see me,' the PM said, with a wry smile.

'No, I . . . I mean, yes, but . . . but it's not just that. This whole situation is . . . I guess I'm just trying to get my head around it, that's all.' Once again Ollie surveyed his surroundings. After everything that had happened, it was hard to tell what was real.

The PM's smile fell away. 'Yes, I . . . I can only imagine what you've been through, Ollie. All I can do is say I'm sorry. Sorry that I didn't help you sooner. And sorry that I didn't listen to you in the first place.'

'Forgive me, Prime Minister, but . . . I don't understand. What's happened? Why did you send the admiral to help us? The last time we spoke, you—'

The prime minister was bobbing her head remorsefully. 'I recall very vividly the way I acted the last time we met. And I can't tell you how ashamed I am of my conduct. But hopefully now I've . . . Well. I hope I've gone some way to making things right.'

Ollie watched as, on screen, the prime minister glanced off to one side. She nodded at someone out of shot.

'I'm afraid I don't have very long,' the prime minister said, turning back to Ollie. 'I'm being permitted to make this single video call. But then . . . then I expect I will be going to a place very similar to the one you've just escaped from.'

Ollie felt his eyes widen. 'You mean *prison*? But why?'

The PM smiled at Ollie's concern. 'Because it's no less than I deserve, Ollie.' She held up a hand as Ollie started to object. 'I told parliament everything,' she explained. 'The whole world now knows about *Deadfall*. There are some who tried to defend the policy, it is true, and still more who continue to insist that the country remains under attack. The poison Sebastian Crowe has allowed to spread will not dissipate easily, I'm afraid.' The PM looked suddenly angry, before her shame reasserted itself.

'However,' she went on, 'there has also been the predictable level of outrage. Everyone who was involved in *Deadfall*, or who knew about it and didn't speak out, will be held to account, and the severity of their punishment will match the gravity of their crimes. And that includes Sebastian Crowe,' she added with a flash of satisfaction.

'You mean Sebastian Crowe's under arrest?' said Ollie, not quite daring to believe it.

'He is. And not just for his part in *Deadfall*. Your friend Montgomery Ross took it upon himself to delve into Sebastian's financial dealings – at significant personal risk, as you can imagine – and he uncovered a sophisticated system of fraud going back years. Sebastian has been taking advantage of his position of power to steal millions of pounds from public funds. Money that was supposed to feed directly into schools.'

'That must have been the secret Maddy Sikes was holding over him!' said Ollie. 'The thing she was using to blackmail him.'

The prime minister frowned slightly. 'I'm afraid I wouldn't know about that. All I can tell you is that Sebastian Crowe is most assuredly going to jail. Probably for the rest of his life. He's already been stripped of his knighthood, and his personal assets seized. Even if he eventually gets released, he will emerge a broken man.'

'And Maddy Sikes?' Ollie said tentatively, already fearing the answer. 'She's the one who was really behind *Deadfall*. Crowe was just doing what she told him to.'

'Knowing Sebastian the way I do,' the PM said bitterly, 'I suspect he wouldn't have taken much convincing. But as for Maddy Sikes, nobody seems to know where she is. And anyway there is no direct evidence against her. Perhaps Sebastian will seek to cut a deal, and implicate her somehow, but unless and until he does, I'm afraid Maddy Sikes will remain a free woman.'

Ollie's hands tightened at his sides. So Sikes would escape yet again. Ollie supposed he should probably have been growing used to it, but that did nothing to diminish his fury.

'I'm sorry, Ollie,' the prime minister said. 'I realise that's not the news you wanted to hear.'

Ollie forced himself to focus on the screen. 'But what about you?' he asked. 'Why are *you* going to prison? If the world knows Crowe was responsible, why are you being blamed?'

'Because Sebastian made sure that *Deadfall* was commissioned in my name,' the PM answered. 'You heard what he said to me: my signature is on every single document in a paper trail a mile long.'

'But he faked those signatures! I heard him admit that, too!'

The PM nodded. 'Indeed. But that doesn't make me innocent, Ollie. *Deadfall* happened on my watch. *Everything* that's happened did so while I was supposed to be in charge. I failed, Ollie. I allowed Crowe and his supporters to hijack my government, and to turn the country into a place of fear and recrimination.' As she spoke, the PM dropped her eyes towards the surface of her desk.

'Why then?' said Ollie quietly. 'If you knew you would end up going to prison, why did you tell everyone about *Deadfall* in the first place? What made you change your mind?'

The PM looked up. 'You did, Ollie. *You* made me change my mind. Do you remember what you said to me, that time in Sebastian's office? You told me I couldn't just stand by and let this happen. And you were right. I realised, belatedly, that *you were right.*'

Ollie was stunned into silence.

'So what will happen now?' he said at last.

The PM straightened her shoulders. 'I have of course resigned my position. My last act as prime minister was to dispatch Admiral Asquith on his mission – and to make this one final call to you. I will face criminal proceedings, and in the meantime, there will be a general election. A highly contested one, I expect, with much more at stake than most people will perhaps realise. Thanks to Sebastian Crowe – and Maddy Sikes, of course, not to mention my own weakness and inaction – this country faces perhaps the most significant decision it has ever had to make. Do we reassert our commitment to the values that have made this country great: freedom, and tolerance, and equality? Or, do we turn in on ourselves, and give in to spitefulness and suspicion?' The PM shook her head sadly. 'I'm afraid I do not know what the outcome will be – for parliament, or for the country.'

Once again her eyes had dipped, but when she looked at Ollie again, she forced a smile. 'But there are positives to take from all of this, as well. The so-called Rat Catchers have been disbanded, and Crowe's Emergency Action Plan has been suspended, pending the outcome of the election. And best of all, of course, everyone who was held captive on *Deadfall* will be set free.'

The image of the prime minister wobbled slightly, as though someone at her end had knocked the camera. The PM's smile faded. 'I'm sorry, Ollie, but I'm being instructed to wind things up.'

'Wait,' Ollie said. 'Is Mr Ross with you? Can I speak to him? I'd like to . . . to say thank you.'

'No, he's . . . to be honest I don't know where Monty is. With any luck, he has taken himself out of harm's way. Monty is a good man,' the PM said. 'He certainly doesn't deserve the same fate as the rest of us.'

She fell silent, and seemed to reflect for a moment. Then she made to rise.

'Prime Minister, before you go, I . . .' Ollie floundered for a moment on what to say. 'Thank you,' he settled on. 'For . . . for doing the right thing.'

The prime minister smiled back at him. 'No, Ollie Turner. Thank *you*.'

Ollie stared out at the churning sea. He was back on deck, as Admiral Asquith prepared HMS *Stalwart* to set a course for home. Most of the rescued prisoners were now somewhere inside, sheltering against the elements, though one or two small groups continued to brave the cutting wind. Mostly they seemed to be looking at the sky. It was dull and grey, like the water, but Ollie suspected they were thankful to be able to see clouds at all after the days and weeks they'd spent in incarceration. Ollie had acknowledged the people he'd passed with a smile, but he'd found a spot at the very aft of the ship where he was able to be on his own.

In front of him, *Deadfall* was a diminishing island. Now, only the control room and the top portion of the derrick remained above water.

'Ollie? There you are. I was wondering where you'd got to.'

Lily leant her forearms on the railing beside him. She joined him in gazing at the sinking oil rig. She'd been smiling when Ollie had turned, but now her smile faded.

'It's not over,' she said. 'Is it?'

For a moment Ollie wasn't sure how to respond. He hadn't told anyone yet the full extent of his conversation with the prime minister, but he knew his friends would have worked out the implications of what had happened for themselves.

'This part is,' said Ollie at last. He smiled at Lily encouragingly.

She nodded. 'Well. I suppose we get to go home, at least. That's something. Right?'

'It's more than something. It will be . . .' Ollie trailed off, changing his mind about what he'd been about to say. 'It'll be good to have you back. We . . . I . . . we've all missed you.'

For a moment Lily held his eye. Ollie was forced to look away.

'Where are the others?' he asked, clearing his throat.

'They're all on the bridge. Flea's begging the admiral to fire that gun again. Sol suggested to the admiral that he should use my brother as a human cannonball.'

Ollie sniffed. 'What about your friend? Kitty, is it? Is she going to be OK?'

'I'm not sure she would call herself a friend exactly. Not yet. But yeah, they've stitched her up, and given her a cabin and everything. It must have been one of the officers' rooms, because it's got a coffee machine, a TV screen, the works. Ember's in there with her, trying to figure out if she can get on to Netflix.'

Once again Ollie laughed. It felt good to do so at Lily's side.

'Listen, Ollie, I just wanted to say . . .'

Ollie waited.

'I just wanted to say, when we get home, I don't think . . . That is, me and Casper, we . . .'

Ollie was suddenly conscious of how closely together he and Lily were leaning on the railing. Feeling guilty, he moved slightly away. 'Look, Lily, I'm sorry I haven't said this before, but I . . . I think Casper's great. I mean, it took me a while to get to know him, but I'm glad you and he . . . that, after Dodge, you've found someone you . . . who makes you—'

'But that's what I'm trying to say,' Lily cut in. 'Casper is a friend. He's always been a friend. I think that's why we ended up together. But I think . . . I don't think I'm being fair on him. I think *friends* is all we should be.'

Ollie's head whipped round to face her. 'You're planning on breaking up with him?' he blurted. The words escaped before he could stop them, and all of a sudden he was sure he'd completely misinterpreted what Lily had been trying to say.

But she nodded. 'I hope he doesn't hate me,' she said, looking down.

'No, he . . . he won't. He's a good guy. A really good guy.' Ollie allowed himself to lean on the handrail. 'And besides,' he said. 'No one could ever hate you.'

Lily turned away then, and once again Ollie was sure he'd said something stupid. But when she turned back, she was beaming, and the world, to Ollie, suddenly felt a whole lot brighter.

Their fingers touched on the railing. From behind the clouds, the sun appeared. They watched it slip slowly towards the horizon, and almost didn't notice when *Deadfall* disappeared beneath the waves.

✠ EPILOGUE

Back in London, night had already fallen, and Maddy Sikes was gazing down at a corpse.

She smiled.

It was true that in one sense *Deadfall* had failed, but in another it had yielded everything she needed. Which wasn't such a surprise. Sikes had christened the converted oil rig herself, and she knew what the name really meant. A 'deadfall' was a type of trap – one from which, once it had sprung, it was impossible to escape. You might wriggle, and squirm, as those wretched Haven children had managed to do, but you would never be able to free yourself completely.

Sikes's husky, Bullseye, growled at her side. Mindlessly she caressed the skin behind her pet's ears, as she continued to study the dead body. Somehow it seemed emblematic. A fitting symbol of everything that had happened. They were now at a transition point, after all. A moment between. In the past lay the world everyone knew, with all its weaknesses and its forbearance and its feeble promise of *democracy*. Ahead lay . . . Well. Ahead lay the world as Sikes would choose to make it.

There were some minor housekeeping issues to deal with first, of course. Crowe would have to be silenced. There was little the man could do to implicate Sikes, but she didn't believe in loose ends. Likewise Warden Bricknell, someone else who had served her purpose. And then, finally, there was the Haven.

They don't make them like they used to. Wasn't that the saying? But Sikes would have to admit that, in her experience, it was the other way round. Ollie Turner and his friends had so far proved much harder to bend to her will than some of the Haven's older members, for example. Or one older member, anyway. The man whose dead body lay before her.

Although in fairness to Montgomery Ross, he hadn't given up the Haven's location easily. In fact he'd resisted to the last. But he'd broken in the end, and when he'd finally felt obliged to tell her, Sikes's only option had been to laugh. It was so obvious. Such a simple solution – one that she really should have guessed sooner. Forest Mount. Of *course* they were in Forest Mount.

So yes, *Deadfall* had in the end given Sikes everything she needed.

A country afraid, and begging for a new style of leadership.

A political vacuum, with nobody but her left to fill it.

And her enemy's most closely guarded secret.

All in all, and apart from a few hiccups, everything had worked out as Sikes had intended. Now all she had to do was wait for the morning, and the darkness it would bring.

PHOTO © JUSTINE STODDARD

SIMON LELIC IS A WRITER OF CRIME AND THRILLER
NOVELS FOR ADULTS — WINNER OF THE BETTY TRASK AWARD,
SHORTLISTED FOR THE CWA DAGGER AWARDS AND
THE GALAXY NATIONAL BOOK AWARDS.

HE LIVES IN BRIGHTON WITH HIS WIFE AND
THREE CHILDREN. OTHER THAN HIS FAMILY, READING IS
HIS BIGGEST PASSION. HE ALSO HOLDS A BLACK BELT
IN KARATE, IN WHICH HE TRAINS DAILY.

 @SIMON_LELIC